SCORPION

BY

JACK STEWART

A BOOTLEG BOOK

A BOOTLEG BOOK
Published by
Bootleg Press
2431 NE Halsey, Suite A
Portland, Oregon 97232

Bootleg Books may be purchased for educational, business, or sales promotional use. For information please e-mail, Kelly Irish at: kellyirish@bootlegpress.com.

First Bootleg Press Trade Paperback Edition.

November 2003

10 9 7 6 5 4 3 2 1

ISBN: 097452462X

Bootleg Press is a registered trademark.

Cover by Compass Graphics

For my very good friend

Devon Paul Adams Douglas

Who is suffering through
His terrible twos.
What a wonderful world
He has waiting for him.

SCORPION

CHAPTER ONE

THE PLANE JERKED with the thundering sound of the explosion, cutting off all talk in the cabin. Broxton grabbed his seatbelt and cinched it tighter. Cold chills laced along his spine. A stewardess going by with a drink tray stumbled. He lashed out with his left arm, circling her waist, and pulled her toward him, spilling the tray from her hand, showering nearby passengers with Coca Cola and orange juice.

"Hey," she said, resisting and pushing against him, but he was stronger. "No," she said, as he pulled her down into his lap.

"Bomb," he whispered into her ear. Her body sagged as he wrestled her into the empty window seat next to him. She grabbed behind herself with both hands, searching for and finding the seatbelt. She buckled up and Broxton saw the color fade from her face. She grabbed onto the armrests, her skin pale as the sky on the other side of the window, her lower lip quivering, her eyes wide.

"Oh, lord," she said, as oxygen masks dropped down from above each passenger, orange, with clear plastic tubes, bouncing and jiggling, like hula dancers on parade. They were flying at thirty-five thousand feet and losing pressure. Broxton reached up, grabbed the mask and slipped it over his head. The stewardess next to him did the same, her hands shaking.

"You okay?" he asked, voice muffled by the mask.

"Yeah," she nodded, but he didn't believe her. She sucked her lower lip between her teeth and clamped down on it to stop the quivering, her auburn hair, long and perfect only an instant ago, now seemed wild and untamed, her flared nostrils accented the freckles around her nose. She had a fawn-like quality that startled him. He forced himself away from the terror in her eyes and looked over her shoulder, out the window. The mammoth wing shuddered and he was afraid the powerful engines were going to break away, but the shaking stopped as the wing tipped earthward, seeming to drag the rest of the plane with it.

"My God!" he said as the plane shuddered again, a great spasm running through it, like a death rattle, as the 747 lurched earthward, seeming to pick up speed. The clouds below were moving in a circular direction, but the pilot straightened the descent, added power and pulled back on the yoke. For a few seconds they were in a steep climbing turn. Broxton felt the G force as the plane fought the pilot. He was sucked into his seat, jaws, arms, hands, even fingers weighed down. He dropped his head, forced his mouth open, fought an urge to scream and grabbed oxygen into his lungs.

Then the plane lost the will to climb and started downward again.

He reached into his pocket, feeling for the engagement ring. He slipped the tip of his index finger through it, satisfied that it was still there. He prayed the pilot would bring them in safely. He twirled the ring around his fingertip. Dani, he thought, and he felt the familiar ache in his heart. He should have married her all those years ago.

The plane shimmied to the left, pulling him out of his reverie as the descent steepened. He was afraid it was too much for the plane. He looked out the window, half expecting the wings to rip away, turning the plane into an aluminum tube, spiraling and spinning toward the ocean below. Then the nose eased up, the pilot had slowed the rate of decent, but the sinking feeling in his stomach told him that they were still going down.

The stewardess gripped his hand, nails digging into his palm. He turned to look at her and she relaxed her grip for a second. He couldn't see her mouth through the mask, but he could tell by the crinkles around her eyes that she was attempting to smile. He forced himself to smile back and he gave her hand a gentle squeeze. He noticed the bruise under her right eye. She'd tried to cover it with makeup. He wondered how she'd hurt herself.

A baby cried, the pressure loss playing havoc on its eardrums. He squeezed his nose, held his mouth shut, and tried to breathe out, equalizing the pressure in his own head. He saw the stewardess imitating him, felt her sigh as the pressure equalized.

A woman's scream shrilled up from deep in second class and it gave him the excuse he needed to turn away from her. He looked around first class. The orange oxygen masks hid the lower half of the faces, but they couldn't hide the furrowed brows, eyes clenched shut against reality, or the stiff hands gripping armrests. Many were holding their breath. But there was no panic. There was no point.

He felt the pressure on his hand lessen, then increase. He turned back to look at the stewardess, caught in her Christmas green eyes, and he tried to imagine what he looked like to her.

Did his eyes show the freezing spark that was running up and down his spine? Did they betray the electric tingling at the back of his neck? The tight heat in the pit of his stomach? Did she know he felt like voiding himself at both ends? Could she feel the invisible claws raking over his skin?

The plane jerked and the luggage locker overhead popped open. He ducked as a briefcase fell out, bouncing off his shoulder, sending a stab of pain through his arm. He saw her wince, as if she felt it too. The briefcase hit the floor and sprang open. Papers, a cellular phone, a pocket calculator and a Barbie doll rolled out. The traveling executive had a little girl.

The doll rolled against his foot. He bent over and picked it up. Wherever this Barbie was, it was always summer. Her hair was always blond, always long, her eyes always blue and she always had on that pert summer dress. Barbie never worried. Barbie never had clammy skin, and Barbie never died.

He inhaled the oxygen, closed his eyes and wrapped his fist around the doll, tiny breasts digging into the palm of his left hand as the stewardess' nails dug into his right. He squeezed harder.

"Hurts," she whispered.

"Sorry," he said and he relaxed the pressure on both her hand and his eyelids. The interior of the plane slid back into focus. They were still going down, but the angle of descent had eased even more. He began to hope as he slipped the Barbie doll into the magazine pouch on the seatback in front of him.

There. She was safe and warm and away from harm.

He leaned his head back against the seat and rolled it slightly to take in the passenger across the isle. She was old, with rouged cheeks and blue rinsed hair, sitting next to a man who looked like he'd been her husband for several generations. Like himself and the stewardess, they were holding hands. She was looking into the man's eyes. The man took off his mask and mouthed the words, "I love you," and Broxton felt the stewardess squeeze his hand. She'd seen it, too.

The plane leveled off after what seemed like a forever down slide on the world's longest roller coaster.

"Ladies and gentlemen," the captain's voice boomed over the plane's speaker system, "I don't know what the problem was, but we have it under control. We've had some sort of malfunction in the rear of the plane that caused us to lose cabin pressure, but we have the aircraft under control."

He was repeating himself. He didn't know what he was talking about. He was lying.

The stewardess squeezed his hand again and he turned toward her. She slipped her mask off and the hairs on the back of his hands started to tingle when she smiled. Full lips, no lipstick, she didn't need it, perfect teeth. She was gently biting down on her tongue, as if she wanted to say something and was holding back.

"What?" He pulled his own mask off. He inhaled and smelled a whiff of her perfume mingled with her fear. It assaulted him like a patch of wildflowers on a windy summer day.

"You didn't check on them?" the stewardess said.

Broxton smiled. "You're very observant."

"I'm married to a cop, it goes with the territory. You've been watching them. Sneaking peaks whenever you think you can get away with it. You're not very good. If they were criminals they'd be on to you." She had a slight Mexican accent that didn't go with her pale skin and green eyes.

"I'm supposed to see that nothing happens to them." He turned and looked over his shoulder at the last two seats in the center of the first class section.

The prime minister's face was ashen, and he was gripping his seat with an intense fervor. His gray skin and gray hair gave off a death-like pallor, only the beads of sweat dripping from his hair line and the weak rising and falling of his chest told Broxton that there was any life there.

By contrast, the attorney general, in the seat next to him, was taking long, slow breaths, sucking the life-giving oxygen deep into his lungs and exhaling in an almost leisurely fashion. He's accepted his fate, Broxton thought, he knows it's out of his hands. He'll take whatever is dealt. He won't show fear. He's a strong man. The prime minister is not.

"He's a good man," the stewardess said. "Tough too. You'd never know he'd had open heart surgery last year."

"I didn't know that." Broxton took another look

at the prime minister's face. He was grimacing, but it could be pain, not fear. Maybe he'd been too quick to judge.

"Looks like he might be in some pain," Broxton said.

"I wouldn't be surprised," she said.

"The attorney general looks pretty calm, though."

"He was an athlete. World famous."

"I've never heard of him."

"Actually neither had I, but the two Trini flight attendants are both gaga over him. He was a cricket player."

"That explains it. It's a sport I don't keep up on."

"They say he's a real ladies man, Trinidad's most eligible bachelor."

"He looks the part," Broxton said, noticing the dark man's expensive suit and salon haircut.

"Are you some kind of bodyguard?" she asked. He turned back toward her and again she was looking deep into his eyes.

"Kind of. I'm supposed to keep Prime Minister Ramsingh alive, only he's not supposed to know it."

"I don't understand," she said. Her nostrils flared, just a little, and the wrinkles around her eyes scrunched together. Little crow's feet. He guessed her to be in her mid-thirties, about his age.

"Someone wants him dead. Attorney General Chandee doesn't take the threat seriously. My boss does." He couldn't believe it. He was telling her about the job. That was forbidden, but he didn't care. They were talking to take their minds off the horrible reality around them. They were whispering.

"Who do you work for?"

"The United States Government."

"Oh," she said.

He turned to look over his shoulder again.

A well built man pushed through the curtain from second class. The sun shining in through the windows on the left side of the aircraft reflected off something shiny in the man's hand. A knife?

Broxton flicked open the seatbelt and charged down the aisle. The man was leaning over the prime minister. Broxton pulled him off and slammed him across the laps of two priests sitting in the seats opposite. The man had a shocked look on his face. Broxton raised his hand to strike, then he saw the chrome flask in the man's hand.

"Sorry," Broxton said, "I thought it was a knife." He held his hand out to help the man up. The grip was strong and firm and a smile glinted out from his pale blue eyes, but it vanished quickly, turning to a cold stare. Not a man to take lightly.

"Brandy," the prime minister said. His mask was off and in his hand. "If I have to take the heart medication I like to enjoy it going down." Broxton noticed the liver spots on the prime minister's hands.

"Bill Broxton," he introduced himself. "Again, I'm awful sorry about the mistake. For some stupid reason I thought I saw a knife. I feel like an idiot."

"Kevin Underfield," the man said. "I work for Minister Chandee." Broxton had to think for a second, then he remembered that in Trinidad the cabinet members were also elected members of parliament.

Broxton turned back toward the prime minister, who continued talking as if nothing had happened. "I used to drink more than my share, enjoyed it. I liked the way it made me feel and usually I could handle it, but from time to time I'd make an ass out of myself. That was before I came into politics, but the press never lets one forget his indiscretions, so now the only time alcohol touches my lips is when I have to take the damn medicine. They still write about my drinking, but now it's a plus because it's the old Ramsingh they're writing about and everybody knows it except them."

"So you turned your drinking and past indiscretions into an asset. It can't be easy to live with."

"So you see the two-edged sword."

"I see it," Broxton said. "As long as you don't drink you can shrug off the past and any man that writes about it unwittingly reminds his readers how you overcame your problem to become prime minister, but if you ever get tanked up again it'll all blow up in your face."

"Yes, they would see me as nothing more than a common drunk."

"A hard way to go," Broxton said. Ramsingh looked up at him through gray eyes that danced around his smile. The man radiated honesty and Broxton couldn't help liking him.

"Are you a cop of some kind?" Underfield asked. He had a British accent and that puzzled Broxton.

"DEA."

"I thought we made it clear to your government that we understand the threat and don't desire any of your help." The attorney general's voice was muffled by the oxygen mask. Broxton was finding it hard to breathe, but not impossible.

"I don't know what you're talking about," Broxton said. "I thought the man had a knife. I recognized the Prime Minister of Trinidad. I made a mistake. I said I was sorry."

"If you're not here to watch over the prime

minister, why are you on this flight?" Chandee pointed an accusing finger at Broxton.

"I'm going to Trinidad to get married," Broxton said, adding, "if she'll have me."

"And the lucky woman is?" Now Chandee had his mask off, too. He pulled his finger back and laced his hands in his lap. He was addressing Broxton as if he was on the witness stand, but it didn't matter, Broxton had an answer for him.

"Dani Street," he said.

Chandee's snarl shifted into a smirk that turned Broxton angry. He wanted to slap it off his face, but he held himself in check.

"The ambassador's daughter?" the prime minister said. "Maybe we've been too quick to judge Mr. Broxton, George. I've told you before, you have to watch that." The prime minister looked at Chandee like a benevolent parent does a wayward child, and the man visibly withered under his stare. His fingers stiffened in his lap as he turned away from his boss and toward Broxton, offering him a thin- lipped smile.

"I think I'll just go back to my seat," Broxton said.

"That would be best," Chandee said, his face tight.

"The ambassador's daughter?" Underfield said, almost laughing.

Broxton nodded, then the plane hit a patch of turbulence and he stumbled, but caught himself, gripping the back of the prime minister's seat. Several of the passengers gasped, but nobody screamed. Most of them kept their masks on.

He looked at Chandee, met his eyes, smiled and said, "You know, George, you really should watch that temper. One of these days it's going to land you in deep shit and the prime minister won't be around to help you out."

"There's always me," Underfield said, his gaze turning to knife blades.

"Right," Broxton said. And he turned away and started back toward his seat.

"I work for the attorney general, you know."

"You said that," Broxton said, without turning around. And he quickly forgot about Underfield when he eyed a little girl sitting next to her father. Her hand was clasped tightly in his and her lips were moving. She's praying, he thought. He smiled at her and she smiled back, lighting up her freckles. Then she gave him a thumbs up sign. He stuck out his right thumb and flashed it back.

He returned to his seat, thinking about the Barbie doll. He took it out of the magazine pouch and fluffed the doll's hair with a finger. Then he straightened her dress. He felt the stewardess' eyes on him. He didn't even know her name.

"Yours?" he said, smiling at the girl. She nodded and he handed it back to her. He was rewarded with a smile back. Would the girl's mother be waiting for her husband and daughter at the airport? Would the airline tell waiting friends and relatives about the trouble on board or would they just say the plane was delayed? Would they make it to Port of Spain at all?

"It'll be okay," the stewardess said, as if reading his mind.

"I know," Broxton said, but he didn't know.

"I'm Maria," she said.

"Bill," he said, "but most people call me Broxton."

"You made an enemy back there," she said.

"Sometimes I have a big mouth, like today. My job is supposed to be kind of secret and not one day into it and I've not only told you, but I've managed to get in an argument with the attorney general."

"It looks like Mr. Ramsingh's being well taken care of."

"You mean the muscle man?"

"He looks like he can handle himself."

"He does at that," Broxton laughed, "and I guess I've upset him a little, too."

"It would seem so," she laughed, and he swore her eyes were sparkling.

"Ladies and Gentlemen," it was the captain's voice over the speakers again, "we're flying at eight thousand feet and although it's possible to breathe without your oxygen masks I would recommend you keep them on. Our speed is two hundred and fifty miles an hour, less than half of our normal cruising speed, and I'm afraid that will put us forty-five minutes behind schedule for our landing in Port of Spain. So our new ETA is 2:45, If you haven't already reset your watches, now would be a good time to do it."

Maria took his hand again and he felt her leg pressed up against his.

"I'm sorry, I shouldn't kid you," the captain continued, "we have a problem and we don't know what it is, but we seem to have control of the aircraft. I don't want to risk climbing or adding any more power. The situation is delicate, but I'm confident we will arrive safely, and in that light I'm requesting that you all, flight attendants included, stay seated with your seatbelts securely fastened until we are on the ground and the engines are off. Thank you very much."

This time he was telling the truth. Broxton preferred the lie.

"It's going to be a pretty tense hour and a half," Maria said. She was still holding his hand. She gave him a half smile, as if she just realized it, and relaxed her grip. He noticed her face turning the embarrassing shade of pink.

He smiled back, "Thanks for the moral support," he said. "I don't know what I would have done without you."

"Thank you for that," she said, her color returning to normal. Then she asked, "Will she be waiting at the airport, your girl?"

"No, she doesn't know I'm coming. It's a surprise. How did you know about her?" he asked.

"You were fiddling and fidgeting with that engagement ring, like it was a hot rock burning your fingers, all during take off, remember?"

"I've known her all my life." He let go of her hand and dug the ring out of his coat pocket. He looked at it, turned it over in his fingers. "Our folks always assumed we'd be married, but things just didn't work out."

"What things?" she said. She pulled her long hair back and met his eyes.

"Another woman," he said.

"Ah," she said.

"But that was over a long time ago."

"She knows this, your girl?"

"Dani? Sure. She never stopped loving me and I guess I never stopped loving her. She's been part of me almost as long as I've been alive. When someone's been that close for that long, well, I took her for granted. I'll never do it again."

"Good for you," Maria said, "I hope it works out for you." And she started to get up.

"Where are you going? The captain said we

should stay seated."

"Someone has to check on the passengers. I'm the senior flight attendant."

"But the captain said."

"He's got his job and I've got mine, and besides you sure didn't stay seated." She smiled.

He unbuckled his belt and stood to let her pass.

"I'll be back soon," she said, squeezing his arm. He watched her make her way back toward second class, working her way down the aisle, steadying herself by grabbing on to the seatbacks.

Then the plane jerked to the right and started to go down again.

CHAPTER TWO

THEY WERE DOING FIFTY on the interstate when the '65 Chevy Impala flew by at eighty-five. Windows down. The driver was sipping a coke. The rider was hunched down low. The car was over thirty years old, but it looked as if it had just been driven off the showroom floor, candy apple red with tinted windows, reverse chrome rims, enough polish to supply a car wash and it was wearing California tags.

"Let's go!" Jackson White said.

"Hold your water." Sheriff Earl Lawson smiled to himself. Speed always got Jackson's heart a pumping. He eased off the gas and let another car pass. Solitude was a small town, most folks knew his unmarked Ford and he didn't want to take any chances.

"Did you hear that engine rumble?" Earl said. "I'll give you dollars to donuts that it's a full tricked out 327 'Vette engine powering that baby and it sounds like he's got glass pack mufflers in front of them chrome tailpipes. I woulda killed for a car like that when I was in high school. Hell, I still might." He laughed. As a kid he loved cars and he'd been particularly partial to Chevys. The first time he'd gotten laid was in the back seat of his own '65 Impala, but his wasn't souped up like that, he couldn't afford it.

"Come on, Earl, you're gonna lose him," Jackson said. Jackson White was the only black deputy on the small force. He was the darkest black man Earl had ever laid eyes on, and although he didn't like blacks in general, he made an exception in Jackson's case. The man was a good deputy, a good friend and knew how to keep his mouth shut. Earl liked riding with him, they made a great team, but he was going to have to talk to him about that newspaper girlfriend of his and her story in last night's *Evening Standard*.

"Stop champing at the bit, Jackson, he's not getting away." The sun was hanging directly overhead. It was August hot, but the heat never seemed to bother Earl. He drove with a casual flair, left elbow flopping over the side of the open window, two fingers on the wheel, seat pushed all the way back, like he was out for a ride in the country.

"They'll be across the line in a couple a minutes, then we'll have to call in the county," Jackson said. He clenched his hands into fists, relaxed them, then clenched them again. He was sucking in deep, fast breaths. He was ready and hoping for a high speed chase.

"Stop talking like a man with a paper asshole,"

Earl said. "He's ours."

"Yeah, he's ours," Jackson said. "I just don't want to give Mayor 'Shit-for-Brains' any reason to be on our case. Things are bad enough as it is."

"It's your fault about Sheeter. Your girlfriend prints that crap and he's all over us like white on rice. Why she believes a coke dealer over me, I don't know." Earl turned and looked sideways at his deputy. Jackson was good looking, the way a woman might call pretty, and he was tall, not NBA basketball tall, but a full six inches taller then his own six feet, and he was certainly dark. Tall, dark and handsome. But his good looks didn't keep his latest flame from printing that cokehead's story.

"I just think we should go by the book for a while, till things cool down. It wouldn't hurt to pull them over before they crossed into county."

"Shit, Jackson, we threw the book away a long time ago, you an' me. Besides I wanna know what their hurry is. And I'd also like to know why Zelda Saul accused me of misappropriating twenty thousand dollars. I didn't misappropriate that twenty grand all by myself, and I didn't hit that asshole on the back of the head neither."

"He's a junkie, nobody's going to believe that story. I wouldn't worry about it."

"People believe what they see in the paper and when the paper says the sheriff's a crook they tend to think about voting for the other guy come election time. You gotta straighten her out, or I will. *Comprende, mi amigo?* And another thing, you gotta watch yourself. You coulda killed him, clobbering him on the skull just wasn't called for."

"He sold dope to kids. He was slime," Jackson said.

"Yes he was, but you don't want to go to jail for the rest of your life over slime. Just cool the violent stuff. *To protect and serve*, remember?"

"I just said that we should go by the book for a while," Jackson said, looking over at Earl, "and I meant it. I know I went too far. I know I got you in trouble and somehow I'll get Zelda to write some good things about you in the real near future. You can count on me. I won't fuck up again."

"I'd appreciate that. Shit, I don't mind taking the rap for the whole twenty large, this time. But if she keeps it up we could find ourselves outta work."

"I'll handle it," Jackson said.

"I don't want to feel that we gotta hand in every dime we grab off these bastards, I mean god knows we get paid shit, we're entitled, but if she's gonna run every dealer's claim about lost money, we'll have to turn into a pair of honest cops, 'cause jail sucks. You get my drift?"

"Come on, Earl, relax. I'll take care of it."

"Why don't you just marry the bitch, then she'd have to do what you say, or else."

"It doesn't work that way for everybody," Jackson said.

Earl was about to respond to that, but the Impala turned off onto Sam Houston Road. He turned to Jackson and grinned out loud, "See, no need to call in the county now, that road stays on our side of the line all the way to the way to Loomis'."

"Think that's where he's going?" Jackson said. Earl glanced over at him again. Not a drop of sweat. No rapid breathing now. No tight fists. Not a shake. Not a shiver, just the animal look of anticipation. No, he didn't particularly like blacks, but if it turned out all wrong, Jackson White would be the man he'd want by his side, newspaper girlfriend or no.

"Nothing else out there," Earl said.

"That old air strip, half mile past," Jackson said.

"Be goddamned."

"Hang back."

"Yeah, good idea." Earl turned the corner and slowed some.

"Dust cloud, they won't see anything in their rearview through that. They must be in a hurry," Jackson said.

Earl added gas and in less than half a minute they reached the spot where the tarmac ended and the road turned into a dirt track. They had no trouble keeping the dust cloud in sight. Another half minute and they were at Loomis' Junkyard and Storage Units. The dust cloud was still moving off in the distance.

"They're going for the air strip."

"Must be an awful important appointment," Earl said.

"Maybe they're late?"

Earl wheeled the car into the shade offered by the new stucco building that was old Loomis' office. Behind, in a fenced compound, were the storage lockers, sixty of them, three rows of twenty, ten on each side, out in the middle of nowhere. Behind them, the vast sprawling junkyard. Loomis had two junkyard dogs. Dobermans, big ones, mean ones. One roamed the junkyard after dark, the other, the storage units.

Loomis slept in the building up front. It was common knowledge that he slept with an AK-47 cradled in his arms. No one stole from Loomis. No one even thought about it.

"Let's see if he's got something cold to drink,"

Earl said, getting out of the car.

"But they'll get away." Jackson jumped out of his side and followed Earl around.

Earl stopped at the door and turned to look at the taller man. "They gotta come back this way, ain't no other way outta here. If we follow any farther we'll spook 'em and their plane ain't gonna land. We'll catch 'em on the way out and see what they're bringing in."

"We don't know for sure there is a plane," Jackson said.

"Go with your gut, Jackson. There's a plane." And as if to underscore his words they saw a small high winged aircraft off in the distance, headed for the landing strip. "Old Cessna 150, looks like," Earl said. Even with the sunglasses he had to squint.

"But what if they're leaving on it?" Jackson held his right hand above his eyes as he watched the plane. He wasn't wearing sunglasses.

Earl shook his head. The man was eager, he was dependable, but sometimes he wasn't too bright. "Wanna get the door?"

Jackson grabbed the knob, then pulled his hand off like he'd been zapped with electricity. "Hot," he said, whipping his hand up and down in a vain hope that the summer dry Texas air might cool it.

"And that's my point, Jackson. You ain't got no common sense. I knew that knob was hot. It's over a hundred degrees out. Common sense told me not to grab on to it." He removed the bandanna from around his neck and draped it over the knob. "This is good for more 'en wiping coke powder off hundred dollar bills." He opened the door and retied the bandanna.

"Hey, Loomis, you have a tall, cool one?" Earl

asked, stepping over to the wall opposite the counter. He stood under the AC unit, letting the cold air flow down over his shoulders as he leaned back.

"Coors for you, Coke for Jackson." Loomis picked cans out of a cooler.

"Sure," Earl said, catching the beer. He rubbed the cold can on the back of his neck as Jackson caught the coke. He waited until Jackson pulled the tab and took a long drink before he asked, "So, Jackson, you know why we're drinking cold ones and not chasing after them boys?"

"Haven't a clue," Jackson said.

Earl shook his head again, pulled his own tab and took a long pull on his beer. "No one's getting on any plane and flying out of that dinky strip. Hell, if a body wanted to leave town he'd drive down to San Antonio and leave on a real plane. No, them boys ain't leaving. They're picking something up. Something dirty. Drugs most likely. So we'll just sit in this cool room, drink with Loomis here, and wait. Shouldn't be long."

"Hey, Sheriff, how's the wife?" Loomis said, then he turned and spit a gob of chewing tobacco into a rusty waste basket.

"Been away for a week, three ta go. She's filling in for a gal on her honeymoon. Doing a international flight down to the Caribbean." He looked at his watch. "Two hours difference, two o'clock where she is. She's in the air as we speak. Should be calling in anytime." She always let him know as soon as her plane was on the ground. He had her trained right. She always called.

"Thought it was her vacation?" Loomis said. "I expected to see her up here sorting through your daddy's things."

"Was, but this offer opened up, and we needed

the money. Gotta pay for that Suburban," Earl said. He didn't want Maria gone a whole month, but the Suburban had oversized tires, chrome rims and a stereo that could wake up the next neighborhood, if he'd a mind to play it that loud.

"What do you want me to do with that locker?" Loomis asked, chewing slow, looking shrewd. "Your Daddy's been dead six months now, sooner or later you gotta toss his stuff."

"We'll get around to it someday soon," Earl said.

"You're two months behind, Sheriff."

"How much is it, Loomis?" Earl balled his hands into fists. The son-of-a-bitch had to ask in front of Jackson, now he'd have to pay, otherwise he'd look cheap. He couldn't afford that. Not in front of any of his men. Especially not in front of Jackson.

"Sixty bucks," Loomis said. That's with your discount and without the late charges."

"Got it right here." Earl felt Jackson's eyes on him as he pushed himself off of the wall and reached into his hip pocket for his money. Earl was moving slow, because he didn't want to pay. He knew his men kidded among themselves about the free lunches he took at Josie's Diner. He knew they thought he was cheap, but they were all younger, just starting out. They didn't know what it was like getting by in today's world. Sometimes he thought about using his secret money to pay his bills, but he never would, because as soon as he started spending more than he made, sure as shit someone, like Jackson's reporter girlfriend, would start asking the wrong kind of questions. That money was going to stay locked away until he was long gone from West Texas.

"Still riding the river?" Loomis asked Jackson, taking Earl's mind off the money and putting it on a subject he loved.

"Every chance I get, but it's not so easy getting Earl down there now that he's putting in those extra hours," Jackson said.

They started riding the rapids in the Guadeloupe River six months ago. They both loved it, but he had to work overtime to make the payments on the new car, he thought Jackson understood that. It had only been a few weeks, and with the money Maria was making on her new job they would get ahead of the payments and soon he'd be back at the river with Jackson on a regular basis.

"You could do it solo, lots of guys do," Loomis said.

"I'm still a little raw, give me a couple more seasons."

"Some guys do it right away. One or two times and they're off by themselves," Loomis said.

"Yeah, and some guys sit on their brains," Earl said, getting into the conversation.

The sound of the plane was above them now and Earl saw Jackson look up, as if he could see through the ceiling. It was definitely landing at the strip. It was obvious that Jackson wanted to get in the car and charge down there, but they'd see the dust cloud coming long before they got close enough to do anything and the plane would be off. It would be better to wait. A Cessna 150 only held two, there were two in the car they were tailing, so even if there was only one in the plane, someone was coming back this way.

"Think they spotted the car?" Jackson said.

"Don't make no difference," Earl said.

"Oh, yeah." Jackson was used to riding in a patrol car. The Sheriff never rode in a black and white, and you never wore your uniform when you rode with the sheriff. The pilot above would see an unmarked Ford parked in front of the storage units. Nothing suspicious.

"They're down," Loomis said.

Earl cocked his head, like an old hunting dog, "Sounds like it," he said.

"Get many planes like that out there?" Jackson asked.

"Some," Loomis said, as he made out the sheriff's receipt. "That's sixty dollars." He looked up at Earl.

Earl laughed, "You know what you remind me of, Loomis?"

"No, what?"

"That skinny old cow over to the Shiller place. The one that's always standing under that shade tree chewing its cud. I swear with your sad cow eyes and chewing that chaw, you could be that cow."

Loomis' eyes narrowed and his face closed in on itself, but it opened back up as soon as Earl counted out the three twenties. "And this is for you, so you don't get charged twice." Loomis handed the sheriff his receipt.

"Nobody ever charges me twice," Earl said, crumpling up the receipt. He tossed it over the counter, making a rim shot into Loomis' rusty, tobacco stained waste basket.

"They're coming," Loomis said.

"That was fast," Jackson said.

The sheriff started for the door when Loomis stopped him with, "That won't be necessary, Earl. They'll be coming here."

"Ah," Earl said.

"They'll use the electric gate opener," Loomis said.

"Which unit?" The sheriff might be cheap, but he was quick.

"Forty-seven, middle of the middle row," Loomis said, then he turned and spit a glob of black tobacco into the waste basket.

"Plane's been here before, hasn't it, Loomis?" Earl said.

"Ain't saying."

"I'm asking."

"Sheriff, you know me. I like to mind my own business. I said too much already."

"You didn't say any more than I'll find out in the next minute or so."

"And that was too much," Loomis said.

The car was just outside now, going past the office. They didn't even glance at the unmarked Ford. Earl heard the car slow and the rubber wheels of the gate roll across the blacktop as it opened. Then the car drove on through and it closed automatically after them.

"We'll give them a few minutes to get settled in, then we'll drive on up like we're going to a storage unit of our own. We'll take 'em quick like, guns drawn, just like cops on TV. Ya with me, Jackson?"

"Yes, sir," Jackson said, and Earl saw that he was pumped. Earl was pumped, too. This was what being a cop was all about. It was the part he loved and craved, but it didn't happen too often, the chance to take the bad guys off the streets, the chance to make a difference. He checked his thirty-eight as he followed Jackson out to the car. He felt the hot sun baking into him. He flicked a fly off his hand and headed toward the driver's side.

"Ya'll can open the gate now," Earl said to Loomis, and the gate started to slide open. Earl cranked the ignition and headed toward the middle row. He took his time as he motored along, whistling, like he was in no hurry. He was enjoying himself.

They came abreast of the Impala and Earl slowly moved on by. The Impala blocked the rolled up door of storage unit 47, but it didn't hide the fact that both men were inside, moving cardboard boxes around.

"Lot of stuff in there," Earl said.

"Yes, sir, lot of stuff," Jackson echoed, hand on the door handle.

"Now," Earl said, slamming on the brakes as Jackson was jumping out the door.

"Freeze!" Jackson yelled. He threw his arms across the top of the old Chevy, elbows on the car, arms extended, holding the thirty-eight.

One of the men started to go for a gun.

"Don't!" Jackson screamed, but the man didn't stop, didn't give him a choice. Jackson saw the man's right arm come out from inside his coat. Saw the forty-five in the man's hand. "No!" Jackson screamed louder, but the man wasn't listening and Jackson shot him before he could bring the gun up to fire.

The sound of Jackson's gunshot ricocheted through Earl, tearing his insides up in a thousand places. It was louder than thunder, more violent than a summer storm, more intense than sex, stronger than passion. Jackson had never fired on a man before and Earl knew that he'd crossed a bridge and that he would never be the same.

The second man threw his hands in the air, grabbing as much sky as he could. "Don't shoot," he said.

"I got him covered, Jackson," Earl said.

Jackson turned away from the man he'd shot, holstered his weapon and tried to fight the rising bile.

He bit hard into his lower lip, then inhaled a deep breath of the hot air. He clenched his fist, exhaled, took in a second breath, deep into his belly. With the palm of his right hand he wiped the sweat from the back of his neck, exhaled, then vomited.

"Sorry," he said wiping his mouth off with the back of his hand.

"Happened to me the first time, too," Earl said. "Nothing to be ashamed of. Ain't a man in the world I wouldn't rather have with me in a shooting situation than you." It was amazing. Jackson could slap around a hooker, push around the high school punks, smack a drug dealer on the back of the head with his pistol, almost killing him, but he upchucks when he has to shoot a man with a weapon. Earl bent low and scooped the boy's gun from the floor. A well used forty-five auto. He was scared, Earl thought, it wasn't the killing that made him vomit, it was the gun pointed at him.

"How would you know? I've never been in one before."

"'Cause you got guts, boy. The way you ran into that fire and brought out them little girls, no one else woulda done that, not me, not their own daddy. We were there, but it was you that charged into the flames." But even as he said it, Earl wondered about the truth of it. It took one kind of guts to run into a fire, another kind to face down a loaded weapon. Still, Jackson took the right action, he didn't flinch, but he was scared, he was shaking now.

"One of them died," Jackson said.

"But one of them didn't. She's a perfectly normal little girl and it's all 'cause a you, so stop beating yourself over the head about the dead one. It wasn't your fault. An' don't beat yourself up over this either.

You did what you had to do. You did good. Now let's just go in there an' see what kind of hornet's nest we stirred up."

The one grabbing for the ceiling couldn't be more than seventeen or eighteen, and it struck Earl that the man Jackson had hit the other day wasn't much older.

"Johnny Lee Tyler," Earl said.

"Yes, sir," the kid answered.

"What are ya'll up to here?"

"Just loading up some things for his dad," the boy nodded toward the body.

"Who is he?" Earl asked.

"Darren Johnson, new kid. He lives with his dad, they only been in town a month." The boy's hands, still above his head, were shaking like palm trees in a hurricane.

"And you hooked right up with 'em?"

"Guess so."

"What 'cha got in all the boxes?"

"CDs. The new Rolling Stones mostly."

"Counterfeit?" Earl asked.

"'Spect so," the boy answered.

"And over there?" Earl pointed to the back wall.

"Porno videos, the kind you can't get at the store. You know, the kind with kids in 'em."

"Shit, Johnny Lee, I know your daddy, we go hunting. He didn't raise you like this."

The boy dropped his hands, then he dropped his eyes to the cement floor. The room was quiet for a few seconds that seem like forever. Johnny Lee appeared to be studying a brown beetle as it scurried toward the cracks made between several stacks of the cardboard boxes.

"All right, Johnny Lee, what did ya'll pick up

from that plane?"

"Two kilos of coke and a briefcase."

"Lordy, Johnny Lee, sex, drugs an' rock 'n' roll. You boys was into it all."

"Not me, honest. It's Darren's dad. I just sorta fell into it."

"Was it the drugs?" Earl said.

The boy nodded.

"Where's the briefcase and what's in it?"

"It's in the car, in the back. I don't know what's in it. That's the honest truth."

"You wanna get it."

"Sure, Sheriff," the kid said, and he hustled to the car.

"You know, Jackson," Earl said. "The hardest thing for a police officer to do is tell a man that his wife just died in an accident or that you've locked up his boy for killing a man. You steel yourself against it, but when you go up those steps and ring that bell, you're quaking inside, like a pup that just shit on the rug and knows he's in for it."

"I can imagine," Jackson said.

"I'm sure not looking forward to seeing Billy Ray Tyler this evening," Earl said.

"And Darren's father," Jackson said. Earl saw him looking at the boy's eyes, wide open in death. Looking at the trickle of blood dripping from a lip that must have been cut in the fall. Looking at the scar under the chin. Looking at the close cropped hair, the white tee shirt, the faded Levi's, the hundred dollar running shoes. Looking at a life that wouldn't be lived.

"Far as I'm concerned, that boy's daddy killed him, not you. I'm ashamed to say it, but it will give me a kind of pleasure telling the man that his boy's dead and that it's his fault. The man sold child porn and drugs. You wanna be there when I take him down. 'Cause that's one arrest that's not gonna go by the book."

Jackson nodded. "I wouldn't miss it."

Earl looked around the warehouse. Not large, thirty by sixty maybe, but it was stuffed full of cartons, mostly compact discs, but quite a few of the video tapes. Darren's dad was in a lot of trouble. Earl didn't think he'd be going to his boy's funeral. He didn't think the man would be too mobile for a while. Not after he got through with him.

He turned his eyes away from the cardboard boxes and the dead body and watched as Johnny Lee Tyler opened the back door to the Chevy and fished out the briefcase. He brought it inside, laying it on top of a stack of boxes. He smiled up at Earl, like a hound dog eager to please.

"Open it," Earl said, and the kid fumbled with the latches.

"Can't, it's locked," he said.

"But you could get it open fast enough if you really wanted to, couldn't you, lad?"

"Yes, sir."

"Then do it."

The boy reached behind his neck, under the back of his shirt, and pulled out a large hunting knife.

"Where'd you learn how to hide a knife like that?" Jackson asked.

"Darren's dad," the kid said, then he pried the tip of the knife under the latches and popped them off the briefcase and opened it.

"Look at all that money," the sheriff said, whistling under his breath.

"Lots of money," Jackson said.

"Way I see it, we got no choice," Earl said.

"No choice," Jackson said.

And Earl shot Johnny Lee through the heart with his friend's gun. The cannon sound of the forty-five roared through the small warehouse like the sound of an exploding jet engine. One second Johnny Lee was filling Earl with those trusting eyes and the next he was flying across the room. But Earl never got to see where he landed because something slammed into the back of his head and the lights went out.

CHAPTER THREE

MARIA LOST HER BALANCE, stumbled and reached out for the seatback behind the prime minister, but she grabbed a fistful of his shirt instead. He pulled her into him, burying her face against his chest, clawing at her, fighting to hold her. She smelled the sweat from under his arms, felt his muscles strain as he fought to keep her from tumbling down the aisle.

She heard someone scream as she wrapped her arms around his chest, straining and struggling to hold on. His knee came up into her stomach, knocking her breath away. She gasped for air, but she was wedged in tightly against the prime minister, her mouth pulled into his clothes. She moaned and felt him relax his hold on her. Then she saw the orange oxygen mask as he wormed it between her face and his chest. She inhaled, quick short breaths, and in seconds she had her wind back.

The noise was deafening, louder than the cranked up volume of any of the Texas honky tonks that Earl liked to take her to, louder than the giant speakers at the Weezer and the Wallflowers concerts she went to with her sister last year, louder than the dragsters at the Southern Texas Speedway, louder than God.

She battled with the prime minister as he tried to turn her around. In her normal, rational mind, she knew what he was doing, but she couldn't help herself, she fought against him, afraid he was going to take the oxygen away. She pushed against his chest, fighting to get up and out of his lap. Then the plane lurched again, as if a giant boy had a giant fist wrapped around his giant airplane toy, and he was shaking it.

She stopped resisting and squirmed around so that she was sitting in his lap, but she lost the mask as she came around. She offered no resistance as he wrapped his arms around her and pulled her in close, grabbing his hands onto his elbows in an effort to form a locking ring around her waist. She felt herself getting light, then heavy, then light again as the plane plunged toward the ground, lurched itself level, then plunged downward again. She grabbed onto the seatback in front of her for added support. Shivers zapped her body, but she fought to control her shaking. Something was smacking her in the head and she reached up and grabbed it. It was the oxygen mask. Without realizing what she was doing, she jerked on it with a maniac force, snapping the plastic tube, destroying the mask and cutting off any more oxygen for herself or the prime minister.

"Please, God," the man next to the prime minister murmured as the plane bucked and slammed through a convulsion from hell. It was a desperate plea, like a puppy dog whine.

She felt the prime minister's hands slipping.

"Help me, George," he yelled, and she felt a second pair of hands wrap around her left arm just as the plane slammed and jerked further to the right. They were still going down. She felt them pull and strain, fighting to keep her in place, as the plane rocked and rolled through the clear sky.

Then the angle of descent slackened and they were flying straight and level again. A collective sigh escaped from first class and Maria felt her breath go out as she sighed, too. She relaxed, her shoulders sagged, her heart slowed its wild pumping. The deafening noise was down to a dull roar.

"Thank you," she said, disentangling herself from the two men by pulling up on the seatback in front of her. The attorney general gave her backside a gentle push. She wanted to be back next to the DEA man with the shaved head, safely belted in. She wanted comfort. She wanted a friend. The DEA man was all she had.

"Sorry folks," the captain's voice soothed through the plane, "I had no control over that, but we have the plane back and she seems to be flying okay. I've alerted Port of Spain and they will have medical facilities standing by should we need any. We're still about forty-five minutes behind schedule. I know it's difficult, but please try and remain calm. We are doing the very best we can."

"It was a bomb," Chandee said. She looked over at the man with the strong voice and the puppy dog whine. He hadn't offered her any help until the prime minister demanded it and she saw why. Sweat ringed his forehead, his eyes were glazed like a rabbit caught in the headlights, his face was ashen, his hands were shaking and it looked like he'd peed his pants.

"Shut up, George," Prime Minister Ramsingh said.

Maria looked down at them. "Thanks again," she said. "You probably saved my life." The prime minister was beaming. The attorney general was not. She watched as he slipped out of his light suit coat and laid it in his lap.

"You should go back to your seat," the prime minister said. He seemed confident now, gone were the knitted eyebrows and the clenched teeth. His neck was no longer bulging and he seemed to be smiling, almost in a state of grace, she thought.

The attorney general, on the other hand, had bitten into his lower lip and drawn blood. A slight trickle oozed down his chin. That, coupled with his glazed eyes, gave him a crazed vampire kind of look. "Yes," he said. "The prime minister is right, you should go back to your seat." The words, whispered above the engine noise, weren't mean in themselves, but the way he said it, they were threatening. She had seen his fear and he was the kind of man who would never forget it. She wanted to be away from him.

She turned to go back to her seat when she heard the baby cry again. A loud, long wail that seared her soul. There was only one lap child on board. A darling baby girl. She remembered seating them in the forward bulkhead position, right in front of the movie screen in second class. Just on the other side of the curtain. She prayed the child was okay, she had to know.

She turned around, away from her seat next to the

DEA man, pushed aside the curtain and stepped into second class and chaos. The overhead luggage lockers had been stuffed to capacity with overweight carry-on bags and many of them had come open during the rapid descent, spilling their contents on the passengers below and out into the aisles.

The baby stopped crying. Her young parents were sharing an oxygen mask, taking turns breathing through it, like a pair of scuba buddies, allowing the baby to wear mom's mask. She felt like reminding the baby's father that they were low enough so that he could breathe without it, but she noticed his shaking hands. Sharing the mask with his wife gave him something to do. Made him feel like he was taking care of her.

"Are we going to make it?" he asked, as his wife was drawing in oxygen.

"Certainly, but like the captain said we'll get into Port of Spain a little late." Maria kept her smile, trying to project an image of calm security to the young couple, just the opposite of how she felt.

The plane lurched to the right and another overhead locker opened. She saw the black bag start to fall and she remembered how heavy it was. Full of bricks, she thought when she'd shoved it up there. She remembered mentally cursing the ground personnel for allowing the passengers to bring aboard carry-on baggage that was obviously too large and too heavy.

She lunged toward the open compartment as the plane careened through more turbulence. Someone screamed. The boy sitting below the falling bag was piercing Maria with innocent blue-eyed trust. The bag was halfway out of the locker. She wanted to scream, tell the boy to move, but she needed all her energy. She slammed her right foot into the deck and dove, hands outstretched. The boy started to look up. The bag was out of the locker. Her stretching fingers tipped it toward the aisle. She tried to loosen her body as she fell, she didn't want to break anything. She hit the deck and wound up wedged between the bag and a seat stuffed with a large black man. Her right ankle was screaming.

"Let me help you," the man said in a rich baritone, and in the fluid movement of a professional athlete he was out of his seat, one hand lifting the bag and the other pulling her off the deck.

Standing, she caught her breath and looked up into his eyes. He looked as if he had played basketball when he was younger.

"I think I might have sprained my ankle," she said. She remembered earlier thinking that it was a shame that such a big man had to be folded into one of the cramped second class seats. "There's an empty seat up in first, if you help me back, you can have it."

"No problem." He looped an arm behind her legs and hefted her off the deck.

"I didn't mean you had to carry me."

"It's the best way." He turned sideways and sidestepped up the aisle toward first class. She pushed the curtain aside as he carried her through.

"Are you all right?" the prime minister said as they passed his seat.

"Sprained my ankle."

"Ouch," he said, and she smiled down at him.

"What happened?" Broxton said, when he looked up and saw her in the arms of the tall man.

"Sprained my ankle," she said again, and Broxton scooted over to the window seat as the big man gently put her down in the seat he'd vacated.

"You can take the seat over there." She pointed to an empty seat in the second row. He nodded, went forward and took the seat.

She buckled up, then wiggled her ankle.

"How is it?" Broxton asked.

"Not sprained, just twisted. It'll be okay," she said.

"That's good," he said. He was holding onto both a tight smile and the ring.

"Squeeze it any tighter and you'll break it," she said. Damn, she thought, that came out wrong. She was always putting her foot in her mouth.

He lowered his eyes to the ring, relaxed the tight expression and slipped it back into his pocket. She wondered if it had a case. "You're right," he said, looking up and grinning.

"I'm sorry," she said, "I didn't mean it the way it sounded. My mouth is always getting me in trouble."

"That what happened to your eye?" he asked.

That got her attention and she bored into his eyes looking for a trace of sarcasm, but found none. She decided to be honest. "Yes," she said.

"The cop husband do that?"

"Yes," she said. It had been over a week ago and she really thought the makeup covered it.

"He do it often?"

"Not so often." She raised a finger to touch the bruise. She winced and she saw that he noticed.

"Once is too often," he said.

"I'm handling it," she said.

"You should leave," he said. "They never change."

She broke away from his stare and looked beyond him, out the window. They were flying smoothly now, but the ocean seemed unnaturally close. She saw a sailboat below and wondered what they thought of the big jet flying overhead, so low and so slow.

"He'll change," she said, still looking out the window, but she felt his eyes even as she tried to avoid them.

"How long have you been waiting?" he asked.

"Twelve years," she answered without hesitation. Everyone on the aircraft was worrying about whether or not they were going to live or die this day, including the man sitting next to her, but he was also concerned about her.

"You could leave," he said, voice barely above a whisper.

"And go where?" she said.

"You're working. You have a glamorous job. You must have some self esteem left."

"I have a lot." She turned toward him, angry now.

"Then you could leave," he repeated.

She bit off her answer by biting into her lower lip. He was right, she had a chance, if only she could be brave enough to take it.

"What is it?" he asked.

"I speak Spanish," she said. "My mother is Mexican."

"And?"

"I have this friend, she works for Iberia, you know, the Spanish Airline. She said I could get on there."

"But?"

"It'd mean moving to Madrid and starting over. No seniority. Less pay."

"Do it," he said.

"I'm thirty-six, three more years and I'll have my twenty in. It would be insane. It wouldn't just mean less money, it'd be a lot less."

"How much do you get to keep now?"

That stopped her. How did he know that Earl took all her money, leaving her only a small allowance for food and clothes? It was one of his ways of keeping his fist wrapped around her.

"Take the Iberia job."

She looked back into his steady eyes. He didn't understand. "He'd never let me," she said. "He'll come after me."

"Maybe, but I doubt it. They get off on the control. If you don't go back, he'll most likely look for someone else to dominate."

"You make it sound so easy."

"It usually is." His hands were folded in his lap. She noticed that his finger tips were white. He was worried, too, but he did a good job of covering it up.

"Do you have a picture of your girl?" She wanted to take his mind off his fear and take the conversation away from her problems with Earl.

"I do," he said, and she couldn't help but notice how his blue eyes glowed as he reached toward his back pocket for a wallet. It was a short struggle because the tight fitting Levi's didn't want to yield the wallet. He had to shift in the seat in order to get his fingers in the hip pocket and she saw a quick grimace as he pulled it out. From the faded condition of the jeans she'd guessed that he'd had them a long time, and from the way they fit she guessed that he'd been a few pounds lighter when he bought them.

"My husband never carries anything in his back pocket." She didn't know why she said it. She was thinking about the bulge the wallet must have made when he was standing and for some reason she'd pictured Earl standing fully dressed in front of the full length mirror in their bedroom, admiring himself, running his hand over his muscular body, touching his chest, his stomach, his ass.

"Why not?" Broxton asked.

"He's proud of the way he looks. He doesn't like to break up the lines."

"Weightlifter?"

"How'd you guess?"

"Weightlifters like to show off."

"He doesn't lift for bulk, he lifts for strength," she said. For some reason she felt like she had to defend him. "He does all kinds of sports."

"Really?"

"Sure, he hunts."

"That figures," Broxton said.

"He goes river rafting every chance he gets."

"Really? I wouldn't have guessed it."

"He's on a softball team, they came in second place last year. He bicycles, runs and he swims everyday," She was rambling and she knew it.

"All right, he's into more than body building and killing innocent animals. I still don't like him."

"You don't know him." Why was she still defending him.

"He beats his wife, I don't need to know anymore."

"How about that picture," she said. Now she really wanted the conversation turned away from her and Earl.

"Here." He handed her the open wallet. "It's my favorite picture of her."

Maria looked at the picture. It was a black and white photo. The girl staring at her from inside the plastic credit card holder was stunning. She had a model perfect face, not a blemish, a perfect roman nose, perfect wide set eyes, gray in the photo, but she guessed they were blue, perfect blond hair flowing past her shoulders, perfect high cheekbones, perfect chin, perfect woman, perfect girl. "What color are her eyes?" Maria asked.

"Blue," Broxton said.

"Perfect," Maria said.

"She sure is," he said.

"She looks happy here."

"It was taken on the day the happiness came back. She went right down to the studio at the mall, no makeup, no fancy hairdo. She wanted her happiness recorded forever, just her happiness, nothing else."

"Where'd it go, the happiness?" Maria asked.

"A drunk driver took it away. She was fifteen and riding in the back seat. That's why she survived."

"Who was in front?"

"Our mothers. Hers and mine. Their lives were snuffed out in an instant."

"I'm sorry," Maria said.

"It killed something inside of her, her father too. For over a year they went through the motions of living. Then finally Warren, her father, started to come out of it, but Dani was lost to all of us. I suppose I could have helped, she was my best friend, but I was suffering, too. When we started living again, Dani was a recluse. She failed her sophomore year in high school and had to be sent back a grade and we just sort of lost touch.

"Warren tried everything—counseling, doctors, shrinks—nothing seemed to help. So he threw himself into his business, built it up, sold it and bought property in the booming Southern California market. He made a fortune, but he still lived next door, in a fifty-year-old home on the edge of the barrio.

"Then it happened. It was Dani's eighteenth

birthday and she was as glum as ever. I hadn't seen her in a while, but I knew what day it was so I went to the pet store and bought a collie puppy. I took it next door after dinner. That little pup took one look at her, jumped in her lap, shook his little body like he'd just come in from the ocean and promptly pissed.

"Warren and I watched in dumb amazement. Then Dani smiled, then she laughed and then the light came back into her eyes. It took three years and a collie puppy.

"After that she threw herself into school. She majored in French, minored in business and studied Spanish and Japanese in her spare time. She managed her father's successful Senate campaign before going into business and making a fortune in her own right."

"Senate campaign, as in the United States Senate?" Maria asked. She wanted to ask more about Dani, because something about her picture was familiar. She knew her from somewhere, but she couldn't put her finger on it.

"Yeah, the U.S. Senate. He went in 1980, a Democrat that squeaked through the Reagan landslide. One of the promises he made during his campaign was that he wouldn't be a career politician. One term only, he promised. He turned control of his real estate empire over to Dani and spent six years on the business of the United States. Nobody could buy him, lobbyists were afraid of him, everybody respected him, because he didn't take a dime. He had no campaign committee to feed, no exploratory committee for higher office to staff, no image to improve. When his six years were up he quit as one of the richest men in America."

"How'd he do that?"

"While he was in office Dani sold all of his real

estate and invested in some computer and software companies. Apple, IBM and Microsoft. She made him wealthy, but in his mind he's still a poor boy from the wrong side of the tracks. He'll never be anything but an aw shucks kind of guy. He couldn't get used to all the money, so when the Democrats finally regained the White House and the President called, Warren went back into government. Three years later he had a heart attack. The doctors said rest, at least a year. But Warren couldn't just lay about and do nothing. The president suggested an ambassadorship, somewhere where he could take it easy but still make a difference. Trinidad was the place. Warren gets a year's rest with an easy job, then he'll probably go back and help the president again."

"Wow, and that's your girl's father?"

"That's him."

They were quiet for awhile, and she took the time to study the other passengers, some staring blankly forward, some lost in their own thoughts, some conversing softly, trying to forget that the plane was flying low and slow. She thought of Rick Nelson and wondered what it was like for him just before his plane plowed into that dark Midwestern ground. She imagined his pure sweet voice singing *Hello, Mary Lou*. She started singing, just above her breath. "Believe me girl, I just had no choice, wild horses couldn't make me stay away, it's all I had to see for me to say…"

"Hey, hey, hey. Hello Mary Lou, goodbye heart," he softly sang in answer.

"I'm embarrassed," she said.

"I was thinking of Buddy Holly and *Peggy Sue*," he said.

The plane lurched downward and she grabbed his

hand without thinking. He felt good and kind and strong and she felt that nothing could go wrong just so long as she held on to him.

"It's all right," the captain's voice said. "We're coming into Port of Spain. We should be on the ground in about fifteen minutes."

Maria heard the landing gear coming down. It locked into place with a slam that sounded like another explosion and the plane jerked to the right again. The wing tipped, straining for the ground below. Someone screamed and Maria knew it wasn't all right. Then the giant aircraft righted itself and she prayed they had it under control.

And for a few seconds they did. They were flying straight up, landing gear down. She let out a long sigh, and started to say that it looked like they were going to make it, when normal sound was erased by the tearing sound of metal. The sound rocketed through the plane, stealing the hopes and draining the dreams of all on board. Now the left wing tipped toward the ground and the nose arched upward for a second, then rocked to the left, following the wing. They were in an earthward bank, making a downward left turn.

She grabbed onto the hand that was still there and looked past the man sitting next to her and out the window, and all she saw was blue. But it wasn't the blue of the cloud filled tropical sky, it was the blue of the ocean below.

The plane banked steeper into the turn. Maria was afraid that they were going to go into a spin, but they gradually eased out of the bank. She sighed again when the view turned from ocean back into sky and they were flying level once more.

"Oh no," she whimpered.

"What?" Broxton said, and he turned to look too. "Shit," he added.

She didn't say anything, there was nothing to say. They were flying over Chaguaramas Bay, barely skimming over the tall masts of the sailing yachts anchored there. She saw the upturned faces on the boats below, saw the rolling waves as the plane blew out of the bay toward Casper Grande Island, level now, but still turning. She saw the Fantasy Island Resort on Casper Grande and she shivered, because she wasn't looking down. A woman behind her screamed as the plane whisked by the tall trees. Then they were headed back out to sea, away from Trinidad, the ocean only feet below.

For fifteen minutes that seemed like forever, they flew low over the ocean as the plane made a wide turn, back toward Port of Spain. Maria held tightly to Broxton's hand and stole a quick look around.

The elderly couple in the center seats across from them were locked in an embrace. The woman in the aisle seat behind was frantically writing in a pocket diary. Probably a goodbye to someone she loves, Maria thought, and for a second she thought about writing her mother a quick note. Just to say she loved her. She hadn't said it in so long.

But she dropped the thought as the blue ocean disappeared and the green tropical jungle of the Caroni Swamp filled the window. They were skimming the trees and Maria knew they weren't going to make it. She wondered what lived in the vast swamp below.

"Bend down and grab your socks!" the captain's voice screamed over the speaker system. "It might be a rough landing."

"He's going for it," Broxton said.

"Good for him," Maria said, but her thoughts were filled with gators and crocks and she wondered if sharks wouldn't have been quicker.

Then she felt the plane crash into the ground with a shotgun sound. They seemed to be sliding out of control. She wanted to cry out, to scream at the cruel death only instants away. Then she realized they were rolling to a stop. They hadn't crashed. They were on the runway. They were safe.

Someone started clapping, then someone else on the other side of the cabin clapped an echo back and she felt a blissful peace and uncanny joy take hold of her as she freed her hand from Broxton's and joined the applause that filled the aircraft.

"Ladies and gentlemen," the captain's voice broke out over the speakers. "Welcome to Port of Spain and thank you for your appreciation."

The applause picked up and someone cheered. Then they were all cheering. The door to the cockpit opened and Captain Roger Herra stepped out followed by his copilot and the cheering increased to a deafening crescendo. Then as suddenly as it started, it stopped.

There was no panic. No one screaming, no one pushing, no one fighting to get off. They'd cheated death and they all knew it.

She watched as Broxton flicked open his seatbelt and stood. He stepped over her and bent over and gathered up the contents of the fallen briefcase and filled it. Other passengers were picking up around themselves, standing and stretching, the dangling masks, the only sign that this flight had been any different from any other.

Broxton gave the child a smile and Maria saw the gratitude in the little girl's eyes. He handed the briefcase to her father and received a smile back for his kindness. Then he pulled his carry-on bag from the overhead locker.

"I'm staying at the Hilton," Maria said. "Maybe we could have dinner or something."

"I'd like that," Broxton said. Then he asked her if she needed any help getting off the aircraft. She wiggled her foot. It didn't really hurt very much anymore, but she nodded anyway. A small kind of fib, but she was still shaken up and she wanted to stay with him just a little longer.

Ten minutes later they were inside the terminal. Broxton had an arm around her waist, even though she didn't need any help walking. She was dragging her bag on its trolley. He had his bag slung over his right shoulder. Then he froze. She saw him bite into his lower lip, saw the smile slide off his face, felt the spike that must be knifing through his heart.

She turned to see what he was seeing.

He was staring at a rack of newspapers, studying the front page of the *Trinidad Guardian*, caught by a color picture of a smiling blue-eyed blonde with her arms wrapped around the man from the plane, the prime minister's body guard, Kevin Underfield. For a second she thought the blonde woman resembled the Barbie doll he'd handed back to the little girl. She was smiling up at the man and he was smiling at the camera, like he was the cat that just swallowed the canary. Then she read the headlines.

ARE THERE WEDDING BELLS
IN DANI'S FUTURE?

"Your girl?" she asked.
"My girl," he said.

CHAPTER FOUR

SHERIFF EARL LAWSON HEARD the buzzing of the flies a few seconds before he inhaled the repugnant odors of dried blood and human feces. The nauseating smells filtered through dry and dusty air and assaulted him as surely as the plague of flies that attacked his face, tickling, biting, itching. Frantically he tried to move his hands to brush them away, but couldn't. He shook his head back and forth, but it didn't seem to bother them. He tried to move, but he was frozen in place, wedged in tight or paralyzed. Shivers tingled along his spine, sweat fed the flies on his neck and face.

He opened his eyes and was swallowed by the darkness. He strained to see, but flies attacked his open eyes and he forced them shut in an effort to keep them out. He fought a rising urge to scream. He squeezed his eyes into slits, trying in vain to see some light. Nothing but flies and more flies. The constant buzzing, combined with the roasting heat, made him feel like he was in an oven being baked alive, the pig in the pit, buried for the luau, flies on his face instead of an apple in the mouth.

He tried to speak, to call out, but couldn't. Something was wrapped around his face, wrapped around the back of his neck, wrapped around his mouth. He forced his tongue between his lips and touched something sticky. Tape. His mouth was taped shut.

He struggled to bring a hand up, to pull it off, but his arms were frozen behind his back. He moved his wrists. Handcuffs. He tried to roll over, to bury his face into whatever he was laying on, anything to keep the flies off. They were at his nostrils. He felt one crawling in and he snorted it out, but it came right back, it or another, there seemed to be thousands. Terror gripped him. They were going to flood up his nasal passages, he was going to drown in flies.

No, the thought screamed at him, no, not like this. He fought for control, fought against the rising panic, fought the fear, fought the terror, and like a scalded snake, he bucked his body and managed to flop onto his side. That chased the flies away from his face and gave him the renewed energy for another jerk and twist. Then he was on his stomach, face against an oily, dusty carpet. In an instant the flies were back, but with his face pressed into the carpet they couldn't get up his nose or into his eyes, but they were at his ears and on the back of his neck, crawling under his shirt.

Where was he? What happened? What went wrong?

Then he remembered the briefcase and shooting Johnny Lee Tyler. Somebody smacked him in the back of the head. Kids must have had an accomplice. How could he have been so stupid? There must have been two cars, of course. Darren's father, it had to be.

He wondered if they got Jackson, too. They must have, otherwise he'd be home counting the cash. They must have come in that garage quiet and careful. Must have snuck up behind them. One clobbered Jackson and the other got him. He tried to slow his breathing, tried to think. There had to be a way out. He wondered again where he was and how long he'd been unconscious.

His legs weren't straight. Before he'd rolled over they were bent at his side, now they were bent unnaturally and uncomfortably against something, a roof of some kind. He tried to straighten them, but they were wedged firmly against whatever he was encased in. He thought of a coffin and shuddered, but it couldn't be, not with the flies. Besides, it was too big.

He heard the sound of an engine starting. Then he felt movement. All of a sudden he knew where he was. The car hit a bump or went down a curb, then accelerated, throwing him toward the back of the trunk and scattering the flies. He smacked into something warm. Not warm like human warm, but not cold like stone either. Something in between. A dead man turning cold.

Johnny Lee Tyler, Darren or Jackson. He wondered who, and he shivered, despite the heat. Maybe all of them were in here with him. Maybe one of them was alive, like him. Maybe Jackson. Between the two of them they could get out of anything. He moaned through the tape, a mournful sound, like a poisoned dog.

No answer.

He moaned again, louder.

Still no answer. Whoever was in the trunk with him was dead. He tried to think. The man next to him was dead, and he wasn't. That was fact. Again he tried moving his legs, but still he couldn't. They were tied together. Whoever taped, cuffed and bound him obviously wanted him alive. That was a good sign. You didn't go to that much trouble with a man if you wanted him dead. He wondered what they wanted with him, what they'd ask of him.

But he didn't wonder about what he'd do for them, because he knew the answer. Anything.

Please, God, let me make it.

A spasm of cold fear shot through him as he sucked hot air in through his nose. The dry air brought along other smells besides the coppery scent of blood and the revolting smell of shit — grease, oil, dust and death. He fought the rising bile. To vomit now was to die. He thought about death for a second and he wanted to scream and rage, but he was trussed up tighter than a rodeo calf.

Please, God, please.

The car accelerated, swerved, fishtailed and he tasted the rising dust as it swirled around in the trunk. He felt something slam into the back of his head and he wanted to cry out, because he was butting heads with a dead man.

Please, God, please.

Then the car was on the pavement and going fast.

It made another hard right and he pulled his head to the side to avoid smacking into the body again, and he banged his head into something harder, something made of metal, like a jack or a tire iron.

"Shit," he murmured through the tape, angry now, and ashamed. He tried to think, but the shame rode over rational thought. He was Earl Lawson. Big Earl Lawson. Sheriff, sportsman, strong as an ox, tough as they come, hale and hearty, leader of men, ex marine, and now a coward. They'd broken him in seconds. All it took was a few flies, a dead man and a trunk and he was whimpering like a woman, praying to a god he didn't believe in.

Please, God, please.

He felt sick. They hadn't put a hand on him and he was a broken man, ready to fall on his knees the minute he met his tormentors, ready to beg for his life. No, that's not the way it was going to be. If he was going to die, he'd go like a man, head up, proud. He was Big Earl Lawson, sheriff, marine, hunter.

No more praying, he told himself, grabbing his fear with a mental fist and squeezing it away. He bit into his tongue and curled his fingers into tight fists. The fear gone now, all he had left was anger, all he had to do was endure. Sooner or later the car would stop and sooner or later he'd get his chance. Nobody fucked with Earl Lawson. He felt an erection building. It happened every time he sighted in on an animal, every time he pulled the trigger, every time he dealt death. It was getting hard. It was starting to throb. He was going to get even. Oh yeah, somebody was going to die.

The car came to a skidding stop, throwing him against the dead man. The scraping sound of the screeching tires echoed through the trunk sending icicles shivering up his spine, but he met the cold terror with hot fury, clenching his teeth and firming his resolve. The car banked quickly right and his head smacked into the hard metal of the jack. He blacked out again.

When he came to he was bent over a round bar or tube, like a dead outlaw slung over a horse. Hands hanging down one side, feet over the other. He heard the rushing of the river and he knew where he was even before he opened his eyes. His hands were flopping below his head, swaying in the brisk breeze. His feet were on the other side of the fence, the safe side. His legs were bound together at the ankles, the ropes were tight, cutting off the flow of blood to his feet. Eyes wide, looking down, he saw the Guadeloupe River. He was just above the rapids.

The afternoon sun was blazing overhead, his view was excellent. He grabbed a breath through his mouth, the tape was gone. He felt the blood rushing to his head. He tried to move his hands. They were heavy, he flexed his fingers, felt the pain. The back of his head was throbbing, his erection was gone. The fence rail was digging into his stomach.

He reached behind himself, stretched out his right arm and wrapped his fingers around the lower rail. He was about to pull himself up when he felt a hand on his leg. Someone was untying the ropes. He felt the fumbling fingers between his legs. He wanted to shout, to tell the man to pull him up first, worry about the ropes after he was on the bridge.

Relief flooded through his legs the instant the ropes came off. "Thank you," he called out as he pulled himself up toward the rail.

"Sorry, Earl," Jackson said. Earl felt his friend's strong hands grab him by the ankles and lift his legs into the air and over the rail. He held on to the lower rail as his legs came arcing over, bound for the river below. He screamed against the jerking pain that shot through his right arm, but he managed to hold on with that lone hand, dangling above the river, face even with the concrete bridge and his deputy's feet.

"Jackson!" Earl cried out, grabbing onto the rail with his other hand.

"I am mighty sorry about this, Earl. I truly am, but sometimes things just get out of control."

"I thought you were dead," Earl said, looking up and into Jackson's eyes.

"The river is going to kill you," Jackson said. He leaned over the rail and smiled down at Earl. "Sorry, buddy."

"Jackson, we're friends," Earl shouted up to be heard above the river.

"Yeah, Earl, we were, but the cash sort of got in the way."

"There's plenty for us both. There always has been."

Jackson ignored him and leaned lower over the rail. For a second Earl thought he was going to pull him up, but instead he grabbed onto his right hand and tried to pry it loose. That was a mistake. He should have stepped on the fingers, like they do in the movies, but he didn't and that gave Earl his chance. Rattlesnake quick he whipped his left arm over and grabbed Jackson around the wrist. The weight of his body pulled Jackson into the fence, slamming his stomach against the bar as he flayed out with his free hand and grabbed onto it for support.

"Pull me up," Earl said.

"No!" Jackson clenched his abdominals against the rail to support himself.

"Come on, Jackson," Earl said. His erection was

returning.

"You're going," Jackson said, and now that he had his balance he was able to let go with his free hand and he grabbed downward, reaching for Earl's hand. He was ten years younger than Earl and had the rippling muscles of an athlete, but Earl was scared strong. The more Jackson tried to free Earl's fingers from his wrist the tighter Earl squeezed.

"I can't hold on much longer. Pull me up or we both go." He was hard now, throbbing and ready.

"No," Jackson said.

"Fuck you!" Earl yelled, letting loose his anger. He let go of the hand that was holding on to the rail and grabbed onto Jackson's dangling arm and now all of his weight was pulling Jackson downward. It was too much, and in the instant it took Jackson to figure out what had happened it was too late. He slid off the rail, tumbling after Earl, and together they fell toward the river below.

"Son of a bitch!" Earl yelled as they fell. He felt Jackson's body jerk, and he let go of his arm just as they hit the water, grabbing a great breath as he slid into it feet first. The cold wet chilled him, body and soul, as he sank like a missile to the bottom, feet digging through the moving silt and into the soft mud. The adrenaline sparking and slicing through his body killed the river cold as he pushed and swam toward the surface. But the rushing river had a mind of his own, dragging him away from the spot where he'd plunged into the water and toward the rapids.

The more he struggled toward the surface the more the river struggled to keep him below, pulling him along, like a leaf on the breeze. His heart was thumping, his lungs were aching. There was a jackhammer pounding in his chest, demanding oxygen. The dark wet of the river engulfed him.

The river hit a bend and something struck him as he made the turn. He couldn't hold out much longer. The thing hit him again. A log, his mind screamed. A floating log. A log floating on the surface. He was close, so close. He couldn't quit now. He wouldn't quit now.

He surfaced, grabbed a quick breath and went under again. If only he could grab onto the log. He could maybe ride it through the rapids. Maybe. He bumped it again and threw an arm around it. It sank some as he pulled on it, but it allowed him to get his head out of the water again, and he grabbed another breath.

Not far now, rapids and rocks.

He knew his chances weren't good. He'd seen what the rapids could do to a man, been present at more then one autopsy. The river broke your bones, lacerated your skin, filled your lungs, then it beat you raw and spit out a thing in the calm below that didn't look human.

And people came from miles around to ride the rapids. They called it a challenge, a thrill. They called it fun. And Earl was one of them. He loved riding the river. Knew its every twist and turn. He'd done it dozens of times. But always in a raft, and never solo.

The first dangerous turn was coming up. There was a large group of rocks to the right, on the outside of the turn, and a smaller cluster in the center of the river. You could either take the turn on the left, close to the bank or take the more dangerous route, between the rocks. He'd done it both ways and preferred to go between the two groups of rocks, because it left you in a better position for the next group. But he was without a raft and there was nobody on the river except him and the log, so he wrapped his arm around it and frantically kicked to the left.

It was a cloudless sky and the sunlight reflecting off the rushing water made the rocks ahead hard to see, but he sensed he was heading right for them. He kicked himself around the log and positioned it between himself and the hazard ahead. The log hit the rocks first, cushioning the collision, and that surprised him, but he held onto it until they were through the narrow gap.

Then for a few seconds it would be smooth, then came the worst or the most challenging part, depending on your point of view. He tried to pull himself up on the log, but it wasn't buoyant enough, and it had more give than a log should have. He turned away from the rocks and rapids up ahead and stole a quick look at it.

And screamed.

The log had a face.

It was Loomis, eyes stone wide in death. He let go of the body, flaying the water and fighting for air. Then something smacked into him. He grabbed onto it, and screamed again. This log had a face, too. But the need for survival overcame his terror and he grabbed onto Jackson's limp body and sucked in a huge lungful of air.

Then he was in it. The river churning and boiling all around him. He fought for air, fought to stay afloat and fought through the gaps, using Jackson's body as a cushion against the rocks. He did it without thinking, his will to survive stronger than the revulsion of hanging on to the dead man.

And even with the body he was still taking a beating. He had to get out of the river. Several homes lined the riverbank at various places, but yelling for help was out of the question. He was in the river canyon twenty feet below. No one would hear.

He tried to form a mental picture of what lay ahead. Not the rapids and the rocks, he knew those, but the places on the side that he might be able to get to, places out of the river rush. There was one, not far ahead, sort of a side pool, blocked by a huge rock that rose from the river. He'd actually seen fishermen in it as he'd rushed by with Jackson in the past.

If he missed the pool there was a section of the river after the next group of rocks that had several overhanging branches on both sides of the river. He remembered having to duck to keep his head as he and Jackson had rafted under them.

He started to make his way to the right as the river rounded another bend. If he could stay far enough to the right, but not so far that he smashed into the giant rock. If he could summon enough strength for a few good kicks, and if his timing was spot on, he might be able to swim into the pool.

It was coming up faster then he anticipated and he was too far to the right. He was going to crash into the giant rock. Frantically he pushed Jackson in front of him, using the body as a shield, as the raging river threw them toward the rock. The dead body careened into the it and he smashed into the dead body. He heard bones crunching and cracking as he lost hold of Jackson. The river picked him up and flung him sideways. He hit the rock back first and slid along it, clawing and scratching for a hold. Then he was past the rock and he kicked and swam for the hole into the pool, but the river was too fast and he didn't have the strength.

He sucked in a lungful of air as the river drew him

under. Now he was going down the river without any protection and he was only halfway through this group of rapids. If he made it through them, he would have nothing but rushing river for a few hundred yards. He'd be able to grab onto the overhanging branches by the riverbank. Then he was in it again, swimming and dodging, holding his breath, lungs bursting, adrenaline flowing. His body took over, it was all reflex now. His experience and memory of the river, its twists, turns, rocks and hazards, all buried in the subconscious that took over. Sheriff Earl Lawson was only along for the ride, the animal within was running the show.

He was an eel, sliding through a narrow passage, then he was a great fish, powerfully swimming toward the next opening in the rocks where he became an eel again. A few times his animal judgment was off and he'd scrape along a rock as he struggled through a slim opening, and once he smashed into a smooth shaped boulder his animal self didn't remember. But he managed to keep his breath, despite the crash, and then he was through it, floating down the rushing river, headed for the next group of rapids.

He fought the pulling river as he pulled in air and he swam toward the side. The next group of rapids would be the last. If he didn't make it this time he was history. He knew it and the animal within knew it. Just as he thought it was all over he saw an overhanging branch within his reach. He gave it his last and his best effort as he thrust his arms out of the water and grabbed onto it.

He didn't know how long he'd been hanging onto the branch, a few seconds or a few minutes, but he had to do something. His arms were straining, he was still in the water from the waist down, and the river was sapping what little strength he had left. He tried to pull himself up and he managed to almost chin himself, holding his eyes level with the branch, knees in the river, stomach muscles screaming as he struggled to get out of the water, but he couldn't do it and he sagged back down. He didn't have the energy or the strength left to pull himself up onto the branch.

The water was rushing around him, dragging him, tugging on him, calling him. He was holding on, breathing like a machine, in and out, taking in vital oxygen for one last try, and then it dawned on him that he'd never be able to pull himself up on that branch, but it wasn't the only way out, there was another way, a simpler way. All he had to do was inch his hands along the branch toward the riverbank.

The wet cold cut through to the bone, the driving river was pulling at his heavy legs, his arms were screaming, his hands aching and his fingers were numb. He was about used up. He was fighting just to hold on. He was afraid if he let a hand go he'd fall back in the river, but he knew that if he didn't move quickly he'd fall back in anyway, and the river would finish him, so he slid first one hand, then the next toward the riverbank.

It was slow going, but he was making progress. He was getting out of the river. Then he couldn't move anymore, something was holding him back. He started to panic, but fought it away. Then he realized what it was. His feet had hit bottom. He was safe. He'd made it. Soloed halfway through the rapids, with a dead body for a raft.

He stumbled out of the water, grabbing onto the tree's root system for support. He was out of the water. Now he only had a twenty foot embankment to claw his way up. He thought about Maria. He thought about the money. And he thought about climbing that cliff. Not so high. Not so hard.

He wormed his way around the tree and started to climb, digging his damaged hands into the soft earth, pulling on small branches, clutching onto small stones, grabbing any and every purchase he could. He moved slowly and deliberately. He didn't want to fall back into the river.

CHAPTER FIVE

"YOU WANT TO HANG AROUND or do you want to get out of here?" Broxton asked, coming up behind Maria. His voice cracked with the words. He sounded like a little boy fighting tears, and her heart went out to him.

"The quicker I'm gone, the better, but I'm the senior flight attendant. I should stay till they release us." She regretted the words as soon as they'd left her lips, but she really couldn't leave. Her life had been split between Earl and the airline and the airline had been the better half. Still Broxton was a man in pain and after their experience on the plane she felt a certain kinship with him. She wished there was something she could do.

"I understand," Broxton said, with sagging shoulders.

He was looking down, at the floor, and she imagined that he was feeling twice rejected. She wanted to fold her arms around him and hug him into her like she would a lost child. She wanted to tell him everything was going to be all right. There were other women out there, she wanted to say, and someday soon he'd meet one and then the heartache would be gone. Instead she said, "I'm ready to go, if you are. I just have to make a quick phone call." She had to call Earl, but she shivered with the thought that it wasn't going to be the kind of call he was expecting.

"But you said."

"I think the airline can probably get by without me right now. They probably won't even notice I'm gone," she said.

"I have baggage, but I imagine I can get it tomorrow or the next day," he said. Then he followed her toward the phones.

"I'm sorry about your girl." They were at the phones.

"Thanks," he said. He turned and faced her for a second with mist covered eyes. The pain there was real and it looked like it cut deep.

"I'll make the call from the hotel," she said. Earl could wait. "Are you going to be okay?" she asked as they made their way to the street.

"Sure," he said. Then he raised his hand for a taxi.

A rusty Toyota pulled up to the curb. The car was fifteen years old, but the tires were new. "You want a taxi?" the driver said. His rich baritone and dark ebony skin conspired to hide his age, but the gray hair and wrinkled hands gave it away. He was old and he reminded Maria of her own father.

"Yes, to the Hilton Hotel," Broxton said.

"I'm your man," the driver said with a smile in his voice.

He opened his door and started to step out of the car, but she stopped him, saying, "That's okay, we don't have any baggage."

"Makes it easy on these old bones," he said. Broxton opened the front door and put his carry-on bag on the front seat. Maria unclipped her small bag from the trolley and laid it next to his. Then they climbed into the back.

"Dependable Ted, at your service." The driver turned and handed her a card. "You need a taxi, anytime, day or night, you call me, hear? I'm dependable, like my name, the name on the card, Dependable Ted."

"I'll be sure to do that." Maria handed his card to Broxton.

"Now you sit back and enjoy the ride. I might not be the fastest taxi in Trinidad, but I'm the most dependable." Broxton laughed for a second, then he turned glum. On the plane he seemed bulldog-strong, now he was puppy-dog meek. She needed to get his mind off that girl.

"Very lush here," she said, making conversation as the taxi started winding its way along the access road, heading for the highway that would take them into Port of Spain, about a half hour away.

"Your first time in the tropics?" Broxton asked her.

"This is my third flight out of Miami, she said, so I guess you could say I'm new to the tropics, if you don't count Texas. You?" He chuckled and she took that as a positive sign.

"I spent a year in Mexico," he said, slipping the

driver's card into his shirt pocket.

"Looking for drug smugglers?" she asked.

"Hardly. All I do is process the paperwork. The most exciting thing that ever happens to me is when the computer crashes. Even that scares me."

"Then why did they pick you to protect the prime minister?"

"Because of who my future father-in-law is, or rather who I thought my father-in-law was going to be."

"I can't believe that," she said with a smile in her voice.

"It's true," he said. "I'm sort of like an analyst. They give me the data and I try to put it all together in my trusty laptop. Some days I never see the outside.

"That explains why you can live a year in Mexico and still be so white," she said.

He laughed, and she felt like she was definitely making progress.

"*Hablas Español*," she said, using the familiar form.

"*Claro*," he answered.

"Most Americans don't bother. They expect us to learn their language."

"Us," he said. "You have a slight Mexican accent, but you're American."

"How can you tell?"

"It's in the way you walk and talk. Like you're sure of yourself. Like you're an American."

"I don't understand."

"Americans stand out, wherever we go. We can't help it. Black, white, red or yellow, we're all the same when you start comparing us with the rest of the world."

"I don't know if I can believe that," she said.

"I'll give you an example. Years ago, when I was a child, I was in Nairobi with my parents. It was the first anniversary of the death of Jomo Kenyatta. People had walked for miles to pay homage to the great man at a rally in this huge park in the center of the city. They were all black and as they passed my dad would say '*Jambo*, Hello,' and they'd say *Jambo* back, and smile at us. But when this one man approached, my dad said, 'Hello,' and he said, 'Hello,' back. He asked where we were from and my dad told him Long Beach, California, and he answered back by saying he was from Portland. He was as black as everybody else, but he was different. He was an American. My dad knew it and so did everybody else."

She thought about what he said. He didn't sound like a racist or a nationalist, he was just telling the truth, and truth was truth, even if it wasn't politically correct. Then she asked, "How about the Europeans? Do we look different from them too?"

"Especially them," he said, laughing. "You should see us blundering around in their countries trying to communicate. When they don't understand we just talk louder, till eventually we're almost shouting."

"Your girl, the one in the paper, she's Danielle Street, the literary agent, isn't she?" She didn't want to put the subject back onto something that would hurt him, but she had to know.

"You're a novelist?" Broxton asked. She saw the way his eyebrows arched and the way he bit into his lower lip. This wasn't a pleasant subject for him.

"I wanted to be once. I sent my manuscript off to an agent in Los Angeles, and shortly after it was rejected I received a letter from Ms. Street in New York."

"And?" Broxton said. She had a feeling that he knew what was coming next.

"The letter said that she was told by another agent that I had a book worth publishing. The other agent was unable to take on any new clients, but felt that my work was worthy enough to mention to the Street Agency and would I please send her a copy of the manuscript right away."

"Which of course you did," Broxton said.

"Of course," she said, meeting his eyes.

"And," Broxton said again. His hands were folded in his lap. The fingertips were white. He didn't want to be talking about this.

"She recommended an editorial service," Maria said.

"And for only four or five thousand dollars they could make your manuscript publishable," he said.

"Something like that," she said. "But there was no way Earl ever would have let me have the money."

"Earl doesn't sound like a man I'd like, but it's probably a good thing you didn't get the money."

"Rip off, huh?"

"Usually." Broxton nodded. "The old Dani never met a manuscript that five thousand in her pocket couldn't fix. She owned the editing company."

"Who did the actual work?"

"College kids mostly. She paid them peanuts. Usually the manuscripts never went anywhere, however once in a while one got published."

"How'd she get my name?"

"She paid the secretaries in the other agencies for a list of all their rejections."

"That's horrible," Maria said.

"She was ruthless," Broxton said.

"But what about Jack Priest? She's his agent, isn't

she? I see his books all over."

"Oh she's had her successes. She's sharp. When she saw a book with potential she ran with it. She's gotten several six figure advances."

"It makes it hard for the person starting out. If someone with a reputation like Danielle Street's rips off new authors, who doesn't?"

"Lots don't. In fact I'll bet most don't. Dani was just hungry."

"Was?"

"She sold the agency. Now she just lives the life of luxury."

* * *

The taxi turned onto the highway and Broxton noticed that the driver kept to the slow lane. Cars and trucks of all ages and sizes flew by them, all in a hurry, junkyard fugitives racing along with cars fresh off the showroom floor. Speed tempered by chaos seemed to be the order of the day, and if Trinidad was governed by any law, it certainly didn't apply to the highway, Broxton thought. Everybody was in a hurry to get somewhere. Everybody wanted to pass the car in front and nobody wanted to be passed.

"Do they always drive like this?" Maria asked the taxi driver.

"Mostly, except me and a few others that have lived long enough to develop common sense. And of course the man that's been following us since the airport."

Broxton turned and looked through the back window. "The green BMW? How can you be sure he's following us?"

"We're in Trinidad. Look how people drive here. That's a new sporty car. How come he doesn't pass?"

"If he's following us, he's following the wrong people, I've got nothing to hide," Broxton said.

"I don't either," Maria said.

"So should I ignore him or lose him?" the driver asked.

"You could lose him? In this?" Broxton said.

"Not if we were racing to the Hilton, no, but I can lose him."

"I'd like to see that," Broxton said.

"So you shall," the driver said, and he settled back and continued on down the highway. "I'm going to pass Port of Spain and go out toward Chaguaramas where all the foreign boats anchor, so take it easy and enjoy the ride."

Broxton and Maria sat back and looked out the windows, the desire for conversation killed by the car following. The scenery flashing by was covered in green and dotted with billboards bearing familiar names—KFC, Pizza hut, McDonald's—and although the billboards were in English, the houses on the side of the road reminded Broxton more of Mexico than America. There were a lot of poor people in Trinidad, and Broxton wondered why he hadn't thought about it before. When he'd first been given the assignment he'd imagined Trinidad as a sort of south seas tropical isle. Tropical it was, but Trinidad was firmly planted in the twentieth century and it looked like poverty was endemic.

"Port of Spain just ahead," Dependable Ted said, slowing down. "We'll be stuck in traffic for ten or fifteen minutes till we pass."

Broxton turned to look behind and couldn't see the BMW.

"He's back there, 'bout ten cars," Ted said. "But not to worry, once we pass the yacht club we be losing him good."

"The city reminds me of Nairobi," Broxton said.

"Why, 'cause we're all black?"

"Maybe, but it's more than that."

"Maybe 'cause we were both colonized by the British."

"That could be," Broxton said.

"We're not all black, you know, 'bout ten percent white and the rest split 'tween African and Indian. That's Indian from India not the American kind."

"I'd never really thought about it," Broxton said.

"But the white people run things," the driver said.

"How's that?" Broxton asked. "Isn't this a democracy? Don't you have elections?"

"We do. The government was African, now it's Indian an' the prime minister's a light skin Indian fellow, but it makes no difference. Once they get elected they think they're white and they start stuffing their pockets."

"That's a shame," Maria said.

"Way it is," the driver said.

"The same all over," Broxton said.

"True, true," the driver said.

Then they were past Port of Spain, the beach still at their left, the sun starting to hang low in the evening sky and the traffic had thinned considerably. Broxton noticed the bars on the windows of the homes that flew by. "It looks like you have a lot of crime."

"Not like you do in most your big American cities. Peoples just over react. Nobody wants somebody breaking into their house."

"A mall," Maria said, looking out at the buildings to their left, between them and the beach.

"We have some malls in Trinidad. Not great big

ones like you do. But they're nice, just the same. And up ahead is the yacht club. We gets a lot of foreign boats in Trinidad."

"We saw some this afternoon," Broxton said, remembering the tall masts he'd seen earlier that seemed to be reaching up from the sea, trying to grab the plane and pull it down.

There was a short bridge up ahead where the road changed from four to two lanes. Cars were putting on the gas. Everybody wanted to pass the slow moving taxi before the bridge. Broxton turned and looked out the back window. Not everybody was trying to pass. The BMW was three cars back, still following. Broxton continued watching as a battered, left-hand-drive American Chevy flew past the car immediately behind them and kept on coming.

"I think he's going to try and pass us, too," Broxton said, his voice rising. He was more than a little surprised that the car wouldn't slow down.

"Can't make it," the driver said, but it made no difference, the car kept coming.

"He's not passing, he's coming in on the left!" Broxton shouted as the car plowed into the left quarter of the taxi, then slammed on its brakes as the taxi lost control. He threw an arm in front of Maria, keeping her pinned to her seat as the taxi spun onto the other side of the road. A pickup truck, coming in the opposite direction, clipped the taxi's rear bumper, tearing it off.

Then they were off the road and spinning through a park toward a soccer game. Children screamed and fled the oncoming taxi and for an instant Broxton thought they were going to roll, but Ted let out a whoop, like an American Indian's war cry, and spun the wheel into the slide, managing to turn the car away from the fleeing children, pumping the brakes all the while, trying to slow the car as they scraped along a huge tree.

Ted screamed again as the car slid by the tree with a soul wrenching sound that shrilled through the evening. The tree slowed the car, but it didn't stop it, and Dependable Ted never stopped working the wheel.

* * *

"Hold on," he yelled from the front seat. Maria looked up and saw what he saw. Another tree, this one, thicker than the last, and it seemed to be charging straight for them as it loomed larger and larger in the front window, a giant, green grizzly, with raking claws on the end of the branches. Claws and jaws, reaching for her, reaching to tear her apart, but at the last instant the roaring rear wheels found purchase in the wet grass. The old Toyota shot forward like a race horse. Ted yelled again, because even though he was heading for the tree, he was back in control.

He spun the wheel to the right, missing the tree, but the branches scraped the side of the car as it headed, like a wild mustang, into a huge mass of green, the very edge of the rain forest. Ted jerked the wheel one last time and stomped on the brakes. The engine died, but the car continued its slide through the lush green vegetation, twice missing trees that would have brought it to a crashing stop, coming softly to rest in an almost anticlimactic absence of sound.

"Sheeit," Dependable Ted said under his breath, but Maria heard.

"Is anybody hurt?" Broxton asked.

"Don't think so," Ted said.

"I'm okay," Maria said, looking out of the car. Seconds ago she'd been on a highway, with cars, houses, stores and people. Now she was surrounded by green—leaves, grass, weeds, bushes and trees. She was in an ancient world, a primitive place, and something deep in her heart told her that man wasn't welcome.

"That car hit us on purpose," Ted said, turning toward them. His smile was gone and there was a glazed look in his dark brown eyes.

"Looked like it," Broxton said, and even as he said it the glaze faded from Dependable Ted's eyes and as they cleared Maria saw anger, bubbling and boiling, raging and ready to burst forth.

"It was an accident," Maria said.

"Wasn't," Ted said, "and somebody is going to pay."

Broxton put his hand to the latch, pulled it and pushed against the door. It creaked and groaned, but it opened. He turned back toward Ted and leaned forward till his face was inches away. "My name's Broxton. Call the American Embassy tomorrow. Tell them I owe you a new car and cab fare. It'll be taken care of." There was something about the way he said it. Low and slow, every syllable clear, even though it was barely a whisper, that told both Ted and Maria that what he said was truth.

"Yes, sir." Ted held his hand out. Broxton shook it.

"Then forget you ever saw me."

"Yes, sir." Ted released Broxton's hand.

"No questions?" Broxton asked.

"You best get going, 'cause I never saw you," the driver said. Then he added, "go straight into the green till you get to the river, ain't far, then turn right and follow it back to the road. Bridge goes under, you come out on the opposite side. It's easy. I used to do it all the time when I was a boy."

"Thanks," Broxton said, and he grabbed both bags, took her by the hand and slipped out of the car, pulling her out after himself. She offered no resistance. He led her around a large teak tree and pulled her further into the tall grass and dense growth. He heard the running water and in seconds he was confronted with a small river that wound from the mountains above down to the sea. Still holding her hand he started to step down the bank.

"Wait," she said.

Broxton stopped.

"Why are we running?"

"I don't know," Broxton said. "Somebody ran us off the road."

"It was an accident," she said again.

"No, someone tried to kill us." Again he was whispering and again she heard truth.

"You can't know that." She was panting and she felt sweat rolling down her back. She wiped an insect off of her face with her free hand and met his eyes.

"I'm an analyst. I'm paid to think and figure the odds, and right now my training tells me that if we don't move we will wind up dead." He was talking fast now, trying to convince her.

"What if you're wrong?" she said.

"What if I'm not?" he said.

"They went in there," she heard a voice say, gravelly and menacing, not friendly.

"You're not," she said, deciding. "Let's go." She felt him tighten his grip. Then he turned back toward the river and started down the bank. The ground was wet, muddy and it smelled. People up in the mountains had been using the river as a dump for too long. The water that should have been fresh and sweet was polluted with litter: plastic bottles, Styrofoam cups, coke cans and other odd bits of trash. The river was taking it all toward the sea.

At the bottom he sloshed through the river, still pulling her along behind. The water was only inches deep, but the mud was tugging at her shoes, threatening to pull them off. The growth was dense and oppressive and she was thankful that he was breaking trail for her. Chills ran up her spine, sliding under the sweat that was running down her back. She was as frightened now as she'd been on the plane. She squeezed his hand tighter as he led her toward the road and safety.

"Shit, I think they're headed back toward the road," the gravel voice from behind said, and Broxton answered her squeeze by gripping her hand even tighter as he picked up his pace through the shallow river, pushing low overhanging branches aside with his other hand.

"Bridge up ahead," Broxton said. "We have to go under."

But when she looked ahead she didn't see a bridge at all, just the highway above the trees and a place where the river vanished into the undergrowth beneath it and he was pulling her steadily toward it.

"No," she said, jerking on his hand and forcing him to stop. "Let's climb up this side."

"That's what they'll expect," Broxton said. "They might even have somebody up there waiting."

"Who?" she asked.

"Don't know and we don't have time to discuss it," he said, then he released her hand and turned toward the spot where the river disappeared under the road. "I hope there's no snakes under there" he said. "I hate snakes."

She shivered. "Me too," she whispered, as he slung the bags over his neck and dropped to a crouch, making his way toward the dense growth.

"Going to have to crawl." He dropped his hands and knees into the water. She watched as he forced himself through the wet and slimy foliage that guarded the area under the bridge, and then she couldn't see him anymore and she was alone. She heard the slight murmuring of people overhead and the sound of a siren off in the distance, but there were no traffic sounds on the highway, no cars whizzing by above. Traffic was stopped. She didn't want to go in there. Maybe she could climb up on this side. There were people there, she'd be safe.

"Hurry up." It was the gravel voice behind her. "Not much farther," it said, and it made her mind up. She dropped to a crawl and scooted through the muck and slime, pushing as much of it away from her face as she could. Her heart was racing, sweat chilled her skin and she felt insects crawling on the back of her neck. She wanted to scream each time her fingers curled into the muck, but she fought it back and pushed forward.

She was closed in by the dark, like a letter in an envelope and she was waiting for somebody to seal her in. Then she felt something else under her hands. The mud and muck had a bottom to it and it was solid. A chill rippled through her as she pulled a hand out of the river. She reached out to her left and shivered when she struck something solid. A wall. She thrust her hand above her head and whimpered when it touched the concrete top.

She was in a drain pipe.

Every ounce and fiber of herself screamed, *Go back*, but she bit into her lower lip, closed her eyes and plunged on ahead. Then she felt sunlight on her eyelids, and when she opened them she saw Broxton. She pushed herself out of the pipe as a great wave of relief flooded through her.

But as quickly as it came, it went, when she saw she had nothing to be relieved about. They'd gone only halfway. They were under the highway, between the lanes. There was another drain pipe on the other side. She was going to have to do it all again. She didn't know if she could.

He leaned toward her and put his lips to her ear. "It's going to be all right," he whispered. "You're doing fine." His whisper calmed and soothed her. She closed her eyes for a second and took a deep breath, trying to get control of herself. "That's the way," he said. "It's going to be all right."

She shivered, but not as much as before. She opened her eyes and looked around. She was in a place where trolls lived. Under the bridge, under the feet of people and the wheels of cars. A mythical, fairytale, dangerous kind of place. There were things here she didn't want to know about. Creepy crawlies and slithering slimies, all chucky jammed full of poison. She wanted out and the only way was to slide through that other drain pipe.

He took her hand again and gave it a gentle squeeze, then he turned away and went back down on all fours. She followed and again she was in the dark and again she felt the chili whillies shoot through her, but this time she wasn't alone, because she grabbed onto one of Broxton's feet as he crawled ahead and not God or the devil himself could have made her let go.

Then they were through it and on the other side. She let go of his foot and he took her hand again and led her up the embankment, onto the far side of the highway. Then she saw why she'd heard no traffic sounds. The car that hit them had itself been rear ended and the result was an accident on the bridge, causing traffic to be backed up in both directions. People were out of their cars, some were helping the victims on the bridge, others were in the park assisting the taxi driver and still others were watching, talking, laughing, having a good time, enjoying the excuse to take a few minutes off toward the end of the day. Most of the drivers were apparently viewing the accident more as entertainment than aggravation.

The BMW was sitting four cars back from the bridge. It was unoccupied.

"Come on," Broxton said, leading Maria over to the car. He peeked in the open window. "Keys are in it. Let's go."

"You're not going to take the car?"

He turned and faced her, smiled, and without a word, opened the door and tossed the bags onto the back seat.

"But that's stealing."

"Better hurry, before they come back," he said, getting in. She hurried around to the passenger side. Broxton had the engine started before she had the door closed.

CHAPTER SIX

BROXTON THREW THE CAR IN REVERSE and backed up till he tapped the car behind, then he shifted into drive, cranking the wheel all the way to the right, moving forward till he bumped the car in front. The accident on the bridge had traffic backed up for miles and the cars were packed in tight. There was only inches between bumpers.

The driver behind saw what he was trying to do and backed up a few inches, giving him that much more room to maneuver. Broxton stuck a hand out the window and flashed him the peace sign and the driver responded with a short honk.

"Friendly people," he said.

"Seems so," she answered. He liked the sound of

her voice. It had a smile in it despite everything she'd been through.

"Stop them," a voice rang out.

"You better hurry," she said and Broxton backed up till he tapped the bumper again, cranked the wheel and moved forward, but he still didn't have enough room to make the turn and get out of the squeeze.

"Two of them and they're running," Maria said. Broxton didn't see them but he heard the urgency in her voice and he jammed the BMW back into reverse, this time tapping the car harder then he'd done the last two times and this time the honk wasn't as short and didn't sound as friendly.

"They're getting closer," she said, as he again cranked the wheel and bumped the car in front, this time pushing it a few inches forward before throwing it back into reverse and hitting the car in the rear. Hard. The driver behind responded with a loud, steady honk, not friendly at all anymore.

"They've got guns," she said and Broxton cranked the wheel and stepped on the gas. He hit the front car's bumper with a hard glancing blow, but he was able to squeeze out and he turned onto the right shoulder.

"They're getting ready to shoot," she said. Broxton put his foot to the floor and the BMW responded like the thoroughbred that it was, tires spinning, sending dirt and grass flying from behind as they flew along the stalled cars going in the opposite direction.

"Cross there," she said, and Broxton followed her pointed finger, spinning the wheel to the left. They charged across the wide center strip. Then they had the two lanes all to themselves as they sped toward the city and away from the danger behind.

"Lookout!" she screamed. Broxton stomped on the brakes and swerved to avoid an old four wheel drive Toyota Land Cruiser that turned onto the highway going the wrong direction. They started to slide toward the car and all Broxton could see was the flashing blue light on top of the Toyota.

The policeman's reaction was faster than his and the Land Cruiser swerved and jerked out of the way as Broxton clung to the wheel. They slid sideways past the police cruiser and Maria screamed, jerking Broxton's gaze off of the whites of the policeman's eyes and back onto the road. He pulled himself back together and pulled the wheel into the direction of the slide as he pulled his foot off the brakes, attempting to bring the car back under control.

But the car resisted and Broxton panicked and jammed his foot back on the brakes, sending the car into a three hundred and sixty degree spin. The outside circled by and he saw lightning glimpses of houses, highway and hills as Maria's scream mingled with the sound of the squealing tires.

Most cars would have rolled, but the stable BMW came to a jerky stop in the center of the road and Broxton quickly shifted into neutral.

"Son of a bitch, you sure know how to scare the shit out of someone," Maria said, as Broxton leaned back and sighed.

"I lost it for a second," he said, ashamed. Then he added, "It's been a few years since I've done any driving on the left."

"But we made it," she said.

He turned to look at her and laughed.

"What's so funny?" she asked.

"You should see yourself." Her blouse and slacks were torn and covered with the drying mud and muck from the river. The stuff was already turning hard on her skin. Her shoes looked like she'd been walking through a cow pasture. She raised a hand to her face, then her hair, and she laughed, too.

"We're a mess," she said.

The police car, small in the distance, turned around, blue light still flashing.

Broxton glanced into the rearview mirror. "He's coming back."

Maria turned around. "But the accident is back there."

"I thing it's time to make ourselves scarce."

"Why? We haven't done anything wrong."

Broxton put the car back into gear. "I don't think they know that," he said. Then he shoved in the clutch and for a few seconds he was a kid again, reliving his high school nights on Cherry Avenue, drag racing all comers, in his souped up '56 Chevy Nomad, on the mile stretch of road that lay straight between the two cemeteries. The never ending everybody cemetery on the right and the perfectly manicured Catholic cemetery on the left.

He felt Maria next to him as she was pushed back into the seat, but he kept his eyes on the road and reveled in the sound of the squealing tires. Then the tires dug into the pavement. Broxton popped the clutch and shoved it into second, grinning as the tires chirped, then he was in third and sneaking a glance in the rearview. The police cruiser was turning into a speck in the distance.

"Another one," she said, her voice calm, like a copilot's, but tense like the plane was going down.

"I see it," he said. The second cruiser was coming head on, driving on the wrong side of the street as the two lanes leaving Port of Spain were backed up because of the accident.

"What are you going to do?" she said, voice still calm, tense.

"See who's chicken," he said, shifting into fourth. He stole a look at the speedometer and he wondered how fast two hundred kilometers an hour was. He didn't have time to do the math, but he knew he was flying. And he was still acting the teenager on Cherry Avenue. Playing chicken with a fast car was no new game to him, but he was gambling that it was to the driver of the blue Land Cruiser that was looming larger in his windscreen with each heartbeat.

"He's not going to turn," Maria said, still calm, but he heard the coffin-like stiffness in her voice as he tightened his hands on the wheel. Any sane man would pull aside, pull over, and pull out his wallet and hope that his California driver's license would identify him as enough of a tourist to be let off with a stern warning, but the memory of the men back at the bridge was still sending shivers up his spine that turned into sparks at the base of his neck.

"Oh my God. This is it," she said. The edge was gone from her voice and he admired her for not screaming and not panicking. Then, at the last possible instant, he pulled the wheel a few inches to the right and the police car flew by, close enough to touch.

"Do you ever know how to get a girl's blood pumping," she said.

He saw a turn-off ahead and he stomped on the brakes, sending the car into a slide, laying rubber all over the road as he flew through a long circular exit behind a soccer stadium. He worked the gears through the turn and he was down to second as they shot out of the exit and into the evening traffic. After a few blocks he turned onto a side road, making several turns until he was confused and lost. Finally he pulled up to the curb and parked in front of a small white house covered with frilly gingerbread lattice work.

"We're here," he said.

"Where?" she said.

"I don't know," he said, opening his door and stepping out of the car.

"What are you doing? Where are you going?" she asked.

"This looks like a nice house." He leaned back into the car. "And I'll bet nice folks live here. I'm going to ask them for directions to the Hilton."

She started to say something, but he turned away from her and started up a flower-lined walkway toward a shaded front porch. A black woman of indeterminate age was swaying in a porch swing, sipping something tall that looked cold, and she was eyeing Broxton coming up her walk like a hen eyeing the fox.

"Evening, ma'am," Broxton said, slipping on his father's Irish smile and his mother's southern accent.

"Good night, son," she said and Broxton stopped, frowned and turned back to the car. "Where you going, boy?"

Broxton turned back toward her, confused.

"I wasn't dismissing you. 'Good night' is a greeting here. You know like, 'good morning' and 'good afternoon'. You say 'good evening', we say 'good night'." Her eyes were smiling at him. "Now tell me why you're covered in filth on such a fine, clean evening and why you're driving George Chandee's car."

"George Chandee, the attorney general?"

Broxton said.

"The very one. That's his slick car that your lady is sliding out of right now."

"I didn't know that," Broxton said. Why had Chandee been following him? Maybe he didn't believe Broxton's story. Maybe he wasn't following him at all. Maybe it was only coincidence that he'd been in the same place at the same time, but whatever the reason, it was a good thing he'd been behind him and that he'd left the car open with the keys in it when he did.

"How's that?" she said.

"He stole it," Maria said, coming up the walkway.

"Stole it?" the woman said. "You stole Chandee's car? The chief law enforcement officer in Trinidad?"

Broxton saw the smile splitting her face and grinned. "I guess so," he said.

"Well, la de da, here I'm sitting on my porch swing and a man with brass balls comes a walking right up to me. Lord I wish I was twenty years younger."

"I do too," Broxton said.

"You're in trouble boy, Mr. Chandee is not a forgiving man."

"We've met," Broxton said. "I don't think he likes me."

"You stole his car. I can tell you right now he hates your guts, pardon my French. And I'll tell you something else. You need help and you need it now, right now."

"Can you help us?" Maria said.

"I can and I will. You come on up here, darling."

Maria brushed past Broxton and made her way up the steps. The woman stood and from the effort it took her to push herself out of the porch swing,

Broxton could tell that she wasn't well. She coughed, then reached out and opened her front door. "Freddy, you get on out here. We got some company." Her voice rang true with the authority of command and when a tall, light-skinned man framed himself in the doorway it was easy to see who was in charge of the household.

"What you want, woman?" He sounded tough, but the love he had for the frail woman was pouring out of his eyes. Then he turned and saw Broxton and Maria. "Lord if they aren't a sight." Then his eyes moved on past them. "Chandee's car," he said, turning toward his wife.

"Does everybody in Trinidad know that car?" Broxton asked.

"Probably," Freddy said, "Trinidad's a small place and Chandee's a popular man, and ain't too many people own a green BMW with AG 1 on the license plate."

"Popular with some," the woman said.

"He's a son-of-a-bitch is what he is," Freddy said. "How'd you get his car?"

"They stole it," the woman said, laughing, then she held a hand out toward Maria, "My name's Bertha, but most people call me Little Bee, or just Bee."

"I'm Maria and that's Broxton."

"What happened to your hair, boy?" Freddy said. "You got cancer?"

"No," Maria said, "he wears it that way on purpose."

"Stupid," Freddy said and Maria laughed. Broxton didn't think it was funny.

"You come in and get out of those clothes and tell me all about it," Bee said, and thirty minutes later

Maria was wearing a spare change of clothes from her flight bag and Broxton was wearing a pair of Levi Dockers and a bright Hawaiian shirt with a busy floral pattern full of yellows and greens. He liked the shirt and he liked Freddy and Bee.

"The shoes are a little tight," Broxton said.

"Beggars can't afford to choose what they wear," Freddy said.

"That's the truth," Broxton said. Then he asked, "How come you don't like George Chandee?"

"He threw a big money cricket game and I lost a bundle."

"Now, Freddy, you don't know that."

"I do, woman. I used to play, dammit. I know the game. He claimed he was sick, but I know better."

"And you better keep your mouth shut about it or you'll be in a world of trouble."

"Hush, woman, it was years ago."

"Can't trust anybody that would throw a game," Broxton said.

"Exactly," Freddy said.

"And they made him attorney general?"

"It's not like the whole world knows he did it, but I know."

"Freddy," his wife said.

"I know I what know," Freddy said.

"I only talked to him for a few seconds and I know I don't like him," Broxton said.

"You going to take his car when you leave?" Freddy asked.

"Not if I can help it."

"You need a ride somewhere?"

"I have to get to the American Embassy."

"What for, you gonna file a complaint?"

"He works there," Maria said.

"You don't say? I had a party at my house two weeks ago and I invited the American ambassador. I know most the people at the Embassy." Broxton watched as Freddy puffed up. He was sitting, but if he'd been standing he'd have been strutting. "I take them out on my fishing boat, usually one weekend a month," he continued. "We go out to Scotland Bay, it's a lot of fun. You'll have to come along next time."

"I'd like that," Broxton said.

"Freddy thinks he's just so important. The ambassador never came to the party."

"But I invited him."

"Yes you did. You invited him. You also invited the prime minister."

"One of these days, woman."

"Hush up, Freddy."

"Where's the little lady going?" Freddy said.

"I'd like to go to the Hilton," Maria said.

"You take the man to the embassy," Bee said. "I'll see to lady."

"Fair enough," Freddy said, and after a few minutes of goodbyes Broxton found himself on the way to the Embassy in Freddy's small Mini. Once there he promised to have dinner with Freddy and Bee a week from Saturday. He'd been assured that several important people were going to be there and he promised that he wouldn't miss it. Then he was out of the car and headed into the embassy as the sun was going down.

CHAPTER SEVEN

DANI STREET RAISED HER WRIST so that the porch light lit up the face of her Rolex. It was the maid's day off and she had two hours before her father came home, plenty of time. She was leaning against the porch swing, long legs barely covered in a bright, very short summer dress. The ambassador would be shocked, she thought, but the ambassador wasn't home.

She looked past the circular driveway and out across the Queen's Park Savannah, the tree-lined park that dominated the center of Port of Spain, on the other side of the street. Although it was just after dark, the lights around the park were on, keeping the night alive, and safe. A young couple was slowly jogging along the Savannah, followed by a pair of frolicking German shepherd puppies. Off to her right a man was selling hot dogs and lemonade. Boys were playing cricket in the park. Lovers were strolling, holding hands. A young Rasta man was sitting, playing the guitar, his case open at his side, and every now and then a passerby would drop some coins into it.

It was a typical Friday night at the Savannah. Cool tropical breezes fanned a myriad assortment of trees after a hot and humid day. People were bustling, the night was alive. The sounds of the Rasta's deep voice drifted across to her. She started to lose herself in his song of love and love lost, when her reverie was interrupted by the black Mercedes rolling up the circular drive.

She looked at the watch again. An hour-and-fifty-five minutes till her father bustled in the front door. The ambassador was always punctual, something that was close to impossible in Trinidad, but it was his punctuality that unnerved the Trinidadian political and social set and gave him his edge. The world, even Trinidad, marched to his drummer. He'd even taught the prime minister a thing or two about being on time.

The Mercedes stopped in front of the porch. She silently watched as Kevin exited the car. He closed the door with a soft push, barely enough to latch it, and even that slight movement made his biceps ripple. He looked over at her and smiled, then he moved toward the back of the car, running his hands lovingly along the top as he made his way. The car was only two weeks old.

"I brought a case of that Venezuelan rum your father likes so much," he said, opening the trunk.

"He'll be home soon." She flicked the long blonde hair from her face. "What took you?"

"We got in late. I'd still be at the airport sweating customs, but I whisked right through with Chandee and the prime minister." He looked at his watch. "We have plenty of time," he said, echoing her earlier thought.

"How did it go?" she asked.

"Good as gold, picked it up on the stop over in Caracas. Carried it in my shoulder bag the whole way, no problem."

"You have a sample?" she said, backing through the doorway.

"Of course."

She turned and he followed her into the house.

"You want me to set this in the kitchen?" he asked. He was holding the case of rum as if it was feather light. He had a good body, the result of six days a week in the gym at Starlight Plaza.

"Sure." She led him through high-ceilinged rooms, first through the entryway, then a sitting room, then the formal dining room.

"The table, is it new?" he asked of a massive oak table surrounded by nine chairs, four on each side and one at the head.

"Yes," she said, without turning around.

"Nothing but the best for old Warren," he said.

"That's right." She pushed a swinging door aside and stepped into the modern kitchen. Her father loved the old house, but he'd had the kitchen completely redone. Cobalt blue tiled floor and counters, stainless steel range and oven that would be at home in the best of the world's restaurants. She spent a lot of time in here with him, cooking, talking, laughing. The kitchen was his unofficial office, and on a small breakfast table sat his laptop and numerous papers.

"He's still working on that book? I thought he'd given it up," Kevin said.

"Still at it," she said.

"Nobody will ever print it," he said.

"I'll get it printed. I still have a lot of clout in the publishing industry."

"Even so, it'll never sell. Nobody cares about a race of people that died out two hundred years ago."

"They're not all dead, but that's not the point. It'll sell because it's good. People will want to know their story, how they lived, what they believed, because through them we learn more about ourselves. This book is so well written it would make you cry. He makes them come to life."

"Give me a break. Nobody wants to hear that Columbus killed the Caribs. Nobody cares about naked Indians. Nobody wants their idols trashed."

"Columbus didn't kill them."

"You know what I mean. He started it."

"That's like saying if my father gets drunk on your rum, your grandmother's responsible. If she hadn't had your mother, your mother wouldn't have had you, and you wouldn't have bought the rum. Where'd you get it by the way? You surely wouldn't try and slip a case of rum by customs while you were smuggling in the coke."

"Margarita, last trip. I stopped by my place on the way over."

"You can set it by the sink," she said, wondering if getting the rum for her father was the only reason he'd stopped off at his apartment.

"Fine," he said. By the time he'd laid the case on a long tiled counter she was leaving the kitchen and headed for the hallway. He turned to follow.

She heard him behind her as she entered the guest bedroom at the end of the hall. She opened a bureau drawer and took out a mirror and handed it to him. She eased the drawer shut with the eager anticipation she always felt when she did a test. It was the only time she allowed herself to use the drug.

"Are they ready to ship?" she asked.

"They sent five kilos with me. It's all up front, to show their good faith. They want my principal to know they're ready to go. Soon as I call them, the goods will be in route." He untucked a shirt tail and wiped the mirror off. Then he blew his hot breath on it and wiped it again.

She pushed the hair from her face and tucked it behind her ears as he lay the mirror on the bureau and pulled out a brown glass vial from his shirt pocket. She wet her lips with her tongue as he unscrewed the cap, and she started drumming her fingers against her thighs as he tapped the vial against the mirror, spilling out some of the white powder.

She sucked in her upper lip and gently bit down on it as he pulled out a credit card and a blue hundred dollar bill from his shirt pocket. He set the bill on the bureau and divided the cocaine into two equal white lines with the credit card. He picked up the blue bill and started rolling it up.

"Put it away," she said. "We'll use mine."

"Got a problem with the local currency?" he said, tucking the bill back into his pocket.

"The paper on these is better, they roll nicer." She rolled the green US hundred dollar bill. She approached the mirror, put the rolled bill to her left nostril and inhaled. Then she did it again with the right. She closed her eyes, inhaled a deep breath through her nose and let the cocaine rush to her brain.

"Well?" he said after a few seconds.

"Exhilarating. You've done very well."

"I try." He sounded smug, and from the tone of his voice she knew the real reason he'd stopped by his apartment. She could never prove it, because she'd never met the Salizars. It had to be that way, both because of her father and because there was no way they'd ever deal with a woman.

She opened her eyes and nailed him with her stare. He met her eyes with his own and for a few seconds they were locked together, a contest of wills. He grinned, looked away and she bit into her lower lip, enjoying the euphoric high and resisting the triumphant smile. The bastard had stolen some of her cocaine.

"You made the papers again," he said.

"Really? What was it this time?"

"Picture of us leaving the Red House Ball last week." His voice had a haughty kind of sneer in it that put her on her guard.

"And what else?" she asked. There was no reason the paper would print a week old picture. She was popular, but not that popular.

"Headline implied that there might wedding bells in our future."

"That's not so bad then," she said.

"Why did you agree to marry me?" he asked.

"You're exciting, you take risks, you're in love with me, you come from a solid British family, you're great in bed and you're the only person in the world that understands me."

"We are good in bed together, aren't we?" he said.

"Yes," she said, but she'd had better. Of course she could never tell him that. Because like all men, when he wasn't serving his ego he was trying to serve his penis. And like most men he never seemed to get either one right, where the penis wanted to go, the ego followed, dragging along the wagging tail of a man, like an eager puppy anxious to please.

"Why do you do it, the coke I mean? Don't you have enough money already?"

"I'll have enough when I'm satisfied," she said.

"I'm sorry, I've spoken out of turn. It's just that it doesn't mix too good with our other business." He looked at his watch. She inhaled deeply and closed her eyes. Life was never simple. She heard the tapping of the vial on the mirror again and exhaled, opening her eyes.

"I won't do another." She was about to say more, but she was interrupted by the phone ringing in the other room. "I'll be right back." She dropped the rolled hundred on the bed. She left the door open on her way out and she was conscious of him watching her backside as she made her way down the hall to the living room. She knew he was licking his lips as her body moved beneath the tight summer dress, not a wiggle, not a bounce, but a natural, almost innocent teenage movement that locked men's eyes onto her like they were radar trained. But she was no teenager and she was no innocent. They knew it and she knew it.

She turned back and saw him as he sat on the bed, she smiled, flicked the long hair out of her eyes again with her right hand as she picked up the phone with her left. "Ambassador Street's residence," she said with a Spanish accent, mimicking her Venezuelan maid.

"Dani Street, please." She recognized the smooth voice of George Chandee, only this night he didn't sound as smooth as usual.

"It's me," she said into the phone with her own voice. She looked down the hall, Kevin was off the bed and leaning in the bedroom doorway, staring down the hallway, watching her. She knew he could hear her every word. He looked at his watch. He wanted to do the cocaine, but he'd wait for her.

"So you have an extra fiancé I didn't know about?" Chandee said over the phone.

"I don't know what you're talking about," she said.

"A man named Broxton."

"Where did you meet him?" her voice turned wary.

"On the plane. He told us about his marriage plans right after the bomb went off."

"Say again," she said.

"He said he was going to marry you."

"Not that, the other."

"The bomb?" Chandee said as Dani clenched her fist around the receiver and shot Kevin a cold glare.

"Yeah, that."

"A bomb went off on the plane. We had a frightening flight. For awhile I didn't think we were going to make it." Now she knew why he wasn't his usual smooth self.

"I'll get back with you," she said.

"Dani—"

"Not now, I'll call you, soon," she said, and she cradled the phone.

She started toward Kevin. "I need a drink, how about you?"

"Scotch and water."

Her silky hair whipped around as she spun on her heels. She put a spring in her step and she knew that Kevin was feeling lucky. She'd never bedded him in the residence before.

In the kitchen she made two quick drinks, then started back to the guest bedroom. He was at the bureau, tapping out more of the white powder, dividing it into four white lines when she came back into the room. She set them down on the nightstand next to the bed, then came toward him.

"Did some while I was in the kitchen," she said. It wasn't a question.

"Small ones," he said, like that made it all right to do more. Then he said, "There was a man on the plane claimed to be engaged to you, so it appears that I'm not the only heart that's fallen under your spell."

"Really?" she said, feigning surprise. "He said we were engaged?"

"Something like that. He said he was coming to Trinidad to marry you."

"And you just assumed I'd say yes and jump into this stranger's bed?" She curled her toes in an effort to keep the anger out of her voice.

"He sounded so sure."

"Does he have a name?" Dani asked, still pretending ignorance.

"Broxton."

"Bill Broxton?"

"That's him," he said.

"He's an old friend."

"He works for the DEA."

"Yeah, I know that. He's a systems analyst of some kind. We grew up together."

"He thinks you're going to marry him."

"Then he's wrong."

He smiled, that seemed to satisfy him. She was beginning to have second thoughts. Maybe he wasn't for her after all. However, as she'd just admitted to him, he was the only man on the planet that could ever understand her. But she didn't like it that he'd pinched some of the coke, the deal was fifty-fifty. He was making enough that he didn't have to skim off the top. And she didn't like him not telling her what happened on the plane. And she really didn't like his smug, holier than thou attitude. This was not going to be a marriage made in heaven, she thought and she wondered if there was going to be a wedding at all.

Then she thought of Bill Broxton. What would her life have been like if he'd married her way back then? Would she be a frumpy stay-at-home mom, or would she be an honest Josephine, balancing motherhood and career? But he'd never asked, he married someone else, and things were the way they were. She could never marry him now. It would be the end of everything.

Still standing, he turned toward the bureau and picked up the mirror with the cocaine on it.

"I won't do any more," she said. She had strict rules and he knew it. Never do the drug, except when testing. She'd done her test, now she would have her drink.

"Relax, these are all for me," he said, as she studied the four lines, little snakes of white powder, on the mirror. He looked toward her, like he was expecting her to hand over the rolled bill. When she didn't, he reached into his pocket, took out the blue hundred, rolled it, and quickly inhaled two lines. Then he picked up the small mirror and offered it to her with hope dancing in his eyes.

"Why does it always come to this?" she said.

"What?" he said.

"You think if you get me high enough I'll hike up my dress right here?" He was a better than average lover, but he was insatiable. He wanted more than she wanted to give.

"Come on, Dani," he said, pleading with his eyes.

"Finish it, Kevin." Why did she always give in? She was a strong woman, she didn't have to spread her legs for him every time he snapped his fingers.

"But they're for you," he said, still trying.

"Finish it," she said under her breath as she turned away from him and moved toward the bed. It was almost an order and, in the wall mirror above the bed, she saw his ears turn red. He'd been in Trinidad long enough to think like a Trini, and Trinis didn't like women giving orders.

He opened his mouth, but stopped as she reached her hands over her shoulders and took her dress by the straps and started to pull it up, revealing first pale pink panties, then her bare back as she pulled it over her head and dropped it at her feet. She turned to look at him, but he couldn't meet her eyes, he was captivated by her breasts.

"Do you like them?" she said. "So round, so perfect, nipples so hard, standing at attention for you. I'm hot for you." She'd learned early on in their relationship that these were the kinds of things he like to hear. She didn't mind saying them, it kept him excited and hard.

He could only nod as she stepped out of her panties and showed herself to him. They stood like that, facing each other for over a minute. She shivered a bit as he drank in her body. Then she hopped onto the bed and pulled her knees up under herself till she was sitting in a full lotus position.

"Aren't I just the most erotic thing you've ever seen?" she said, and using both hands she brushed her blonde hair, silky with a little sweat, off her breasts and back behind her ears. She looked at him, her full lips curved up in a half smile, her mouth partly open, her clear blue eyes, unblinking. He was hard in a heartbeat.

"Say it, Kevin, do you like what you see?" She'd turned her voice from the cool businesslike tone she usually used into an animal husky kind of thing that was like a razor shooting down his spine to his erection. He looked like he was going to explode, just looking at her. She was excited too, but she couldn't get that stolen coke out of the back of her mind.

"Go on, say it, do you like what you see?"

"Yesss," he hissed, sounding like the snake that tempted Eve. He couldn't take his eyes from her breasts.

"Then finish it." She nodded toward the cocaine on the mirror still in his hand.

"Yes," he said, obeying her. She was still glorying in the rush she received from the two lines she'd done earlier, reveling in the electric tingles that danced on her skin and shivered down her spine. She took a deep breath, held it and lay back on the bed, arms behind her head, legs spread wide.

He pulled at his clothes.

"Hurry," she said, "I want you in me." Now the words were for her as well as him.

He kicked off his loafers, ignored the socks and pulled his trousers and boxer shorts down, shaking them off as he made his way toward the bed. He left the silk shirt on, but she ripped it off him as he climbed on top of her.

"In me now," she urged, and she took hold of him

and guided him into the heat of herself. She thrust up at him and he pounded down. Her nails raked along his back, drawing blood.

Time stood still as he thrust himself at her, seeming to push himself in deeper and deeper. She was engulfed by pleasure, lost in it, surrounded by it. She was on the edge, straining, close to the mountain top, but unable to take that last step. She felt like he was going to burst inside of her, but she kept him on the razor, slowing her movement just when he was about to blast off, making it last longer for him and for her, until there was nothing she could do to stop him and he exploded with a sigh. But she wasn't there yet so she dug her hands into his buttocks, pulling him into her, pumping, keeping him hard. She wouldn't let him quit, and to her amazement, he didn't. She was on the edge of exhaustion, panting heavily, every muscle taut, every nerve glowing, drenched in sweat and her heart was thumping, threatening to beat out of her chest.

And then it happened.

She screamed as the orgasm shot through her, lightning quick and thunder deep. Then it was over and she knew exactly why she was marrying him, but she had to get some things straight first.

"Good lord," he muttered, as she rolled him off. He flopped over onto his back, staring up at the ceiling, panting and gasping for breath as she willed her heart to slow it's rapid breathing.

"Cocaine and sex, a powerful combination," she said.

He pushed himself into a sitting position. "It's never been that intense for us before," he said.

"Darling, would you cut me a couple of lines."

"But your rule?"

"I think I can break it today. What do you think?"

"Sure." He hopped off the bed and went to the bureau.

She reached a hand behind herself and snaked it under the pillow while he was tapping out the cocaine. When he looked up she was back in the lotus position, but his eyes were glued to the chrome-plated thirty-eight police special she held in her left hand.

"Don't point that thing at me," he said, stepping back.

"I give the orders around here," she said. Whatever happened, their relationship was forever altered.

"Yes, okay."

"Make four lines," she said.

"Yes, sure, anything." His hands were shaking as he tapped more cocaine out onto the small mirror. "Shit," he said, "too much."

"That's all right. Now divide it up."

"All of it? There must be close to a gram here."

"Yes," she said. "All of it."

He made the lines, licked his finger and tapped it into some of the residue on the mirror and then rubbed it across his gums. She saw his quaking shivers.

"Do two of the lines," she said.

He picked up the blue hundred, and made two of the white snakes disappear.

"I killed the last man who disappointed me. Do you believe that?"

He looked at the steady way she held the gun, as if it was an extension of her left hand, and nodded.

"Look at my breasts."

He moved his eyes away from the gun.

"See how the nipples are hard. See how you make them stand up." She pinched her left nipple with the thumb and index finger of her right hand. The gun never wavered. "They are very hard. I'm still excited. Do you believe that?"

He nodded.

"Do the rest of it."

He hesitated.

"Do it," she said and he quickly inhaled the rest of the cocaine. Now he would be flying and too shit scared to lie.

"This isn't right," he said. She knew he was trying to figure out what went wrong, trying to figure out an angle. He was slippery, but tonight he was out of grease. "What's going on?" he asked, melting under her stare.

"My bomb went off on the plane."

"I was going to tell you about that," he said.

"When?"

"As soon as I got here, but you looked so good in that dress I forgot."

"You said that wouldn't happen."

"I was assured," he said.

"I don't want to hear about your assurances. I want my bomb."

"I'm sorry," he said.

"When they start reconstructing things, they will find the bomb maker and through him, you, and through you, me."

"Not a chance," he said. The man I hired is first rate. He's a stand up guy, from the IRA. I know him. He'd do the time before he ratted."

"At least it wasn't one of your Middle East terrorist friends. They give up their mothers the second someone shines a light in their eyes."

"No, no, he's IRA, those guys never talk. They won't find him," he said.

"I hope you're right."

"I'm right," he said, sweating. "Come on, put the gun down."

"You stole my cocaine."

"Bullshit."

"That's why you stopped by your apartment."

"I stopped by to pick up the rum and my neighbor. He followed me over in your surprise. The poor guy had to take a taxi back."

"What are you talking about?"

"Go look out the front door. It should be parked behind my Mercedes by now."

"You didn't," she said, lowering the gun.

"I did." He grinned.

She dropped the gun on the bed, put on her dress, and ran to the front door. "Kevin, it's gorgeous."

"Is the color all right?" It was bright red.

"It's great." She approached the new Porsche convertible.

"Now say you're sorry about sticking that cannon in my face," he said.

"Oh forget about that," she said, turning toward him. "And get your clothes on so we can take it for a spin."

"About the bomb," he said ten minutes later as they approached the light before Western Main Road, "do you think that way is wise? You've been pretty lucky with a rifle all the other times."

"Senator Rowland's car went off a cliff," she said.

"That's different," Kevin said. "You were supposed to make that one look like an accident."

"I can't shoot Ram," she said, downshifting. It was a risk telling him. She hated to show weakness, but he had a right to know why.

"There's too much at stake," he said.

"I didn't say I couldn't kill him. I just can't shoot him. I've tried. I had him lined up with the crosshair between his eyes, but I couldn't pull the trigger. He's a friend. Like a wise old uncle. I know him. I like him. I almost admire him. It's not like the others."

"We can't back out now," he said.

"I know that. That's why I want to use a bomb and a timer. I'll be long gone. It'll be out of my hands."

"There's someone here that can do it. I can have you fixed up by tomorrow evening. I didn't want to use him, because he's so close to home. But now I guess I don't have any choice."

"Good," she said. "Then we don't have a problem."

CHAPTER EIGHT

"YOU'RE LOOKING FIT, WARREN," Broxton said, holding out his hand. The handshake was strong, but not overpowering. Warren Street was a man who was sure of himself and his place in the world.

"And you. I'd ask about the flight, but I know about that." The ambassador gestured toward two bamboo style chairs away from his desk. Broxton smiled. The office had a tropical flavor to it, and the bamboo furniture, the parquet floor, the indoor plants and of course the floral prints, all conspired to camouflage the century old oak desk that Warren took everywhere his office happened to be.

"A bomb," Broxton said. "Too small to bring down the aircraft, but large enough to poke holes through the sealed baggage compartment and through the plane's skin. We were lucky. The pilot was great." He decided not to tell Warren about the accident and the car chase. Warren was a great friend, but he was also a great worrier.

"Who would do such a thing?"

"Someone who doesn't care how many people he kills," Broxton said.

"Have you made any progress?"

"Not really. A Colombian picked up during a drug bust wanted to deal. Miami heard what he had to say and called in the FBI. They believed the story and State issued an invitation to the prime minister to visit Washington where they laid it all out."

"And?" Warren asked.

"As long as the government went after the users and the dealers, the drug cartels didn't care, but when Prime Minister Ramsingh started going after the money they decided he had to go."

"So they've hired a professional, someone like Carlos the Jackal?"

"They've hired Scorpion," Broxton said.

"I've never heard of him."

"Since Carlos' capture the Scorpion is number one on the assassin's hit parade. No political affiliation, an equal opportunity killer. He's taken out a right wing presidential candidate in Uruguay and a left wing one in Chile. He's even killed in the United States."

"Who?" Warren asked.

"Senator Rowland."

"That was an accident," Warren said.

"It wasn't," Broxton said.

"How do you know all this?"

"Couple of guys from Langley came to the office

and filled me in. Until then I'd never heard of Scorpion and I certainly never thought of major drugs going through Trinidad. I was just a lowly DEA guy back from a year in Mexico.

"So why you? Is it because of me?"

"Sure it's because of you. When Ramsingh turned down American protection they went scrambling around for someone they could send in that wouldn't attract too much attention. Someone that could hang out where Ramsingh does, go to the same parties, attend the same functions, meet the same people, that sort of thing, and when they found out how close we are, well, all of a sudden I filled the bill."

"You have backup of course?" Warren said.

"If I do, they didn't tell me, but who knows? You know how they are."

"And you're supposed to prevent this Scorpion from assassinating the prime minister?"

"That's what they said."

"How are you going to do that?" Warren asked.

"I don't know. I'll figure something out, but it won't be easy after what happened on the plane," Broxton said. Then he told Warren about the silver flask that he'd mistaken for a knife.

"So you're not very undercover," Warren said when he'd finished.

"Not at the moment."

"I'll have Dani throw a party. You can meet Ramsingh under different circumstances, cozy up to him, make him like you."

"Thanks," Broxton said. Then he asked, "How is she?" He dreaded the answer. Sooner or later they were going to have to talk about the story on the front page of the *Guardian*.

"Just watch." Warren picked a video tape from

the bookcase. He went to a bamboo cabinet, opened it to reveal a portable television and a video player inside. He slipped the tape into the player and punched the play button.

Broxton was drawn into the beauty that was Danielle Street. Flowing blonde hair the color of honey mixed with straw, sparkling blue eyes, flawless skin, like a child's, and her beguiling smile.

The camera cut away to reveal a small black child in her lap. The little girl had her hair in braids and wore a bright smile, her wide brown eyes stared up at Dani. The background could have been a village anywhere in Africa. The camera panned over villagers going about the daily business of living. Broxton saw a man herding scrawny cows in the background, a woman pounding grain with a mortar and pestle, another sat with her and they were talking. They seemed happy.

The camera left them and came back to Dani.

"What you see behind me," she said, "is a village that works. People here contribute. They help their neighbors, grow their own crops, tend their own cattle and raise happy children like Amanda." She bounced the girl on her knee and the child giggled. "But it wasn't always that way. Before Save the Children got involved there were no crops to tend, no cattle to herd, no happy children. Amanda was sick and wasting away, her parents had no food or shelter, they'd already lost two children and Amanda was close to being the third. Then you helped through Save the Children, but we can do so much more. So if you're not one of our sponsors, please help. You can do so much for just pennies a day."

The camera pulled in for a close up and Dani reached a hand to her forehead and pushed some hair out of her eyes, then she wiped away a tear. "We need your help. Amanda needs your help. I need your help." Then the screen faded to black.

"I can't believe it," Broxton said.

"A powerful ad," Warren said.

"Better than any I ever wrote. I almost started crying when she wiped that tear away," Broxton said.

"She's the perfect spokesperson. She's doubled the income for Save the Children in less than a year and she's hoping to double it again."

Broxton stepped toward the pictures on the wall behind Warren's desk. "A who's who of world politics," Broxton said, as his eyes moved from a picture of Warren and the President of the United States to one of him with the Prime Minister of England. "When was the one of you and Aaron Gamaliel taken?"

"In Paris. Dani took it. A few hours later he was dead."

"Killed by the Scorpion," Broxton said. Aaron Gamaliel had been the Israeli Defense Minister. "Him, too." Broxton pointed to a picture of Dani and President Jomo Seko of Zaire.

"He was assassinated while she was up country doing one of the those commercials for Save the Children," Warren said.

"Poor Dani," Broxton said. "It must have been horrible to have been with two such men hours before they were assassinated.

"She's had horrible nightmares about it," Warren said. "It's really shaken her."

"I won't mention it," Broxton said.

"God, I hope not. She's just starting to act like her old self again. Let's just say you're here on vacation."

"That's my cover story," Broxton smiled. "I'll stick with it." He was quiet for a second. "You're right, Save the Children couldn't have found a better spokesperson. I can hardly wait to tell her how proud I am of her."

"You can do it over dinner. You'll be staying with us, of course," Warren said.

"How is the palace Street?" Broxton said. It would be pointless arguing, Warren always got his way.

"It's just a simple home," Warren said.

"Warren, if you're living in it, it's a palace."

"I have brought over a few of my little luxuries," Warren said, and laughed.

"Like the grand piano, the walk-in wine cellar that's bigger than a garage, and the drive-in movie screen that you call a television."

"Well yes, I brought those."

Broxton followed Warren out of his office and through the embassy to the garage in back. He watched as Warren ran his hands along the walls as they went from room to room, almost like he was trying to reassure himself that he wasn't dreaming, that he really was out of the Washington mad house. Broxton knew that Warren loved being Ambassador to Trinidad as much as he'd hated being National Security Advisor.

In the garage Warren went to the driver's side of a two-year-old left-hand-drive Ford, and Broxton was reminded about the left-hand-drive car that had run them off the road.

"What happened to the Silver Cloud?" Broxton asked, looking over the roof of the car at his friend.

"Left it at home," Warren answered.

"That's not like you," Broxton said.

"This is still a third world country. It wouldn't do

for the American ambassador to go driving about in a Roller."

"Doesn't Dani miss it?" Broxton was looking at Warren over the roof of the car. Warren Street was still as handsome as ever, his jaw still firm, his eyes still crisp. He was fifty-four, rich, an American ambassador, Dani's father and his best friend.

"Miss the Rolls? I don't think so. She always thought it was a bit conspicuous. Thinks my left-hand-drive Ford is, too. She usually endures the press and grind of the maxi taxies."

"What?"

"You'll find out about the maxies soon enough. Yellow mini vans, they cram as many people in them as possible and zoom up and down the streets at something just short of the speed of light. It's like a local bus system."

"And Dani rides in them?"

"Every day. She's become quite a woman, my daughter."

"Do I hear a but in there?" Broxton said.

"I hate it that she has to travel so much. She used to enjoy spending the new money. I loved it. We'd go out and just buy things, rich is so much better then poor. And then she made a pile in her own right, but now sometimes I think she's ashamed of all the money. I think it's why she goes traipsing all around the third world."

"It looks like she does good work," Broxton said. He was proud of her and it pleased him. He'd always loved her, but he could never remember a time when he'd been proud of her. She'd always used her ruthless beauty and fierce determination to get ahead. Now she was applying her looks and will for the benefit of others and it made Broxton feel good.

"I can't argue with that," Warren said. "I love her," he added, "but I'll never understand her. You know she works in the embassy four days a week for no pay. She's my unofficial press secretary. Nothing goes out of that place without her looking it over first, and if it looks like it might harm me in any way, ever, she cuts it. You can't believe the amount of paperwork she wades through just to make sure my image isn't tarnished. As if I really cared about my image."

"Nobody will ever understand her." Broxton sighed. "That's what makes her so unique." The two men climbed into the car. Broxton settled down into the passenger seat. He thought about the story in the newspaper, but he was afraid to bring her up.

"She's always loved you, Bill, but I think you waited too long," Warren said, bringing it up for him.

"She looked happy in the picture," Broxton said. He didn't have to tell Warren what picture.

"It happened so fast." Warren took a right out of the driveway and headed for the long cool ride around the Savannah. "One minute she's the social butterfly of Trinidad, then Kevin starts acting serious all of a sudden and the next thing you know they're an item, and I mean an item. Kevin must eat at our place five nights a week. Not my favorite person in the world, but he's okay.

"Kevin Underfield, the guy with the flask on the plane. I saw it in the paper."

"Yeah, him."

"Sounds like a mortician."

"Used to be a newspaper reporter, now he's working with Chandee, helping him modernize the police force. Comes from a good family. Big bucks," Warren said. Broxton smiled. Despite his wealth,

Warren still thought like a middle class kid from Long Beach.

"She knew him from before?" Broxton asked.

"She was his agent."

"He wrote a novel?"

"No, he wrote that book defending the Hezbola. Said it was their right to take hostages. Claimed they had just as much right to torture and kill their captives as those early American terrorists had dumping tea in the ocean. His words, not mine."

"I remember now, he was on all the talk shows. The guest everybody loved to hate."

"That's him. Only he's not that guy you remember from television. He's tamer now, talks like a scholar."

"I remember him on *Cross Fire*. He seemed more like a rabid dog than a college professor."

"That was all Dani. Theatrics to sell his book. Remember how she used to be?"

"Yeah."

"She spent a lot of time with him in Lebanon, helping him with the second draft. I think the book was as much Dani as it was Underfield," Warren said.

"I didn't know that," Broxton said. He'd lost touch with her during his marriage. While she was making her mark on the world, he was wallowing in a dead end job with a woman that wanted his boss more than she'd wanted him. Dani was making her fortune while he wrote bad copy for bad ads touting bad products.

"He can't write. Dani can. His thoughts, her talent. It was a controversial book. Did well."

"I read it," Broxton said. "I thought it was a load of crap."

"Yeah, well I guess I did, too, but one good thing

came of it."

"What's that?"

"After that horrible book tour was over Dani lost all interest in making money. She sold the agency and came to work for me in Washington."

"National Security Advisor to the President of the United States," Broxton said. "Pretty important job."

"Yeah, well I was kind of tired of it. My heart problem was a good reason to walk away."

"Big job to walk away from."

"Not when you don't see eye to eye with the boss."

"I thought you two got along great."

"We did, we do. He listened to everything I said. Then most of the time he went and did the direct opposite."

"He's the one that has to answer to the voters."

"So he's told me. More than once."

"You going back?"

"Next year, but not in an official capacity. I've had my fill of that. I'll just sort of hang around and nag at him when I think he's screwing up."

"You can do that?"

"Probably not. He wants me for State in the second term."

"You're shitting me?"

"No."

"That's pretty official."

"If I take it." Warren slowed the car and turned up a circular driveway and parked behind a red Porsche convertible. The porch light was on, the front door was open and the light inside the house framed Dani in the doorway. She was wearing a white silk blouse and faded Levi's. She wasn't wearing shoes.

"We have company," Warren said.

"Billy Boy," Dani squealed.

"Dani," Broxton said, and she was in his arms, squeezing tight. She gently bit into his neck, as she used to do when they were children, and he answered her squeeze with a bear hug of his own, pulling her off the ground and twirling her as if she was still a little girl.

"No Kevin tonight?" Warren said, after Broxton had set her down.

"He bought me a car." She pointed to the Porsche.

"Kind of fancy for the proletariat," Warren said, kidding, but she wasn't laughing anymore and Broxton looked into her eyes, clear as cut glass, and shivered. For an instant he thought he caught a glimpse of wild desperation. Then it was gone and she looked hard, old beyond her thirty-six years. Tiny crows feet crinkled out from those eyes, long eyelashes adorned them, a hint of baby blue eye shadow covered their lids. She'd been driven when she ran the literary agency, but never desperate. She'd been ruthless, but in a soft kind of way, never hard.

"It's been a long time, Bill" she said.

"Almost two years," he said, relaxing as her stare mellowed into a welcoming smile. This was the Dani he knew, the Dani he loved.

"A lot can happen in two years," she said.

"I saw the television commercial for Save the Children. I was proud of you." He wondered if that was it. Sure, he thought, seeing all those poor kids in those poor countries would harden anybody. His heart went out to her.

"Thanks, I enjoy helping out and it's made Daddy proud of me."

"I've always been proud of you, dear," Warren said.

"Not always," she said, and Broxton thought of her literary agency.

"Always," Warren said. "You proved you can be a success in a tough field. What father wouldn't be proud? Then you gave it up and came to work for me and made me even prouder. I've always felt like I'm the luckiest man alive."

Her smile toward her father was warm and genuine, her eyes now a window to the Dani of old. She was a little girl pleased that her father was proud, then something happened, her eyes appeared to glass over for a second, like her mind was elsewhere. He sensed that she wanted to be somewhere else, that she had other plans, that he was interrupting, intruding.

"I'd love to sit up and talk the night away, but I've been up for the last twenty-four hours. I'm about to pass out." It wasn't exactly the truth, but he wanted to give Dani time to adjust to his being in Trinidad and he needed time to adjust to Dani engaged to someone else.

"Of course," Warren said. "Your room is at the end of the hall."

"Wait," Dani said, sharp, quick, almost a shout. Broxton stopped, set his bag down and met her eyes. "Not that room," she said.

"Why not?" Warren said.

"I think he'd be more comfortable upstairs with us. Not down here like a guest."

"But I am a guest," Broxton said.

"No you're not. You're family."

"It's a better room," Warren said, "with a bigger bath."

"No, Bill should stay upstairs, with us, not in the

stuffy guest bedroom."

Warren shrugged, looked at Broxton and smiled. It was a good sign, Broxton thought. She wanted him upstairs, close to her, not on the opposite end of this big old house.

"Upstairs is fine, as long as it's got a bed. Who needs a large bath anyway?"

"Then it's settled. Follow me, Bill." She spun around and started for the staircase.

"She always gets her way," Warren said.

"She always has." Broxton picked up his bag and followed her up the steps and then into a large bedroom with a king-sized bed.

He set his bag at the foot of the bed and peered into the attached bathroom. "This is about the size of my apartment in D.C. and you say the one downstairs is bigger. I'm beginning to feel slighted."

She laughed and he enjoyed the sound. Now she appeared open and vulnerable. He wanted to ask her about the story in the newspaper, but he was afraid that it would spoil this moment between them.

"It's good that you're here, Bill," she said. "I've missed you."

"I've missed you, too," he said.

"Look, I've got some things I have to do tonight that I can't get out of, so why don't you get some rest and tomorrow maybe we'll go sailing."

"Sounds good to me," he said. Then she was gone. He looked over at the bed. He was tired. He felt the mattress, firm, comfortable. He stretched out on it without removing his clothes. He'd only intended on a few minutes rest but in seconds he was asleep, dreaming of Dani, the ring in his pocket, and the desperation in her eyes.

CHAPTER

NINE

EARL WOKE TO THE SMELL of his own sweat in the tall grass. Shivering, he brushed an unseen insect off his neck as he sat up. He looked to the sky, now covered in clouds. It was either very late or very early. He checked his watch, 5:30. He felt a sharp pain at the base of his skull. He ran a hand back there and found a large bump. It wasn't cut, and for that he was thankful, but it hurt.

"Are you okay, mister?"

He turned toward the sound of the voice.

"I thought you were dead, but I felt your neck pulsing, like they do on TV, and I knew you weren't."

The insect was this boy's finger searching for life.

"That's good," the boy said, "'cause I sure didn't

want to get the police."

"Why not?" Earl asked. He was cold and wet. His body ached from the thrashing it had taken in the river. His head felt like it was being used as a snare drum, and he had to piss like a pent up storm, but he'd been too many years a cop. He wanted to know what a child was doing out by the river, so far from town, alone.

"I'm running away from home," the boy said.

Earl's skin crawled and he shook with the cold. "Not very warm out," he said.

"Don't I know it," the boy answered. "It rained while you were asleep, but the sun will come back. It always does."

"Your parents must be worried."

"They're getting a divorce. They don't care about me."

"How long do you think you can live out here?"

"Oh, a long time. I got a two man tent and a sleeping bag over there." He pointed toward the falling sun peeking through the clouds. "I got enough canned goods for a couple of weeks and I got friends that'll sneak me more when they run out. I can stay hidden forever."

"It sounds like you've thought of everything."

"I've been planning a long time," the boy said. Then he added, "Are you hungry?"

"Powerfully," Earl said.

"I thought you would be. I saw you climb out of the river. Then you crashed. I thought you might be dead."

"I'm not dead," Earl said.

"My name's Mick," the boy said. "My mom named me after Mick Jagger. He's in the Rolling Stones. That's a rock band."

JACK STEWART

"I've heard of them," Earl said, smiling despite his suffering body.

"Can you get up? Can you walk?" Mick asked.

"I think so," Earl said, and he pushed himself to his feet.

"Okay, follow me. We're having hot dogs for dinner." The boy walked with a self assured swagger. He was at home by the river and Earl guessed that he was a veteran of many camping trips with his father.

He groaned when he walked, but the boy didn't look back. He ran a hand over a pain in his side and winced when he remembered slamming into a rock. He flexed his fingers, then his toes, then ran his head in a circle. Everything ached, but everything seemed to be working.

"You got a nasty cut over your eye," the boy said without turning around. Earl reached up and felt the scabbing wound. "And a bad bruise on your chin," the boy said, with his eyes still forward. Earl moved his hand to his chin. He put a little pressure on it and grit his teeth against the tenderness. "I can imagine what the rest of your body looks like," the boy added, as he moved into a clearing.

"Nice place," Earl said, admiring the tent and the small cook stove in front of it. "Nobody would ever find you out here."

"That's the plan," Mick said, then he crawled on his hands and knees into the tent, the flap closing behind him. In a few seconds an eight pack of hot dogs appeared out of the flap, followed by a hand that quickly vanished back inside. Then came the buns sitting on top of a plate. Then butter, mustard and ketchup on another plate and a quart of orange juice.

"Pretty good, huh?" Mick said, crawling out of the tent.

"How do you plan on keeping the meat fresh?"

"I don't, it's only for today. From tomorrow on I'm eating out of cans."

"How about water? That juice won't keep."

"Come on, there's a whole river down there," he said, pointing. "You should know that."

Earl watched while the kid lit a can of sterno. The boy was an experienced outdoorsman, the kind that only another who loved living out of doors and camping could appreciate. Earl pulled off his wet shoes as Mick smeared some butter on a fry pan and set it on the stove. He was taking off his socks as the boy cut the wieners in half and dropped them in the pan. The sizzling meat had him salivating in seconds. He was hungry and the boy was cooking up the best dinner possible, fried hot dogs, out-of-doors, nothing better.

After he'd eaten his fill, he lay back and closed his eyes. He faded off to a quick but restless sleep. Random thoughts turned into short dreams and faces kept flashing beneath his eyelids, Johnny Lee, Maria, Old Loomis and most of all, Jackson. Then finally he sank into a deep sleep, where his only dream was of the flowing river. The dark river. The dream turned into a nightmare when the river grew hands, clear water dripping hands, reaching for him, tugging at him, pulling him under. He screamed himself awake.

He jumped up to the setting sun, pushing himself from the ground to his feet with athletic grace. He rubbed the confusion and delirium from his eyes, blinked, squinted, then turned away from the sun and faced the river below, and it all came rushing back to him.

"Hey, Mick," he said, turning around.

The boy was gone. He'd moved his campsite like

a true woodsman. Only a pro, like himself, would ever know a tent had been there. His socks had been laid out and were dry. Mick must have dried them over the camping stove. He sat back down and tugged them on. His shoes were still damp, but he put them on anyway. He wished the boy hadn't gone, but maybe it was for the best. He didn't think he could kill a child, but he would have given it some thought, because he hated the idea that someone had seen him climbing out of the river. It was lucky for the boy that he was gone.

First order of business was to get himself back to the bridge and his car. He pushed back to his feet and brushed off. He couldn't go walking around wearing wet, bloodstained, and torn clothes. He was going to have to do something about that.

He walked to the edge of the cliff and looked down at the river, trying to get his bearings. He'd been down it so many times, but he'd never looked at it from this perspective. He tried to imagine himself down there, rushing on the raft, paddling furiously on the right, Jackson digging his oar into the water on the left. What would that bend up ahead look like if he was down there? Then he saw it, pictured it in his mind as clearly as if he was flying over the water.

Right around the bend there were a couple of houses overlooking the river. He started walking. The green river grass grew high and the trees he wound through often blocked his path and confused him, but he kept the river at his left as he pushed through the thickening woods, thinking of the money in that briefcase. It had to be in the car, but was the car safe? Could he get back before it was towed away, or worse, stolen? And then, just as his anxiety was reaching a fever pitch, the woods fell away into clear ground and he saw a neatly manicured front yard.

He studied the house. Then the one next door, looking for signs of life. He found none. Both homes faced the river. Both were built in log cabin style and Earl guessed that a man must be mighty rich to have an extra home, just for the weekends and holidays.

He crossed the front yard and made his way to a garage between the two homes. It had no windows and the door was locked. The chances were slim, but he needed to know if there was a car in there. The door was too thick to kick in and he didn't have his weapon. He checked the lock, a dead bolt. The garage was locked good.

A bird called overhead and Earl turned, quickly spooked. He looked out toward the sound of the rushing river, then back toward the first of the two vacation homes. His mind made up, he crossed the lawn to the front porch, taking the steps two at a time. He tried the door. Locked. But not deadbolted. He thought about that. Maybe there was a car in the garage after all. Then with a swift side thrust kick, made powerful by twenty years of Shotokan Karate workouts, he blasted the lock and the door flew open.

Too easy. Inside, he went straight toward the bathroom, dropping his wet shirt as he crossed the hardwood living room floor. He kicked his shoes off in the hallway, and stepped out of his pants as he faced the tub. He reached in and turned on the water. Cold only, but that was all right, he'd had plenty of cold showers in his lifetime.

Once the dirt was off he padded to one of the bedrooms and rifled through the bureau drawers and closets. He found a pair of Levi's a couple of sizes too big, but a thick leather belt took care of that, and a white sport shirt made him look close to presentable.

He stared at his reflection in a mirror above the bureau as he buttoned up the shirt. The scabbing cut above his eye and the black and blue bruise on his chin made it look like he was the loser in a heavyweight battle, but there was nothing he could do about that, so he left the mirror.

There were several pairs of shoes in the closet, both men's and women's, but the men's shoes were several sizes too small for Earl's size twelve feet, so he put his own wet shoes back on. Then he made his way to the kitchen, scooping up his wet clothes as he went.

In the kitchen he made a beeline for the refrigerator, but stopped dead when he saw a ring of keys on a wall hook. People could be so stupid. Lock up the garage, then leave the keys in plain view. In the garage he found an almost new Jeep, gassed up and ready to go. Ten minutes later and still hungry he parked it behind his unmarked cruiser.

He wiped his prints off the wheel and the door handle before stepping out of the Jeep. He looked around. He was alone. He closed the door and hustled over to the unmarked. He looked through the open driver's window and saw the briefcase and a surge of relief flowed through him. The money was still there. He tossed his wet and dirty clothes on the floor in the back. Then he stepped back from the car and moved to the side of the bridge, to the spot where Jackson had draped him over the rail, not so long ago, and looked down into the river.

Jackson was dead, Loomis was dead, the boy Darren and Johnny Lee Tyler were dead. He thought about Johnny Lee and he examined himself for signs of remorse and was surprised that he couldn't find any. He'd killed for money before, but doing Johnny Lee wasn't quite the same.

The first time it was a spaced out drug dealer that had been dealing to the kids down to the junior high. Earl had been so pissed off he put three shots into the fucker's chest. Then Jackson had calmly gone to the car and fetched a throw down, fired it once and put it in the bastard's hand. They split forty-five hundred dollars. There wasn't even an investigation.

The other time was after a high speed chase. They caught up to the two out-of-staters that had robbed the Farmer's and Merchant's bank after their car slid out of control and crashed into a tree. One was dead, the other barely alive when they arrived on the scene. Without a word Jackson lifted the money bag from the back seat, and Earl smacked the driver on the back of his head with his pistol, hastening a certain death. Then they torched the car. They split thirteen thousand and again there wasn't an investigation.

But Johnny Lee was different, it was hard to rationalize that. He'd known the boy all his life, and although he wasn't a particularly good kid, he wasn't a bad kid either. If he had it do to over he might not act so hastily, but when he saw the money he'd gone nuts. He supposed the first two killings kind of conditioned him.

He thought of the dead at the warehouse. He knew what had become of Loomis, but he wondered where the bodies of the two boys were. Did Jackson throw them in the river too? And he wondered how much trouble he was in. The boy Darren had been shot with Jackson's gun, he'd killed Johnny Lee with Darren's gun. He didn't know how Loomis had died, but Jackson had probably done him with his own piece. Maybe he could walk away from all of this. Maybe all he had to do was claim that Jackson and

Loomis cold cocked him and hightailed it with the cash. When their bodies were found it would look like one of them got greedy and decided he wanted all the loot for himself, they had a fight and they both lost. Not the best scenario, but not bad.

He needed to see what was what down to the junkyard and the warehouses.

It was dark when he got there. Clouds still covered the moon and the hot Texas air smelled like rain. The electric gate was closed. He parked to the right of it and got out of the car, leaving the headlights on. He whistled, but the dog didn't answer. He wasn't surprised. Loomis' dogs were well trained. They would wait for him to enter, then be on him like a wraith.

Earl turned away from the gate, sniffed the air, looked at the sky, then quick stepped to the office. He tried the door. Locked and barred, a side thrust kick wasn't going to get him in. Shit. There was no way he was getting inside the office without a key. Then he saw Loomis' aging '59 Chevy Biscayne.

The car wasn't locked, no reason to, everybody knew that the driver's window had been broken out years ago. The keys were in it, but usually that wouldn't have made any difference, because usually it was inside the fence with the dog, and usually Loomis was asleep in the bedroom behind the office with that AK-47. But he wasn't sleeping in his bed tonight and Jackson had forgotten to put away the car. Maybe he forgot about the dog, but Earl didn't think so. Jackson wasn't stupid, he would have wanted it to look as natural as possible. He would have let the dog loose.

He climbed into the car, started it up, took a breath, put it in gear, cranked the wheel, pointing it toward the gate, and floored it. The impact stopped the car, the gate held and the dog went crazy, barking and snapping on the other side of it like a saber-toothed hell hound. He threw the car in reverse and backed away. Then Earl looked to the office, put the car in gear and braced himself for a second impact. The barred door crumbled under the car's onslaught. He backed away, climbed out of the car and started toward the office. The dog was howling now, angry and raging, sending chills charging up Earl's spine.

He knew Loomis kept a pair of bolt cutters, so that he could remove the lock if your rent was two weeks past due and put his own lock on. If you wanted the key to Loomis' lock you paid your rent. He found them behind the counter, next to the AK. He picked them up along with the rifle and started toward the gate.

"Hey, you wanna fuck with me now, boy, you wanna fuck with me."

The dog became silent as Earl approached, glaring.

Earl clicked off the safety, raised the rifle in a smooth one-handed motion and put a bullet between the dog's eyes. It went down quiet and quick. Then the other dog, the junkyard mate, started howling like a werewolf, but it didn't matter to Earl, because they were at least a couple of miles from the nearest human being. The fucking dog could howl itself to death for all he cared.

The lock snapped in the bolt cutter's jaws like spaghetti sliced by a scissors. The stench hit him before he hit the light. Blood, urine, feces, but no bodies. The counterfeit CDs, the porno videos, the cocaine were still there, along with his weapon, sitting on an open box of compact discs. He picked it up, glad to have it back.

He didn't know what Jackson had done with the bodies, but it was a fair guess they'd never be found. Not a bad plan. When Earl washed up at the bottom of the river with Loomis the investigation would eventually get the police to the warehouse and his gun. Still a good plan, only now it would be Jackson's body along with Loomis' floating in that river.

But then he thought about the broken lock, the dented gate, the smashed in office, and the dead dog. He had to destroy any evidence that he'd been there, and he remembered the two out-of-staters that he and Jackson had torched. He had a siphon hose and an empty gas can in the unmarked.

An hour later he was home, dying to get his aching muscles under a hot shower. A shower would also wash his conscience clean and clear his mind. Just a little hot water, that's all it would take, because it wasn't the first time he'd shot someone for the money. But before, a voice in his head told him, it was a drug dealer and a couple of robbers, men he didn't know, with families he'd never see. But that time, he answered the voice, he'd only netted peanuts.

The briefcase in the back seat of his unmarked must have a half million or more in it. For that kind of money he'd go hunting with Johnny Lee's daddy for six months of Sundays and never even think of the boy. He looked at his feet and frowned. He'd tracked in some dirt on the new carpets. He'd have to clean it up as soon as he got out of the shower. He wanted everything to be perfect for Maria when she got back.

He slipped off his shoes, careful not to get any more dirt on the rug. He had his hand on the belt buckle, when he saw the flashing red light on the answer machine. He stepped out of the jeans and went over to the phone.

"Earl, it's me," Maria's voice came soft and low through the small speaker. "I won't be coming home. You can feed yourself, or let Josie down at the diner feed you, or starve for all I care, but you've seen the last of me."

He stood there in his jockey shorts, jeans under his left arm, right fist clenched and listened to the silence after the message. He had a car full of cash. Josie was young and luscious, he had a good job, he was looked up to. He knew he should be satisfied, but no woman walked out on Big Earl Lawson.

"Son of a bitch," he said as he threw his jeans onto the carpet. He picked up the phone and called the airline. It didn't take him long to find out about the bombs on the plane or where she was. Shit, the plane was on the ground for less than an hour and she was calling it quits.

CHAPTER TEN

"THEY STOLE MY CAR." The blue veins on his forehead were pulsing, his neck cords were throbbing, his hands were shaking, but his speech was clipped and calm. "I don't care if he is your friend, I want him arrested and slammed in jail. I want him put so far away that I'll never have to hear his name again. I want him buried so deep, that he'll wish he was dead. I want him to suffer for the rest of his life. Do you understand what I'm saying?"

"Calm down, George. This is another day. It won't do any of us any good if you have a stroke," Dani Street said. She'd seen him mad, never heard him swear.

"Don't tell me to calm down. You aren't shit

without me."

"Cool your jets, George, and try to remember who you're talking to." He bit into his lower lip. She knew he was a man who suffered orders and taking them from a woman tripled the salt.

"Sorry," he said, the color beginning to fade from his face.

"That's better," she said.

"But he stole my car," he repeated, and she shook her head. He was a smart man, but he was bullheaded, like a lot of Trinidadian males. She was afraid he'd worry about his car like an old woman until it was a festering sore that he had to do something about, and she couldn't allow that to happen.

"We need you, George," she said. "It's your plan. We can't make it work without you. I can take care of Ramsingh. The Salizar brothers can move the coke. I can bury the money so deep the US will never figure it out. Kevin can whip your armed forces and police into shape and guarantee that they remain loyal. But without you we might as well fold our tent and take the show on the road." She reached into him with her steady gaze and held his eyes. She waited a few seconds, blinked and turned away. He liked to think he was the stronger of the two and she saw no harm in letting him believe it.

"What about your friend Broxton?" he said.

God he was stubborn, she thought.

"He did steal my car."

"Come on, you had no business having your security people go chasing after him like that. Bill Broxton may not be the smartest man on earth, but he didn't get where he is by being stupid. Credit him with a few brains. And why did they have to use your car?"

"Not enough cars to go around," he said.

"And whose fault is that? You have five thousand police and only a hundred cop cars. It's a wonder the criminals don't rule the island."

"We'll get more cars when I'm prime minister."

"Every election they say that and the police are still walking."

"Can we talk about Broxton? He's here to keep Ramsingh alive."

"Of course he is. Credit me with a few brains, too. He won't be a problem. When the time comes he'll go one way, Ramsingh will go the other, and Ramsingh will die."

"When?"

"Soon." She couldn't blame him for being upset. She should have done it by now. But she had that thing about Ram. He was her father's friend. He was her friend.

"If I didn't know better, I'd say you're stalling. But you wouldn't stall, would you?"

She clenched her fists. She'd been so stupid. The odds that anyone would put her travels together with the Scorpion's jobs were one in a hundred thousand, maybe one in a million. But it had happened. George Chandee had been captivated by her, probably because she was that rare thing in his life. A woman that wouldn't go to bed with him.

He sent flowers. Took her to dinner. Offered her all the right complements. But his old magic failed to light her fires. And the more she refused, the more he desired her. He asked if there was someone else and she'd said there wasn't. Maybe that was her mistake. Maybe she should have told him about her relationship with Kevin a lot sooner, then maybe he would have gone away. But she didn't. She said there was no one, but he didn't believe her. So he watched her.

He didn't say anything when she'd returned from Zambia. She'd done a wonderful shoot for Save the Children just hours before the president was assassinated.

He was silent when she'd come back from a shoot in Ecuador. They'd gotten great footage of her with a pair of paper thin twin boys, but no one got footage of the leader of the opposition when he was gunned down leaving for work only an hour before she left for the airport. He didn't come calling and confront her till she returned from Sierra Leone the day after the new President was shot during dinner.

Once was coincidence, he'd said. Twice was circumstantial, but three times was the clincher, the next best thing to a smoking gun. He was too smart to threaten her, or to blackmail her, instead, he said, he had a plan. She could have more money than she'd ever imagined. She'd never have to work again, never have to do another hit. All she had to do was something she was good at. Assassinate the prime minister. Shoot Ram and she got a hefty share of the spoils. And the spoils: A small oil rich country, ripe for the plucking and the profits gained from laundering the money of one of the biggest drug cartels in Colombia. Too much money to walk away from. It was just too much.

* * *

Earl wiped the sweat from his forehead. He was sweating like a stuck pig and he hadn't cleared customs yet. He was standing behind a large black man with no neck. The son-of-a-bitch must spend his life in the fucking gym, Earl thought, as he concentrated on a fly that was moving downward over the ripple of muscle on the back of the man's head. No Neck swiped at it without looking, moving hand and arm like a giant paw. Earl jerked his head out of the way, barely avoiding the grizzly strike. The fly turned to mush and blood on the hump that passed for a neck. It didn't have a chance.

"Watch it," Earl said, without thinking.

No Neck turned and smiled at Earl. "Sorry." He pinched the fly between thumb and forefinger and flicked it onto the floor.

"Just missed me," Earl said.

"I'll try to be more careful," the huge man said. The encounter was over as No Neck moved up to the customs counter and Earl realized that like the fly, he was out of the man's memory, no more important than the dust on the floor. He was brooding, thinking of home, not even gone a day and he missed Texas.

"Next," the custom's officer said, and Earl felt relief flood over him. He was tired of the line, tired of the dingy airport and tired of the sweat pouring down his back. The sooner he got Maria and got out of Trinidad, the better.

An hour later the road weary cab pulled up in front of the Hilton Hotel. Earl couldn't get out of the car fast enough. Less than two hours in the country and all he wanted to do was go home. He was disgusted by the run down buildings, the fading paint, the litter in the street and the sea of black faces. This wasn't the good old U. S. of A.

"Don't you just love it here?" the driver said. "Everything is so laid back. No pushing and shoving, everybody has a smile on their face."

"Nice," Earl said, wondering if the idiot was seeing the same things he was.

"And it's so clean."

"Clean?" Earl said, he had his hand in his hip pocket, digging for his money. He wanted to pay the sorry excuse for a cab driver and have him on his way.

"Air's fresh," the cab driver said.

"Bullshit," Earl said, money in hand.

"Eighty dollars," the driver said.

"Eighty dollars? You must think I'm nuts. No way. That's robbery."

"It's not robbery. It's the normal charge. If you can't afford it you shoulda taken the bus."

He started to say something, then he remembered the cash in the briefcase by his foot, and he smiled. He'd brought the money with him, because he couldn't think of anyplace to leave it and there sure as shit wasn't anybody he could trust with it. If he'd had time he'd have gotten himself three or four safety deposit boxes down to the bank, but everything happened so fast.

"You're right," he said, counting out four twenties. The cab driver's eyes went white and wide and his hand started shaking as he accepted the money.

"Thank you, sir, thank you very much," he said.

"Now get the bags." Earl felt more important than he'd ever felt wearing a badge in a small Texas town. He was going to like having money.

Once in the hotel he walked briskly across the lobby toward the reception desk. The young man behind the counter looked up as he approached, pulled his face out of a ledger and closed it.

"Can I help you?" he asked. He was an African Trinidadian with a wide smile and pointy ears that looked like they were cropped close to the head, like they came off of a Doberman pinscher.

"You have a Maria Lawson staying here?"

The clerk punched a few keys and studied a computer screen. "Yes we do," he said through his ear to ear smile.

"Can you give me her room number?" Earl asked.

"Can't do that. It's against the rules, but you can use the house phone over there. The hotel operator will put you right through."

"I don't want to be put right through. I want her room number." Earl balled his hands and felt the blood rising under his collar. He wanted to wipe the grin off the young man's face.

"I'm sorry, would you like me to get the manager?"

"I guess you don't hear so good. I don't want the manager. I don't care about your rules. I don't want to talk to her on the phone. I want you to give me her room number." The blood was in his head now and he felt himself turning hot, despite the air conditioning that kept the lobby only slightly warmer than a frozen North Texas winter.

"I'll get the manager," the desk clerk said, spinning around. He opened a door behind him. In seconds he'd have the manager. Well that was all right, Earl thought, he knew how to deal with hotel managers.

"I'll be right back," Earl said. He picked up the briefcase and felt a sort of ecstasy with the weight of it, almost as good as sex, then he was off toward the men's bathroom. Inside he entered the first stall, closed the door, and sat on the toilet with the briefcase on his lap. He opened it and fondled the contents with his eyes before he removed a bundle of hundreds, peeled off ten and put them in his hip pocket.

He inhaled deeply, feeling the air flow deep into his belly. Then with a satisfied grunt he closed the case, left the stall and the restroom and headed back to reception. The man was different, but the question was the same.

"Can you give me Maria Lawson's room number?" Earl slid a hundred dollar bill across the counter.

"Four-eighteen," the manager said as he slipped the bill into his pocket.

"Does four-sixteen or four-twenty have a connecting door?" Earl asked.

"Four-twenty does, but it's occupied," the manager said, staring at a computer screen. "Looks like it's going to stay that way for about a week."

"I'll take four-twenty." Earl counted out five more hundreds and slid them across the counter. Probably more than the man made in a month.

"I can't," the man said, but Earl could see greed tugging at his conscience. "I wish I could, but the room is already occupied."

"You could tell them there's a problem with the plumbing and upgrade them, give them a better view." Earl passed over two more hundreds.

"I could do that." The manager covered the seven hundred dollars with his palm.

"I'll be back in an hour," Earl said.

"It won't take that long. Have a drink in the bar. By the time you finish the room will be ready."

Five minutes later he was drinking a rum and coke in the restaurant bar when he saw Maria out by the pool, having lunch with a man. He slow sipped his drink and started drumming his fingers on the bar. So that's why she'd left him, she was seeing someone else. He wondered how long it had been going on and why he hadn't been able to see it.

"Another?" the bartender asked, jerking Earl's attention away from the couple on the other side of the window.

"No, I've gotta go see if my room is ready." He didn't know what kind of man shaved his head, but he sure planned on finding out.

Fifteen minutes later he was back in the restaurant, the money safely up in the room, and this time he was sitting at a table instead of the bar by the window, and he was staring at his wife and her man friend. He wanted to squeeze the bastard till he popped.

"What joo having?" Earl turned away from the scene outside and faced a young waitress. She was short, dark, and obviously Puerto Rican.

"A rum and coke," he said.

"Joo know Kojack?"

"The ugly one with the shaved head?"

"Sure, him."

"Never seen him before," Earl said. "Who is he?"

"He's American, I heard the accent."

"Really?" Earl said. How long had Maria known the man? "And the woman?" Earl asked. "She's a looker."

"She's staying solo. I think she's a stewardess."

"Can I have my check?" The voice was melodic and belonged to a stunning woman at the next table. Normally Earl would have noticed her first thing, but he'd been so caught up with the idea of Maria and another man that he'd missed her completely.

"Would you like another, ma'am?" Earl offered, ever the gentleman.

"No thanks, I have to get back to work," the

woman said. Her blue eyes twinkled, clear as the South Texas ocean, and her smile promised hidden delights.

"Maybe I'll see you again," he said. He couldn't help himself. When he saw a pretty woman he had to flirt, and if she was receptive he had to give chase.

"Maybe," she said. "I come here a lot." She handed the waitress a blue bill. "Keep the change, Elena," she said.

"What did you pay with?" Earl asked.

"TT hundred dollar bill."

"How much is it worth?" Earl asked, a funny feeling rising in his stomach.

"About eighteen dollars US," she said. "There's about six TT per US dollar."

"Shit." He felt dumber than a roadkilled skunk.

"Why?" she asked.

"I paid the cab driver with green money."

"He must have been very pleased," she said.

"He was smiling," Earl laughed. Then he added, "Name's Earl Lawson."

"Dani, Dani Street," the woman said, holding out her hand. "Are you staying here at the Hilton?"

"Sure am." Earl beamed, thinking he was making headway.

"Then maybe we really will see each other again." She smiled and took her hand back. He watched her shapely walk till she was out of the restaurant. When she was out the door he turned his attention back toward the pool, but Maria and her boyfriend were gone.

He spent another twenty minutes nursing three rum and cokes. Normally he was a scotch and soda man, but he was in the Caribbean and rum seemed to be the drink of choice. At first he didn't like the sweet taste of the Coca Cola, but he found he was warming up to it.

"Joo going for another?"

"I'd sure like to, but then I'd follow it with another, then another, and you know how that goes."

"Sure do."

"So I guess I'd better pay and get on my way."

"Joo can sign for it, if you're staying in the hotel."

Five minutes later he opened the door and instantly grabbed for a gun that wasn't there.

"Stay calm, Earl, and stay alive," Dani Street said. He relaxed his hand and let it fall to his side. She was sitting at the desk by the window. Her handbag was on it and a chrome plated thirty-eight police special was sitting next to the purse. She was still wearing her smile and by the tone of her voice he knew she could pick up the gun and use it before he got close to her.

"What's going on?" he said, trying to sound calm. His money was piled on the center of the bed, still wrapped in ten thousand dollar packets.

"There's more going on than you could possibly understand," she said.

* * *

Dani looked at Earl's strong jaw. His deeply tanned face looked like it belonged on a movie poster. He was a man used to the sun. His eyes bore into her, but he was restraining himself. She took in the cut above his eye and the bruise on his chin. He was no stranger to violence. He was going to be perfect, she just knew it. She wanted someone else to pull the trigger on this one. The job was too close to home.

"Sit down, Sheriff." He stared at the gun on the desk and she could see the calculations going on in his head. "Try it."

"I been around a long time. I know when to fish and when to cut bait. I'll sit and see what you have to say."

"You're not as dumb as you look, Earl," Dani said.

"It was my questions about the man with the shaved head, wasn't it? You were watching him, too?"

"In a way," Dani said. "You were kind of clumsy."

"I got my way of doing things," Earl said.

"The money is counterfeit," Dani said.

"What?" Earl grabbed a bundle from the stack. He pulled a bill out and looked at it against the light. "Looks okay to me," he said, but she saw his furrowed brow and his shaking fingers.

"The serial numbers are all the same, Earl, and the paper is wrong. They have two dollar marking pens all over the world that will tell even the most unaware kid behind a register that you're passing bad money. You might as well burn it."

He peeled off another bill and compared them. "Shit," he said.

"But you have bigger problems," Dani said.

"I can't wait to hear."

"The manager told me you were a big tipper, when he figures out you tipped him with funny money he'll be up here and after your balls."

"Shit," Earl said.

"You'll have to go down and make it right," Dani said, opening her handbag. She pulled out a roll of hundreds and counted out twenty bills. "Here's two thousand. When you buy back your bad money give the man an extra two hundred. That should satisfy him and it'll leave you an extra thousand for walking around money."

She got up and handed him the money. She left

the gun next to the handbag on the desk.

"You're awful sure of yourself," Earl said.

"You're not a stupid man, you're curious," Dani said.

"I'm curious," Earl said.

"Stick with me and I'll turn that pile of paper on the bed into the real thing. You can leave Trinidad a wealthy man."

"I'd like that," Earl said, as Dani turned her back to him and moved back to the desk. "I'd like that a lot."

"I knew you would." She dropped the gun into her purse.

"Who do I have to kill?"

"The Prime Minister of Trinidad."

"I could do that."

CHAPTER ELEVEN

"GOOD MORNING, SIR," Broxton said, rubbing sleep from his eyes as he smiled at the Indian Trinidadian behind the counter. "Do you sell breakfast here?" He was still half asleep. He'd been up most of the night talking and reminiscing with Warren.

"We see a lot of Africans with shaved heads," the Indian said, ignoring Broxton's question, "but I've never seen a white man with one, only on TV. Looks good on you. Looks like you can fight, too. Plenty muscles."

"About breakfast?" Broxton said.

"Do the girls like that head, or is it just you?" the Indian said. He had flashing white teeth flapping inside of withered gums and Broxton caught the laughing twinkle in his eyes. If he wanted breakfast he was going to have to play with the man.

"I think the girls like it," he said, running his right hand along the side of his scalp. "And it's easy to keep up, I start shaving from the top and just keep going." He put his hand back to his head, thumb and index finger together, like he was holding a razor, and brought it from the top of his chrome dome down along the side, where sideburns would be if he had any, over his cheek and down to his chin, imitating a man shaving. "And no barber bills either, very economical."

"I like you. I'm called Davidnen." The Indian stuck his hand over the counter. Broxton shook it and Davidnen laughed. "Tough guy handshake, like a real American," he said.

"Do you always say whatever you want?" Broxton asked.

"I'm ninety-six, almost a century old, a century," he said, emphasizing his speech the way Trinidadians do. "I'm entitled, I've earned the right."

"Yes, sir, you have," Broxton said, nodding. "Now about breakfast?"

"Bakes is the best I can offer. Sort of like a pita bread sandwich. I can make you one with ham and eggs. No charge today, because you really didn't come here to eat, but I might charge you for whatever it is you want to know."

Broxton laughed again, but this time it was forced. "You're pretty sharp."

"Not really. You don't work over there," he said, looking through the front window toward the American Embassy on the other side of the street, "and if you had business there you'd come later, after they're open. You don't look like you're on vacation, and besides we're off the tourist track. So what is it, are you some kind of spy looking for information?"

"It's not like you're thinking," Broxton said.

"I'm hearing you good," Davidnen said. "Keep talking."

"It's about a woman."

"Ah," the old man sighed, then twinkled, "which one?"

"Dani Street."

"And why are you wanting to know about her?" the Indian asked, his eyes narrowing.

"I came to Trinidad to marry her," Broxton said.

"I see, so it's Kevin Underfield you're wanting to know about?"

"Yes, no, I don't know. I was just going to sit here and watch her come to work, that's all." He was talking like a man wearing his heart on his sleeve and he knew it, but he couldn't help it.

The Indian put a hand up and played with his mustache as he studied Broxton. After a moment he said, "You should have come sooner if that's what you're after." And the room was quiet save for the sound of the Indian sucking on his upper lip as he tried to reach his mustache with his teeth.

"There were problems," Broxton said, continuing to confide in a man he didn't know.

"Yes, for sure, you married the wrong woman, Mr. Broxton."

"How do you know my name, and how do you know about me?" Broxton asked.

"We talk, me and Dani. We're good friends. She eats here every day, most of the other Americans from the Embassy don't. They go to Rafter's or one of the finer restaurants. I guess they don't much like the local food."

"Is he a nice guy, this Kevin Underfield?"

"Not so nice, I don't think," the Indian said.

"What do you mean?"

"I think I've said enough, but Dani says you work for the DEA, you'll be able to figure it out." He paused and ran his tongue over his mustache, like he was checking to see if it was still there, then said, "And as we speak of the devil, he arrives."

Broxton turned back toward the window again in time to see Dani kiss Kevin Underfield firmly on the lips. Then she turned and walked into the Embassy and Underfield started off down the block. He was wearing a sweatshirt with the sleeves cut off, sweatpants and running shoes. He looked like a Nike commercial, with his poster boy good looks and strong athletic build.

"I think I'll go," Broxton said, thinking that Dani must place a lot of trust in this old man. She even told him that he worked for the DEA.

"That would be wise, and remember one thing."

"What's that?"

"I wasn't telling you anything here. For myself I don't care, but I have children, grandchildren and great grandchildren, them I care about. Trinidad is a small place."

"I wasn't even here," Broxton said, starting for the door.

"And we never met." The Indian winked.

Broxton closed the door behind himself and started off after Underfield. It was a cool morning, promising to be a hot day, and Kevin Underfield was walking at a brisk pace with the morning sun at his back. That was an advantage for Broxton. If Underfield looked behind he'd be staring into the light.

He half wondered why he was following the man. He also wondered why he showed up at the Embassy and hid in the small restaurant across the street. It didn't seem right, snooping around after Dani. They'd been friends since they were children. If he wanted to know about her relationship with Kevin Underfield all he had to do was ask. But there was something about Underfield he didn't like. Maybe it was just the fact that he'd stolen Dani's heart, but maybe it was something more.

Underfield stopped, waved, and met a *cafe au lait* colored woman with a drop dead gorgeous face wearing black Danskins that hugged her curves like the white line hugs the center of the highway. Just the sight of her set Broxton's heart pumping. Like Underfield, she was wearing running shoes. It took Broxton less than a second to figure out that they'd be coming back his way, because they were probably going to the Savannah to run. He looked left, then right, then dashed between a small auto parts store and a bakery three doors back, toward the embassy.

They jogged by seconds later and Broxton let them get down the block before leaving his hiding place and going after them. Two blocks brought them to the ring road around the Savannah. He watched while they crossed it and turned left. From where he stood it was about three quarters of a mile across the large park. He guessed that it would take them longer to jog the two miles around it to get to the spot where he'd be if he kept straight on at a brisk walk.

Twenty minutes later he was sitting on a bench, looking up the hill across the street at the Hilton Hotel as the pair came jogging toward him, but they didn't pass, instead they turned left, crossed the ring road, and continued jogging on up toward the hotel.

"Shit," he muttered as he pushed himself up from the bench. He'd been so sure that they'd jog on by without noticing him, but then he felt the morning sun on his shaved head and he knew that Underfield would have pegged him right away.

He started to cross the street when he saw a group of young people headed his way. They looked like they were between fifteen and seventeen, four boys and three girls. One of the boys was wearing a New York Yankees baseball cap. He sat back down on the bench and waited for them to approach.

"Wanna sell the Yankees cap?" he said when the group was within hearing distance.

"Not really," the boy said.

"Fifty US, right now," Broxton said.

"It's yours." The boy tossed Broxton the cap. Broxton reached into his back pocket and pulled out his wallet.

"You're crazy, right?" one of the girls said.

"No, I just like the Yankees." Broxton handed the kid a fifty.

"I like 'em, too," the kid said.

"Yeah, about fifty bucks US worth," another one of the girls said and they all laughed and continued on their way.

Broxton set the cap on his head, looked both ways, remembering that they drove on the opposite side of the street in Trinidad. Then he crossed and started toward the path that led up to the hotel. His underarms felt like Velcro as they attempted to stick to his skin with each stride. He tried holding them straight, without swinging them, but it was no use.

They were out of sight, but that didn't worry him. They'd probably gone to the restaurant for a quick bite to eat or a cold drink. It didn't dawn on him that they might be in one of the many rooms till he entered the lobby.

He pulled off the cap and looked around. He headed toward the restaurant, glanced in and didn't see them, then he put the cap back on and started toward the front desk, ready to pay for information from the desk clerk, when he saw the girl's picture encased in glass on the wall outside the restaurant.

She was wearing a skintight, hip hugging formal in the black and white photo, and she looked like a glamour queen. The caption on the poster read, 'Stormy sings the blues live at the Hilton every Sunday night.' Stormy. Broxton wondered what her real name was. He knew he couldn't go to the front desk and ask about her. Any questions he asked, no matter how much he paid, would be repeated back to her and he didn't want that. So he turned back toward the restaurant, went in and took a seat by the back wall, facing the door.

Thirty minutes later, as he was finishing his ham and eggs, she stopped by the front of the restaurant wearing tight Levi's and a pale pink, loose fitting silk blouse. She was beauty personified, she could make old men quiver and young men swoon. Broxton was neither young nor old though, so he raised his hand to get her attention, but he dropped it as quickly as he'd put it up when Kevin Underfield came into view wearing a beige suit and tie.

Not the running sweats he'd come in with, Broxton thought. He watched as Underfield gave her a slight kiss on the lips and he looked away when the man roamed his eyes around the room. He turned his head back as Underfield patted her on the rear, before turning and walking through the lobby and out the front door. Then he raised his hand again as she entered the restaurant.

She saw his waving hand, caught his eyes and started toward his table. He stood as she approached. She was stunning and each step she took stole more of his breath away. Her deep brown eyes were clear as windows and they seemed to be laughing, and her perfect teeth, gleaming from her smile, seemed to light up the room.

"You look better without the hat," she said, as she pulled a chair out from the table and sat down.

Broxton sat and stared.

"Come on, put your eyes back in your head. I'm good looking, but I'm not that good looking."

"You're for sure the prettiest woman that's ever sat down at a table with me," Broxton said, meaning it.

"You've been following me," she said. "Why?"

"Not you. Him," Broxton said. He reached up and jerked the hat off his head.

"Your hands are shaking. Are you nervous?" she asked.

He held his right hand out in front of himself for a few seconds and watched it. It was indeed quivering slightly. "It must be you," he said. "Do you always have this effect on men?"

"I hope so," she said. "Now why are you following him?"

"You wanna go see Tammy Drake at the Normandy tonight?" he asked. "It's a special show for the diplomatic corps. I've got a couple of tickets." Warren had given him the tickets because the prime minister was supposed to be at the dinner concert. He'd planned on asking Maria during lunch, but the woman sitting across from him shot out an aura of sex and danger that tingled his spine and set his feet to tapping under the table. He couldn't help himself, something about her just reached out and grabbed at him, tugging at all the right places.

"Maybe. You're kind of exciting, but first why were you following Kevin?"

"I came to Trinidad planning to ask Dani Street to marry me," he said, "but when I get here I find she's engaged to somebody else. I'm curious about him, and I have to admit, I'm curious about him and you."

"That's it? That's all? You're only interested in him because of Dani? Nothing else?"

"Isn't that enough?" he said.

"I'd love to go with you," she said, "but you know Kevin is going to be there with Dani."

"I know," Broxton said.

"I'll meet you here. Tonight at eight. At this table," she said. Then she stood, and in a second was gone.

Broxton sat for a few minutes, musing over his strange morning. He thought about Dani and he thought about Maria. He was in love with the former and beginning to care about the latter. There wasn't any room in his life for a woman named Stormy who sang the blues. He told himself he was only going out with her to find out about Kevin Underfield, but even as he finished the telling he knew it was a lie.

He raised his hand to get the waiter's attention, then made the international sign for asking for the check by holding one hand flat and pretending to scribble on it with the other. He accepted a knowing smile from the young man, left a generous tip and made his way out of the restaurant. Most of the staff watched him as he left and his waiter flashed him the thumbs up sign. It took him a few seconds, but it finally dawned on him. They all knew Stormy. They were giving him the recognition young men give other young men when they think they've scored with a beautiful woman. He shook his head and left.

As he passed the house phones he thought about calling and inviting Maria to lunch, but he didn't want to have lunch with one woman while he was thinking about dinner with another.

Eleven hours later Broxton drove a rented Nissan Sentra into the parking lot of the Normandy Hotel, and although it was only a few minutes drive from the Hilton, Broxton felt he knew Stormy's life story. She had been talking nonstop the whole way. She managed to tell Broxton that she was twenty-five years old, her name really was Stormy, she was born in Port of Spain just after all the lights went out because of a tropical storm. She had a younger sister, Jenna, and a brother, Gary, living in Canada. She had been singing since she was a little girl. Tammy Drake was her idol and the two women were very good friends. But about Kevin Underfield, not a word.

He parked the car and went around to the passenger side to open the door for her, but she was out of the car before he made it around. "What a lovely night," she said and she inhaled deeply. She was standing under a light that wasn't doing a very good job of illuminating the parking lot, but it was doing a superb job of illuminating her. The soft light reflected off her bare shoulders and winked through her long hair, giving her an angelic halo that contrasted greatly with the devilish look in her shining eyes.

"Before we go in," she said, "I just want you to know that Kevin and I were an item a while ago, but we went our separate ways. Today at the hotel was sort of a test. We both needed to see how it would go. It didn't. It's over now, we both know it. I think we both knew it before we started, but we had to give it one last try just to make sure that none of that old flame was still there. It wasn't. It's gone. What we did is nothing to get excited about and Dani never has to know about it. It would only hurt her."

Broxton nodded, but he thought what they did was wrong. If Kevin was really in love with Dani he didn't need to test himself by sleeping with another woman. But he held his tongue. He didn't want to argue with her.

"Let's go in," he said, and she took him by the arm and allowed him to lead her into the restaurant. They were late and Tammy Drake was already on stage, singing a slow ballad. There were people on the dance floor and tables off to the right and outside on the large balcony.

"Isn't she beautiful," Stormy said.

"She is," Broxton said back, "but she can't light a candle next to you."

"That's nice of you to say, but she's an international star. She sings all over the world. Everybody knows who she is. I'm barely noticed outside of Port of Spain."

"Let's find a table," he said.

"No, let's dance first." She lead him onto the dance floor, where they spent the next forty-five minutes slow dancing to a string of ballads. Every dance brought her a little closer until they moved as one. Tammy's voice and Stormy's lithe body pressing against his combined to make Broxton feel like they were alone on the dance floor. He was a teenager again, biting his lip to control an erection. He wanted her badly and he sensed that she wanted him.

Then the last ballad was over and the lights went on. People started returning to their tables. He was fantasizing about what he could be doing with Stormy afterwards when he was shocked out of his reverie by Dani's glaring stare.

"How could you?" she said, through tight lips.

"What?" he said.

"Her," Dani said. Her face was red and her nostrils were flaring. For a second he thought she was going to slap him, but she turned on her heels and started for the door. He looked around the room to see if anyone had noticed and he locked eyes with Kevin Underfield. The man smiled, then saluted him with a loose hand, before turning and following his fiancé out the door and Broxton knew he'd been set up.

He turned toward Stormy, "Why?" he said.

"She hates me. Kevin wanted to make sure you were no threat."

"I could tell her."

"Tell her what? You're the one that invited me tonight, remember?" she said, then she stood on her toes and pecked him on the cheek. "I guess I'll go too. Don't worry about getting me home, my car's in the lot."

CHAPTER TWELVE

BROXTON WOKE WITH A HANGOVER and a picture of the fire in Dani's eyes burning through the pain in his head. He'd lost her again, and again he blamed himself. He ran his hand over his scalp and down the back of his neck, wiping the sweat off. It had been a hot night and the fan overhead did little more than stir the hot air.

He stumbled out of a hard bed, regretting the bottle of Scotch he bought at the bar, before checking into the hotel. He drank himself into a stupor and now a hangover kept his broken heart company.

He studied the bags under his eyes in the bathroom mirror and splashed some water on his stubble covered face. He wished he had something to shave with. He wished he hadn't slept in his clothes, and he wished he had gone back to Warren's mansion, instead of spending the night with a bottle of Scotch.

He sighed, dropped his clothes on the floor and stepped into the shower with his mouth turned into the spray, soaking up the water into his dehydrated system. After he'd satisfied his thirst, he turned the heat up and let the hot water cascade down his back, soothing the aches and pains caused by his trek along the river and through the drain pipe. If he could have his way he'd stay forever under the spray, but sometimes you just have to face the music. He shut off the water, toweled off and got back into his rumpled clothes. Then he went to the phone and called Warren's. Dani answered on the first ring.

"It's me," Broxton said.

"It's amazing," she said. "You're the only man in the world who could ever get me to act like that. How come that is?"

"Just my lovable good nature," he said, relieved that she wasn't still angry. Maybe there was hope yet.

"How come you brought that slut to the concert?" Dani asked.

"Slut's a little strong."

"You're right. I'm sorry. She used to date Kevin. We don't get along."

"No kidding, you could have fooled me."

"How'd you meet her?"

For a second he debated not telling her, but he'd never lied to her before and he wasn't going to start now. He also wasn't about to tell her that her fiancé was sleeping with his old flame. He decided to hedge. "I saw her poster up at the Hilton, just before I saw her. The restaurant was full. I asked her to join me.

Then I asked her out. She said yes, no big deal."

"So you brought a date to a function you knew I was going to be at?"

"Why not? You brought one."

"Oh shit, you're right," she said. "It's none of my business. Did you have a good time after I left?"

"Ask my hangover," he said. Let her think what she wanted.

"Where are you?"

"The Normandy." Now she definitely was going to assume he spent the night with her.

"Is she there now?" Did he detect a note of jealousy in her voice? Maybe, he couldn't tell.

"No."

"Good, you wanna go sailing on Daddy's boat this afternoon?"

"I'd love it, but my hangover wouldn't. I'll have to pass."

"It'll be your last chance to see me for awhile."

"What are you talking about?"

"The sail this afternoon. It's a sea trial. I'm sailing up island Saturday morning with some friends. I'll be gone for four or five months. It's a long vacation."

"I'm sorry, I'm really in horrible shape. If I'd only known." He wondered if Kevin Underfield was going along.

"Think you might be better by five or six?" she asked.

"Probably."

"Then you wanna go to Margarita tonight?"

"As in Venezuela?"

"Just for one night. I need to go shopping. I need some new clothes for the trip and there's a few things I'd like to have on board that you can't get here."

"I can't. I've got to work, sorry," he said.

"Daddy said to tell you that Prime Minister Ramsingh is going to be on the same flight. He made me promise to introduce you."

"Then I'd love to go," he said, thrilled at the prospect of spending a night with her. Maybe he really did have a chance after all.

"I'll think of your hurting head as we tack and jibe the day away."

"Kevin going?" he hated asking, but he had to know.

"Nope just me, Daddy and *Sea King*."

"A new boat?"

"Yes, *Wind Dancer* was just too small. *Sea King's* sixty feet and fast."

"The two of you can handle it?"

"Electric winches, roller furling sails, even the main, sure no problem."

Broxton didn't know what she was talking about and didn't care. All he wanted to do was drink a gallon of water and go back to sleep. "What time's the flight?" he asked.

"Seven-thirty, but it's a Venezuelan airline leaving from Trinidad, so plan at leaving around eight or nine." She laughed. "I'm already packed and I'll have my bag with me, so I'll go straight from the dock to the airport. Why don't I meet you there at six, then we'll drink till takeoff."

"I'll be there, but don't expect me to be drinking much. I'll probably never drink again."

"That's my Bill. See you tonight."

"See ya," he said. His hat was definitely still in the ring. Kevin Underfield watch out, because Bill Broxton is back in the game, he thought. Then he lay back, closed his eyes, and fell asleep.

* * *

He settled in and had just fastened his seatbelt when his senses went on alert.

"Well, Mr. Broxton, how nice to see you again."

"Good evening, Mr. Prime Minister." Prime Minister Ramsingh was the last to board the plane and he was standing over Broxton's seat with his hand on the headrest.

"Call me Ram, all my friends do."

"I don't know if I can, sir," Broxton said.

The prime minister was smiling, amused at Broxton's discomfort. "Sure you can. And please don't call me sir. I'm just plain Ram. I insist. I really don't like this sir business, especially from my friends. And we better be friends, because I'm not the one paying you to keep me alive."

"I thought—" Broxton stammered, but the prime minister cut him off.

"The attorney general was a little impetuous when he told your secretary of state that we didn't want American help. He embarrassed me into agreeing to go along with his ridiculous notion that we should handle the situation by ourselves, but only a fool would shun the help of someone who was trying to keep him alive. I've been called a lot of things, but nobody's ever called me that, at least not to my face."

"Yes, sir."

"Ram, no more sir," the prime minister said. "I'll have an office set up for you next to mine when we get back to Trinidad and I'll clear my itinerary with you every morning. You can call your people and tell them I'll cooperate fully. They can send over any help they think you might need. Our goals are the same, to stop the flow of Colombian cocaine through

Trinidad, and of course to keep me alive." He chuckled.

"Yes, sir, I mean, Ram."

"I'm staying at the Sans Souci. You can stay with me. The presidential suite has two bedrooms. It's very up scale, with an ocean view. I think you'll like it."

"I'm sure I will," Broxton said. Then he asked, "Where's your security?"

"I don't have any. Mr. Chandee booked this flight under an assumed name and he has me flying second class. He said I shouldn't worry, anybody wanting to assassinate me wouldn't expect me to be in Venezuela."

"When someone tells me not to worry, that's when I start worrying."

"Exactly," the prime minister said.

"Sir, would you please take your seat," a young stewardess said.

"You can ride to the hotel with me," the prime minister said.

"It would be my pleasure," Broxton said, and the prime minister turned and let the stewardess guide him to an aisle seat four rows forward.

"He's going to Venezuela to sign a treaty concerning fishing rights. There's been problems between the Venezuelan Coast Guard and Trini fishermen," Dani said. Her lips were tight and bloodless and Broxton wondered what she was upset about.

"They shot up a fishing boat," Broxton said. "I read about it in the paper."

"I knew it was something like that," she said, tight lips relaxing, forehead scowl easing. The little crow's feet around her eyes were hardly noticeable, unless she smiled wide or was angry.

"You okay?" he asked.

"Yes, I was thinking about Dad's birthday. I haven't bought anything yet."

"Damn, I forgot all about it," Broxton said.

"It's not the kind of thing a man would remember," she said, again relaxed. "You want me to exchange places with Ramsingh?"

"Yeah," he said, and he stepped into the aisle to allow her to slide out from her place by the window. He remained standing as the plane taxied, while Dani moved up to the prime minister's seat. He watched her bend down and whisper in his ear. Then she took his seat and the prime minister moved back toward Broxton.

"I usually sit in the aisle seat," Ramsingh said.

"Not today," Broxton said.

"Of course. You want to be between me and everybody else." Ramsingh took the window seat.

"Something like that," Broxton said. Then asking as Ramsingh fastened his seatbelt, "You really have no security on this trip?"

"None. Both George and Kevin Underfield said it wasn't necessary. Nobody knows I'm here."

"Give me a few minutes to digest this." Broxton leaned back and fastened his own seatbelt. It clicked closed with a snap that sent visions of his last flight flashing through him and he grabbed onto the armrests with a tight knuckled grip. He'd never been afraid of flying, but that last flight was too close in memory for him to be at ease during takeoff.

"You have about forty minutes before we land in Margarita, unless someone kills me on the plane first," Ramsingh said, as the plane started its takeoff roll. His voice had an amused ring to it and Broxton was impressed. Ramsingh was obviously taking the threat on his life seriously, but he wasn't letting it dull his sense of humor.

Once they were airborne Broxton was able to breathe easier. He relaxed his grip on the armrests and started to think. When he'd been given the assignment it was an outside chance at best that he'd be able to do anything more than observe the events in Trinidad as they unfolded. It was an easy job, given to him both because of Warren and as a reward for work well done. A short assignment so that he'd be able to say he'd been in the field. Now it was a real job and Ramsingh was his responsibility, at least until he was able to get help.

"I'm not a field agent," Broxton said, voice barely above a whisper. He didn't want anyone else to hear.

"What do you do?" Ramsingh asked, speaking as quietly as Broxton.

"I read books, reports, newspapers, anything that has to do with cocaine or Colombia. I analyze what I read, I summarize it for people who don't have the time to read, then I go back and read some more and do it all over again."

"And who reads your stuff?" Ramsingh asked.

"Probably nobody."

"And they made you a bodyguard?"

"You have your attorney general to thank for that. He made it clear your government wanted no interference. So the only thing they could do was send me."

"Because you're engaged to Warren Street's daughter."

"That's a sore point with me. We're not exactly engaged. Yet," he said.

"But that's why they picked you, because of Warren?" Ramsingh asked.

"Exactly. They figured I couldn't do much, but I was better than nothing."

"Not a comforting thought."

"But now it's my job to keep you alive."

"Think you're any good?" Ramsingh said.

"I don't like to fail," Broxton said.

"Let's hope that's good enough."

An hour and a half later the three of them were sharing a taxi to the Sans Souci. Broxton was sitting in front with the cab driver, Dani and Ramsingh were sitting in back.

"I hope you don't mind my stealing Mr. Broxton from you," Ramsingh said.

"Not at all. I've got a lot of shopping to do and he'd only be in the way."

"It's a shame you think you have to leave Trinidad to do your shopping," Ramsingh said.

"It's a shame you have a fifteen percent value added tax added on to such a high duty. It keeps your people poor and your goods inferior," she said.

"Government has to run."

"Not on the backs of the poor. Government should encourage full employment so that it can survive on a graduated income tax. The rich need to pay their fair share."

"I can't change the system overnight. Some things are just going to have to wait until after the election."

"You promised you'd get rid of the vat before the last election. I didn't hear you saying, 'Elect me and I'll coast through my first term and if you reelect me I'll do something about these unfair taxes'."

"The government was in much worse shape than I thought before I took office."

"That's an old story. Every third world government uses it."

"It's true."

"Can you two cut it out?" Broxton said. "You sound like you hate each other."

"Not really," Ramsingh said. "This is an old game between us. Nobody else has the courage to talk to me like this, except the loyal opposition and the press, and they don't count. I enjoy Dani's wit. She's made a difference."

"Anybody can agree with a prime minister," Dani said. The cab turned right onto a short palm tree lined road on the Sans Souci property.

"Why don't you check in and we'll see you later for dinner," Broxton said after the cab had stopped in front of the lobby.

"I can't. I have someone to meet, then it's off to Ratan's," Dani said.

"Ratan's?" Broxton asked.

"Very large supermarket," Ramsingh answered.

"Where you can get all those American goodies you can't get in Trinidad, because it's not a free market economy," Dani added.

"She never quits," Ramsingh said.

"That's why we all love her," Broxton said, and they all laughed.

"Okay, dinner in an hour," Dani said. "Then it's off to Ratan's for me."

"Won't they be closed?" Ramsingh said.

"They stay open till midnight. When you have a duty free economy people have more money and stores can afford to be open later."

"The Venezuelan economy is in the toilet," Ramsingh said.

"Not Margarita's. If they ran their whole country like they run this island everyone would be better off."

"All right, no more, please," Broxton said.

"He's not very political," Dani said.

"Doesn't sound that way," Ramsingh said.

At reception Dani checked in first, then headed off toward the elevators promising to meet them in the restaurant in an hour's time.

"I believe you've the presidential suite reserved for me," Ramsingh told the desk clerk.

"We'd also like something smaller, two single beds on the same floor," Broxton said, "and a lot less expensive. You have something like that?" Broxton felt Ramsingh tense up next to him, but it couldn't be helped. Everything was happening so fast. One minute he was heading for a short vacation and the next he was not only in charge of the prime minister's security, he was the prime minister's security.

Ramsingh didn't speak until they were up in the small room. "This is it? We're staying here?"

"It's not bad," Broxton said. "Modern, clean, view of the beach, very touristy."

"And not very presidential."

"Did you book your room yourself?" Broxton said.

"No."

"How many people on your staff know where you're staying?"

"They all do."

"And your attorney general thinks you're secure?"

"Surely you don't think?"

"I don't have the training or the insight to know who to trust, so I'm going to compensate by not trusting anybody."

"How about Dani?"

"Not even her. Certainly she's not going to try to kill you, but who knows who she might talk to. She could easily slip and say the wrong thing. So until we get some real professionals, it's better not to trust anyone."

Then the bomb went off.

Broxton threw himself at Ramsingh, pushing him onto the floor and covering him with his body. The room seemed to vibrate, but the windows didn't break and the explosion was muffled.

"I'm all right," Ramsingh said. Broxton eased himself off and helped the prime minister up.

"It won't take them long to find out you weren't over there. Then they'll come here," Broxton said. "We have to go, now."

Ramsingh reached for his bag.

"Leave it."

"I can't, it's got government papers in it."

"Your life's worth more," Broxton said on his way to the door.

"I'm leaving it." Ramsingh stepped into the hall behind Broxton. The doors to every occupied room on the floor were open and the hallway was teaming with people in various stages of dress and undress.

"What happened?" a female voice said.

"Sounds like the boiler blew," a man said.

"They don't have boilers anymore, at least not on the fifteenth floor," another voice said.

"We'll take the stairs," Broxton said, leading Ramsingh toward the stairway at the end of the hall."

"Billy." Broxton recognized Dani's voice and stopped.

"Are you all right?" he called toward her.

"What happened?" she said, pushing her way through the throng toward them.

"I don't know, but we're leaving."

"The elevator's the other way."

"We're going down the stairs."

"Let's go." She followed them through the excited crowd toward the end of the hall and the staircase.

The stairway was lighted and empty. Broxton took the steps two at a time, the prime minister and Dani doing the same as they passed floor after floor. They were four floors down with ten to go when the fire alarm went off and Broxton quickened his pace. They were five more floors down with five to go when they met the first panicked person entering the stairway.

"Is the hotel on fire?" she asked. She was a young mother, with a baby in her arms.

"I don't know," Broxton said, stopping and gathering his breath. He was panting heavily, but both Ramsingh and Dani looked like they'd just been out for a short walk. "We have to go."

"I can't go down with the baby."

"Give it to me," Broxton said. The woman handed over her child and Broxton again started downward. Three more floors and the stairway started filling up. Broxton pushed into the panicked people, yelling out, "Please make way, my baby's not breathing, please make way," and the frightened people moved aside as Broxton, the baby's mother, Ramsingh and Dani hurried down the stairs.

Broxton burst through the door at the bottom and jogged through the lobby with his troop still following behind. The fire alarm was still wailing, short, steady blasts, but the people in the lobby appeared more curious than panicked. A few were headed for the doorway, but most were standing around like they were at a garden party, talking, laughing, wondering what the fuss was about.

Outside, Broxton saw a couple getting out of a late model Mercedes. A man in an evening jacket was holding the door for a woman dressed like she was going to the Academy Awards. The parking valet was standing solicitously to the side, waiting for the keys.

"You're safe now," Broxton said, handing the baby over to the young mother.

"Thank you," she said.

"Dani, see that she's all right," Broxton said. Then he stepped over toward the Mercedes as the overdressed gentleman was dropping the keys into the valet's hand and he snatched them out of the air.

"I'm going to borrow the car for a bit. Don't worry, I won't hurt it."

"See here," the man said. Two words and Broxton knew he was British.

"Life and death, forgive me," Broxton said. Then he turned away from the man and held the door as Ramsingh slid into the passenger seat.

"Life and death?" the man said. Broxton nodded and noticed a big man leaning on a palm tree, watching him. He was speaking into a handheld radio and Broxton had the impression that he and the prime minister were the subject of the conversation. They locked eyes for an instant, then Broxton hustled around to the driver's side of the Mercedes.

"Yes, sir." Broxton opened the door. "I don't know where I'll leave it, but I'll try and leave it safe."

"Don't worry about the car, just keep the prime minister safe, son."

Broxton hesitated and met the man's wolf gray eyes. "You know?"

"I can guess, now go."

Broxton slipped into the car, started it and spun the wheels.

CHAPTER THIRTEEN

"**HE JUST SPLIT** with the baggage in a black Mercedes and he's headed out." Earl was talking into an miniature handheld VHF radio. He was broadcasting on 01, a channel seldom used by boaters in Venezuela, and the radio was fitted with a scrambler. No one was going to eavesdrop on his conversation.

"This is Undertaker, I have the Mercedes. I'll take it from here." Earl didn't know who his backup was and he didn't care. He'd done his part. It wasn't his fault if the woman couldn't get it right.

"This is Lawman. Am I out of it now?" Earl said into the radio.

"You are not. Get your car and follow. Undertaker will give you directions. Black Widow out."

"Copy," Earl said. He respected the authority in her voice and he sprinted toward the parking lot and the small Ford Escort. Usually he liked bigger, faster cars, but the Escort was in the lot with its windows down. Easy to get in. Easy to get the hood up. Easy to hotwire. Better than a rental.

"He's turned left out of the parking lot. I'm right behind him," his backup said over the radio.

"Undertaker, drop back, give him some room, and remember, nothing happens to Broxton." She called herself Black Widow and just by hearing her voice, Earl knew she was capable of eating her mate, her young, too.

"I see them, up ahead, they're turning again. Left, toward the marina," Undertaker's voice came over the radio. Earl wondered if the British accent was real.

"Copy," he said into his radio.

"Copy," Black Widow said. He wondered where she was. Probably still back in the hotel. What a looker, he thought. What a straight on good looking piece of deadly work.

"I think he's spotted me," Undertaker said.

* * *

Broxton saw the headlights behind and stepped on the gas. He couldn't be sure the car in back was part of the assassination attempt, but he couldn't be sure it wasn't either. Trust no one, suspect everyone, get away. He was racing along the beach and the full moon lit up the phosphorus in the breaking waves. The car behind accelerated too, and then Broxton was sure.

The Mercedes gobbled up the road, blurring the broken center line. Broxton checked the rearview mirror. The headlights behind were fading. They were moving away from their pursuers.

"The road ends," Ramsingh said. Broxton snapped his eyes back to the road, and slapped his foot onto the brakes.

"Shit," he said, as the car slid out of control, leaving the road and heading toward the water. Frantically he spun the wheel away from the beach sand and back toward the center of the pavement. Instinctively he knew it was the wrong thing to do. He should be turning into the slide. But that was book learning, this was real and he'd just fucked up.

The right wheels left the ground and Broxton yelled out, "We're going over!"

Then he stiffened his hands on the wheel, bracing himself as the big car continued its two wheeled spin onto the sand. Ramsingh's side of the car was up in the air and the prime minister wasn't wearing a seatbelt. He struggled to stay in place but the force and surprise of the slide sent him sliding down into Broxton as the two right wheels slammed back onto the ground, cushioned by the beach sand.

They'd spun around a hundred and eighty degrees and were off the road, facing the headlights racing toward them out of the night. The engine was still running and Ramsingh scooted back over toward his side of the car. "We should go," he said. "Now," he added.

"Yeah," Broxton said, adding gas. Then he was back on the road, charging toward an enemy car again. After so long, now twice in the same week.

"What are you doing?" Ramsingh said, voice cool, like he was sitting in a bar ordering a gin and tonic.

"Playing chicken," Broxton said. "The last time I did this was a couple of days ago, with one of your police officers." The back tires kicked off the last of the sand.

"Who won?" Ramsingh said.

"He did," Broxton said, eyes glued onto the rushing headlights. Now, for him, there was no beach, no crashing waves, no lonely road, no prime minister. There was only the headlights, twin beams of death, racing toward him faster than his heart was racing out of control. Twice in the last week he'd taken a car into a spin and twice he'd panicked and done the wrong thing. Last time he told himself it was because he was driving on the left, this time he didn't have that excuse, he just blew it.

And again he was back on Cherry Avenue, back in high school, playing chicken, only this time it wasn't with a macho third world cop who would rather die than blink. This time he was playing with an assassin, and this time Broxton wasn't going to blink.

He braced himself for the collision, but the on rushing car turned. Broxton grabbed a quick glance as they flew past. The driver jerked the wheel too fast and too far to the left. Broxton slammed on the brakes as the other car, a Jeep, left the road on its side. He heard the thunderous scraping of metal against concrete and then the car slammed onto its top, then over onto the other side, bouncing and sliding through the sand.

Broxton saw the headlights up ahead, "Another one," he said as the Jeep hammered into the sea. It went into the water on the driver's side, and Broxton shuddered for a flash of a second, thinking of the water rushing in around the man. Then he whipped the Mercedes around and accelerated away.

"Remember the road ends," Ramsingh said.

"Yeah." Broxton shifted into low, then he was

going through a screaming right turn, following a sign with a long pointing arrow and the single word, 'Marina.' He didn't know if the marina offered any help, or shelter, but he damn sure wasn't going to charge another car. Not now, not ever again. He was going to quit that game while he was ahead. He was on a wide four lane road and the Mercedes was a thoroughbred. If the other car was another jeep he would have no trouble outdistancing it.

The engine was racing and Broxton grabbed the stick to shift out of low. "Shit," he said.

"What?"

"Stuck." The thoroughbred was stuck in low, it was rushing out of the starting gate, but it wasn't going to canter or run. No way was he going to out distance anything.

"Maybe it's just someone out for a late night drive," Ramsingh said.

"They didn't stop for the car that went off the highway," Broxton said, pulling the wheel to the right and following another arrow, another marina sign, this one pointing left, and all of a sudden the heavy Mercedes was humping and bumping on a dirt road.

"Slow down," Ramsingh said, but Broxton already had his foot off the accelerator and he was gently tapping the brakes when the Mercedes coughed and died.

"Shit, shit, shit," he said as he tried the key.

Nothing.

"We're out of here," Broxton said, opening his door.

* * *

Earl spun out of the parking lot and stepped on the gas, going through the gears like a pro.

"Take the first left," Undertaker's voice cracked over the radio. He slammed on the brakes, skidding around the turn. He'd almost missed it. Then he was racing along a dark road, the pounding surf to his left, bare fields on the right. Up ahead he saw the two sets of headlights charging toward each other, like two bulls, fighting over the herd.

"That's some kind of crazy," Earl said, and then Undertaker's Jeep swerved left. The sudden jerk was too much for the top heavy car and it rolled onto its side, then onto its top as it slid off the road, toward the breaking waves. He slowed down, taking his foot off of the accelerator, downshifting into second as the Mercedes ahead spun around and took off like a rabbit running from the fox.

Unlike the Jeeps sold in America, the one sliding into the sea was built with a hard, square, boxy back. Earl noticed the hardtop right off. If his backup survived it would be the hardtop that saved his life.

"Undertaker is down. Lost a game of chicken with your boy and is sliding into the surf as we speak," Earl said into the radio. "Should I stop and offer assistance?"

"Negative, keep after your quarry. I'm a minute behind. If he's alive I'll assist."

More like put a bullet in the poor bastard's brain, Earl thought, but "Affirmative" was all he said, as he stepped on the gas and took off after the Mercedes. It was about a quarter mile ahead. Earl punched the button on the glove box and took out her chrome-plated thirty-eight. Looked liked a pussy weapon, he thought, pretty and glittery, but deadly.

Up ahead the Mercedes squealed around a corner, headed toward the ocean. He wanted more speed, but his foot was on the floor. Then he was at the corner.

He gave the brakes a quick tap, slammed in the clutch and threw it down into third, screamed around the corner and lost control as the Escort howled in protest, bouncing and slamming on a dirt road. The small car whipped around in a tight circle, but Earl managed to stop it without rolling it.

The road ended at the beach. The Mercedes was stopped ahead, with its doors open. The two men were running toward a dark group of abandoned buildings.

* * *

Broxton ran toward a Budget Rental sign, Ramsingh ran along with him, matching him stride for stride. The building was boarded and vacant, they hadn't been renting cars for quite a while. Broxton tried the door, but he knew it was futile before his hand touched the knob. He was heaving air in and out and he could only imagine how the prime minister was doing.

"I'm okay," Ramsingh said, as if reading his thoughts.

"We gotta move," Broxton said. Then he heard the roaring engine and was captivated by the scene before him. The small Ford Escort spun around and was charging backwards toward the Mercedes. If we're lucky, Broxton thought, but they weren't lucky and the car stopped before the collision.

"Quickly," Ramsingh said, jerking Broxton's eyes away from the two cars.

"Right," Broxton said, and together they ran along a series of closed, boarded and graffiti covered buildings. A small book store, a beauty shop, a tee shirt and dress shop, and a souvenir shop. Then he saw it. A huge monolith extending into the night sky.

Dark, with a single light winking out from about the fifteenth floor. A failed hotel sitting smack on the beach, and there was a door on the ground floor, open wide and inviting. There was no place else to go.

"I can make it," Ramsingh said without waiting to be asked, and together the two men sprinted toward that door. Somewhere inside, down a corridor, a dim light beckoned. There was somebody in there. Hopefully not a trigger happy security guard, Broxton thought, as his feet slapped the hard ground. He was worried about Ramsingh, but the prime minister actually quickened his pace and Broxton had to fight to keep up, pumping his arms, forcing his feet to keep the rhythm.

Ramsingh burst through the door first as a gunshot ricocheted through the night and off the wall above the door.

"Down," Broxton screamed, diving forward and tackling the prime minister. They were both in the building, both down, both scrambling forward on hands and knees, when two more shots rang through the night. Broxton heard the bullets slam into something ahead in the dark.

Ramsingh crawled through a door on his right and Broxton pushed in after him. Ramsingh was on his feet first and he offered Broxton a helping hand. "We should keep moving," he said.

"Yeah," Broxton said, and he led the way across a darkened banquet hall that must have hosted many conventions in the past. Would it ever host another? The moonbeams slicing through the hall gave the room a ghost-like quality, as if it was set up for a party that never happened. They weaved through chairs and tables to a door on the opposite side of the hall. Ramsingh pushed on through a swinging door into a full kitchen.

Bright, clean, stainless steel counters reflecting the moon's rays gave the kitchen an even more supernatural appearance than the dining room. Spotless white tile, stainless steel pans hanging on stainless steel hooks around two stainless steel stoves, wide overhead skylights and spotless, white porcelain sinks all combined to chill Broxton's spine.

The hotel had obviously been closed for a long time, judging from the state of the graffiti covered businesses outside, but someone was keeping it up, keeping it ready.

He heard the sound of running behind them and Broxton tapped Ramsingh on the shoulder. They crouched behind a long counter that ran through the center of the kitchen, almost to a second door at the other end. The door that Broxton and Ramsingh were going to have to get through if they were going to get away.

"Lawman, Lawman. Undertaker here, how copy?" Broxton heard the unmistakable sound of a radio. There were more of them.

"I thought you bought it, good buddy," Lawman said. Now he had a name, Broxton thought and he recognized the Texas accent.

"Where are you?" Undertaker's voice cracked over the radio.

"There's a big abandoned hotel, real spooky, down by the beach. I've got them trapped in the kitchen."

"Remember leave the bodyguard alive," Broxton heard the radio voice crackling through static. He thought the accent was White Trinidadian, but it could have been British.

"Shithead," Lawman said into the radio. "He

might have heard."

"Fuck," came Undertaker's reply.

"You coming?" Lawman said.

"Two minutes," Undertaker said.

There were cabinets under the counter and Broxton started feeling around for a door handle, found it and eased a door open, hoping it wouldn't squeak. Inside he found plates and bowls, enough to set table for an army. He picked up one of the plates and tapped the prime minister's arm to get his attention. Ramsingh turned and Broxton showed him the plate. Then he pointed, first to the other side of the room, then toward the door, a long ten or fifteen feet away.

Ramsingh nodded, understanding the message.

Broxton didn't know what kind of weapon the man had and he didn't know if he had spare ammunition. He figured six shots for a revolver and eight, possibly more, for an automatic. The man had used up three. Broxton was counting on a revolver. A lot of counting, a lot of hope.

He held his breath for a mental four count. *One for the money.* He grabbed the plate, like it was a Frisbee, firmly in his left hand. *Two for the show.* He raised his head till his eyes were barely above the counter and he saw the man standing in the doorway on the opposite side of the room. He wasn't looking in his direction and he held a shiny gun in his right hand. Shiny meant revolver, at least Broxton thought it did. *Three to get ready.* He stood, loose as an alley cat, surprised that he wasn't afraid, surprised that the tingling at the base of his neck was gone, surprised that he was calm under fire. *Four to go.* He flung the plate across the room and it sailed as true as any Frisbee he'd ever thrown on a Southern California beach during a hot Sunday afternoon.

Then he slapped Ramsingh on the shoulder as the plate crashed through a window on the opposite side of the room, but the prime minister needed no urging, he was up and running as gunshots rang through the ghostly kitchen. Broxton heard both the shots and the explosions the bullets made as they ricocheted off of stainless steel pots and pans. He counted three and he hoped that meant the man was out of ammunition, because he was running right behind Ramsingh, protecting the prime minister with his back.

Ramsingh flew through another swinging door with Broxton right behind. They ran down the hallway, sprinted through a door at the end of the corridor and found themselves in another banquet room. "There," Ramsingh said, and they dashed toward a door on the far side of the room, dodging and weaving between more tables and chairs, with Broxton again protecting Ramsingh with his back.

"Stop," Broxton said as Ramsingh reached the door. "Me first, in case there's someone out there." He opened the door to the outside and set off a loud wailing alarm.

Ramsingh bent, pulled off his shoes and took off across the sand.

"Shit," Broxton said, grabbing at his own shoes, then he ran toward the sea, chasing after the prime minister.

"Can you swim?" Ramsingh asked, standing in wet sand at the water's edge. Sweat glistened on the prime minister's forehead and his silver hair gleamed in the moonlight. It was quiet, the only noise other than their labored breathing was the gentle sound of the lapping surf.

"Sure," Broxton said, and Ramsingh pulled off his shirt and grinned. "We never give up," he said. His lips were tight. His eyes looked like he'd seen the very fires of hell. He was tense. He was rock hard and Broxton was impressed with the old man's full chest as he took in the scars left by the heart surgery. The man was battle weary, battle scarred and battle tough, and Broxton knew that his first impression of the man was way wrong as Ramsingh turned and loped into the black sea.

"There's gotta be a better way," Broxton said under his breath, wading into the water. Maybe if they just swam out a little way and floated, just beyond pistol range, till they gave up and left, but Ramsingh was swimming like he'd been born to the water, striking out toward the sailboats anchored almost a quarter mile away.

"There they are," Lawman said, his smooth drawl up an octave. He was a big man, big, excited and deadly, and he was less than a hundred feet away. Broxton wanted to strike out after Ramsingh, but he was frozen in place. He felt the sea swirl around his legs as the sand seemed to be pulling his feet down under. He was like a tree, planted in place, his sunken feet as solid as any root system.

There were two of them. The second one had to be Undertaker. He was masked. Fear, mingled with the cold, sent icy tingles rippling over Broxton's skin. He had never known real fear, never been under fire, never been in an accident, had barely ever fired a gun. His stomach cramped. His bowels felt like they were going to cut loose. He couldn't move.

Undertaker probably had a gun, he thought. Then gunfire answered the thought, shocking the quiet night. In an instant he realized he was in no danger. Undertaker was shooting out toward where the prime minister was swimming, and he remembered what he'd heard earlier. *Leave the bodyguard alive.* The electric tingling vanished. The queasy stomach calmed and his bowels clamped closed.

He felt like he was having an out of body experience as he studied his pursuers. He inhaled the sweet night air and pulled a foot out of the sucking sand and moved backwards, toward the deeper water. Then he pulled out the other one. One step back, two, three, he kept easing away from the enemy, all the while watching them, as they were bathed in the overhead light that framed them as they stood just outside the doorway.

Lawman was wide in the shoulders and lean in the waist, like a quarterback. Although the overhead light cast harsh shadows, he could see that the man was shit handsome, a lady killer, big, tough and good looking. Undertaker was wearing a black ski mask and Broxton shuddered at the terrorist look. "Oh, shit," he moaned as the masked man pointed the gun toward him. But lightning fast Lawman snatched it from his hand, sending a scream curdling from Undertaker that raised the hair on the back of Broxton's neck.

Part of him screamed, *turn away, swim for it,* but he couldn't. He was once again planted in place, feet being sucked into the swirling sand below, but this time it was more curiosity than fear that kept him rooted to the spot.

Lawman crouched low, presenting as small a target as possible. Just in case I have a gun, too, Broxton thought. Then the big man clasped his left hand around his right wrist, holding the weapon in his right hand. He was assuming the classic shooter's position and one word shot through Broxton. *Cop.* Lawman aimed both his body and the gun out into the dark where Broxton imagined Ramsingh might be, but he didn't fire, probably because he couldn't see the prime minister. A cop for sure. He held his gun like a cop and he held his fire like a cop. Like his name, Lawman.

The big man stepped out of the crouch and waved to him with his right hand, the gun hanging loosely on his trigger finger, telling him it was over for now. Telling him they were safe, for now. Safe from them, but not safe from the dark sea. Broxton couldn't help himself, he waved back. He didn't want to follow the prime minister blindly into the dark ocean, but he didn't want to face those men either. He wondered why they spared him, why they wanted him alive, but when the man in the mask showed him the middle finger of his left hand, he decided he didn't want to stay around and find out. So he turned back around, and like a dolphin he slipped into the cool, dark water and started out after Ramsingh.

CHAPTER FOURTEEN

EARL KNEW BETTER than to waste ammunition firing at things he couldn't see. He stood out of his crouch, letting the pistol hang off of his trigger finger and waved to the bodyguard. To his surprise he waved back. The man had balls. Most men he'd known would be swimming away to beat the band, but this one was cool, standing there in water up to his chest, watching him, burning everything into his memory.

And here he was, standing under the lights, like a rookie out of the academy. The bodyguard was getting a good look and all Earl saw was shadow. Better to kill him now, but the woman said to leave him alive and that's what he was going to do, although he felt that one day he'd regret it.

The night was quiet again and Earl listened for the sounds of sirens, high pitched voices or running feet. He heard nothing except the gentle surf. He looked out into the dark and saw nothing except the lapping waves, reflecting the moonlight.

"Let's move out of the light," he said, and he moved a few feet away from the doorway. After a few seconds his eyes started to get used to the dark. There were several boats at anchor, but his more immediate concern was the four thatched hut restaurants lining the ocean less than a hundred yards off to his right. He kept his eyes on the tropical buildings, looking for movement. But if they had people in them, they were minding their own business.

"We have to get him," the man next to him said. Earl didn't know him, but when he came flying into that kitchen shouting, 'Undertaker, Undertaker' at the top of his lungs, Earl figured that he'd met his backup. And after the man allowed Earl to snatch the gun from his hand, Earl knew that he'd met a coward.

"Can you swim?" Earl asked, turning to the man in the ski mask that Dani had dubbed the Undertaker.

"No."

"Well I can and I'm here to tell you that I'm not going after them. It's a big ocean and even with the moonlight we'd never see them out there. We won't get them tonight."

"We have to," he wailed.

"He's right, Kevin," Dani Street said, stepping through the doorway and instantly moving out of the light.

"We can't let them get away." Kevin was holding his right hand with his left and now Earl could see why. He'd broken the man's finger when he snatched the gun away.

"Hurt much?" Earl said. The index finger on his right hand was swollen, already black and bent at an odd angle.

"Hurts, like a bitch, you asshole."

"He woulda shot the bodyguard if I hadn't grabbed his gun," Earl said. He felt sand fleas biting into the fleshy part of his ankles. They'd gotten through his socks. He resisted scratching. He didn't want to look at all vulnerable to her.

"Really," she said. Then she pointed her index and middle finger at him, thumb up, turning her hand into a child's gun. Earl got the message and shot him once, straight to the heart. Clean, small entry, no exit wound. Earl saw the man's eyes go wide in disbelief, then he sank to the ground, dead before he hit the sand.

Earl looked around to see if anyone had heard the gunshot, but the night still remained quiet. Now that he could see them, he worried about the anchored boats, but they were pretty far out, and even if they did hear, what were they going to do? What could they do?

"He was stupid. I told him to leave Broxton alone, but like a hyena chasing a wounded animal, he just couldn't help himself," she said, as Earl continued to scour the dark for signs of life. But all remained quiet.

"Better this way," he said.

"Why'd you stop him?" Dani asked. He watched as she raised her left foot, using it to scratch her right ankle.

"When I give an order to my men back home I want it obeyed. I don't want excuses and I don't want no buts. I'm working on your nickel now, so I'm giving you the same respect I want when I'm in charge. No more, no less."

"Why, Earl, I think you and I are going to get along even better than I originally thought."

"You wanna leave this?" Earl said, looking down at the body.

"I don't see why not." She bent over the body and pulled off the ski mask. Then she picked a wallet and passport out of a back pocket. She stood and smiled at Earl, "There's a national guard post not too far from here, but I doubt that they'd investigate, even if they heard the shots."

"There must have been someone in the hotel, that door didn't get open by itself. And what about those?" Earl nodded toward the beach bars.

"They all have someone sleeping in them," Dani said. "But like the security in the hotel, they're not a problem."

"Why not?"

"When there's a shooting in Venezuela, the police round up everybody connected, witnesses included, and throw them all in jail. Then they wait and see who starts talking."

"Won't get many witnesses that way."

"Exactly," Dani said. "When shots are fired people start running. Nobody sees anything. But we should leave anyway."

* * *

Dani sat back as Earl drove back toward the Sans Souci. She marveled at the way he'd sauntered away from Kevin's dead body. It was no more in his mind than yesterday's trash. "Want me to drive, or you?" he'd asked. "What about your car?" she'd said. "Stolen. Better that way, no paper trail," he'd said and she handed over the keys. She usually liked to be in control, but she was at ease with this big man. He was not the lumbering ox she'd first thought. He was smart, cagey, and ruthless. A lot like her.

"Up ahead," he said.

"I see it," she said. They were on the long strip of road with the pounding surf on their right. And ahead, losing its battle with the sea, surrounded by a crowd, was Kevin Underfield's Jeep, still lying on its side as the waves washed around it.

"He was lucky to get out of that alive," Earl said.

"He was climbing out the passenger window when I came by," she said, remembering the way the white moonlight played of off Kevin's blanched face. It was at that exact moment that she knew he had to go. She'd turned a blind eye to his rabid jealousy, and she could forgive him trying to take a few shots at Bill—he hadn't succeeded after all—but she could never forgive the fear that radiated from his eyes when he climbed out of that Jeep. A man afraid was a man that would talk.

Earl slowed, then stopped behind a police car with flashing blue lights, telling the world that there was danger here. He leaned his head out the window and asked, "*¿Que pasa, agui?*" What's going on here?

"*Accidente,*" a young policeman answered back.

"*¿Es alquien lastimado, muerto?*" Is anybody hurt, dead?

"*No veo a nadie, nadie esta aqui,*" I don't see anybody, nobody's here, the policeman said.

"*Esta bien que nadie esta lastimado.*" It's good that nobody's hurt, Earl said.

"*Claro,*" the policeman said, then he moved away and Earl slowly maneuvered around the police cars and the crowd.

"The Mexican accent was a good touch," Dani said.

"I'm from Texas," Earl said. "It was natural."

"Whatever, that policeman will remember a Mexican, not an American," she said, and she caught him looking in the rearview mirror. "Is he writing down the tag number?"

"No, but you should turn the car in first thing in the morning, because when they find that body they're going to be interested in any cars that were seen coming up this road. Especially after they link our undertaking friend to the Jeep back there."

"As I said earlier, I'm going to like having you around, Earl." She was mildly surprised to find out that she meant it. She was more than a little attracted to him. Although she'd known him for only a very short time it was plain that he understood her better than anyone she'd ever met, better than Broxton, her father and even better than her ex-partner, the late Kevin Underfield.

"I have another room, besides the one you booked for me, at the Dynasty across the way. Room six-fourteen," he said. "Not that I didn't trust you, but if things didn't go as planned, I didn't want to be where anybody might be looking."

"Booked in another name, of course?" she said.

"Of course," he said. "I carry a couple extra passports, just in case."

"Earl, you continue to surprise me." Both her admiration and infatuation with the West Texas Sheriff were growing. "But why are you telling me about the other room now?"

"I was kind of hoping you might like to spend the night there," he said. His eyes were straight ahead as he took the corner and aimed the car down the road toward the Sans Souci on the right and the Dynasty on the left.

190

"I have to see someone at the Sans Souci," she said.

"I understand," he said. There wasn't a trace of disappointment in his voice. She liked that.

"I'll try to cut it short. Can you take a raincheck for a couple of hours?"

"I'm a light sleeper," he said.

"I'll bet you are." She laughed, and he turned into the Sans Souci parking lot. She jumped out of the car, tossed him a promising smile and said, "Keep a light on for me."

"Count on it," he said. Then he put the car in gear and in a few seconds was gone.

In the lobby, Dani went straight to the elevator. There were no police, no firemen, no reporters and no milling or panicking people. She punched the up button and looked at her watch. Less than an hour and everything was apparently back to normal. Kudos to the staff, she thought, nothing must be allowed to interfere with the comfort of their guests. The door opened, she stepped in and punched nine. She studied herself in the mirrored wall on the trip up. She was definitely flushed. She was excited and couldn't wait to get the unpleasant business with George over with so that she could keep her appointment with Earl, the small town sheriff with so many surprises.

She stepped out of the elevator on nine and straightened her blouse. Then she took a deep breath and went to his room. He answered while she was still knocking.

"Well?" he asked, his deep brown eyes sparking.

"It didn't go well," she said. Then she told him everything.

"Did you have to kill Kevin?" he asked after she was finished.

"Yes," she said.

"What a cock up!" He waved a newspaper like it was a signal flag. He looked ready to explode. His alluring eyes were glazed and hard.

She wanted to tell him to calm down, but he had every right to be mad. She'd abdicated her responsibility. Turned the job over to someone else. Although she was confident that Earl was up to it, his failure was her failure. It damaged her reputation and by extension, her.

"What were you thinking of?" He met her straight on, eye to eye. His gaze was fierce and she felt like taking him down a peg or two. She knew she was capable, but she couldn't do it, because he was right.

"I wanted to be with Broxton when it happened," she said.

"Lord why?" he asked.

"Two reasons. One, I didn't want him hurt, and two, it was the perfect alibi. If I was with him every second for the three or four hours leading up to the blast then I couldn't have done it. I'd be in the clear, but things didn't happen the way there were supposed to. I didn't expect Ram to start taking Broxton's advice right off the bat. He was supposed to be up in that room alone while the two of us were having dinner. And it's not Earl's fault. He couldn't have known Broxton would change rooms on him."

"You're worried about being tied into it?"

"Not this one, no. I had larger considerations."

"My ears are burning, but I'm listening," he said.

"I was worried about the future. Thinking someday someone might connect my travel itinerary for Save the Children with the close proximity to the Scorpion's attacks, just like you did. I decided to buy myself a little insurance."

"You thought that if you were with Broxton when Ramsingh was hit that you'd be in the clear. If Scorpion killed Ramsingh and you had an alibi, then you couldn't be him.

"Something like that."

"But the idiot set off a bomb."

"At my instruction. When they reconstructed it they'd have found out that I was in an airplane sitting next to the man sent by the United States to protect Ramsingh when the bomb was set."

"And what about your wayward sheriff?"

"He's still useful," she said.

"You're sure?"

"I need him," she said.

"I just hope you know what you're doing," he said through pursed lips. He reminded her of a snake.

"So do I, George."

"And I hope I don't ever have to regret recruiting you."

"And I hope you don't mean that as a threat. This whole thing was your idea."

"I want him dead before he can make the police dedication speech next week," he said. "He plans on announcing a new drug treaty with the United States. Once he tells the world, I'd have to sign it, even if he dies."

"What's the treaty entail?"

"It allows America's drug agents free run of Trinidad. We can't have the DEA over here arresting anyone they want. We might as well be in Washington.

"He'll never announce the treaty, George."

"I have your word?"

"You have it," she said.

* * *

Earl had just poured himself a stiff Scotch when he heard the rapping. He was waiting on room service. He'd only ordered for one, because he was convinced she wouldn't come. He lumbered across the room with an eye on the tube. Rocky was playing on one of the hotel channels, and although he'd seen the movie dozens of times it still hit him in the heart. He was addicted to courage and he loved happy endings.

"You wanna take a shower?" she said when he opened the door.

"Sure," he said. She swept past him heading for the bathroom. He heard her start the water as he picked up the phone and canceled his order of steak and fries.

"Come on, big guy," she said from under the spray.

"Coming," he said, cradling the phone. He stepped into the bathroom and stepped out of his Levi's, noticing her jeans neatly laid across the back of the toilet. She wore Levi's too. He liked that. Then he pulled his tee shirt off and stepped into the shower and the time of his life.

Forty minutes later he was flat on his back, looking up at her firm breasts as she slid back and forth, attempting to make him come for a third time. He hadn't had sex like this since he was in high school. She'd attacked him the second he slipped into the shower, draining him in less time than it took a jackrabbit to jack. Then she led him, still wet, to the bed, where they did it long and slow and she opened the heavens for him. And now she was rocking above him, looking like an angel, and then he spasmed and shot into her for that third time.

"More?" she said, giggling.

"I'm lucky I survived that."

"I wanted it to be good for you," she said. "I wanted it to be the best."

"Baby, it was," he said.

"Good, let's take another shower. And then we have to talk."

Twenty minutes later she told him about the plans to take over a country, and how he could help.

CHAPTER FIFTEEN

BROXTON STRUCK OUT, swimming toward the deep water. Ramsingh must be heading for one of the anchored yachts. It was the only thing that made sense. He stopped, treading water. But which ship? The closest? He was shivering cold and at a complete loss. From the beach the yachts were barely visible, but out here, closer, he could see that they were as thick as trees in a forest. His chances of picking the right boat weren't good, but he couldn't stay where he was, so he started for the nearest yacht.

The black sea chilled him to the bone, his wet clothes became his enemy now, making it harder for him to move through the water, pulling at him, slowing him down. He stopped again, treading water.

He was farther out, the wind had kicked up, and it was harder for him to stay afloat. He had to get rid of his pants or he wouldn't make it.

Treading against the sea with only his left arm he loosened the top button of his Levi's with his right. He popped open the four buttons, but the pants, wet and tight, fit him like a second skin. Try as he might, he couldn't slide them down. Maybe if he was in a quiet bedroom with his rump on a soft mattress, but not out in the cold sea, while he was treading water with only one hand.

A chill, colder than the sea, gripped his spine and squeezed it. The Levi's had to come off. If not he was going to die. He was out of breath, out of strength and his waterlogged jeans were pulling him down sure as cement shoes on a snitch's feet. He wanted them off, had to get them off. But no matter how hard he tried he couldn't force them down with only one hand.

He grabbed a deep breath, slipped his thumbs between flesh and denim and curled himself into a sinking ball. He was alone in the dark as he grabbed the jeans tighter at the hips and wiggled them off. Then he started toward the surface, fighting to hold his breath against the pressure pounding in his chest.

He broke through, taking in air, before he sank back down. He windmilled his arms in an effort to stay afloat. Then he felt something hit him, something grabbing at him. Shark was his first thought, and he lashed out at it, but it moved away. He tried to turn, to face it as it came at him again, and it did, grabbing at his back, tugging at his shirt. He threw a hand over his head, trying to get at it, but he couldn't reach.

"Slow down! Don't panic!" Ramsingh shouted.

"I've got you." The prime minister's steady arm wrapped around him. "It's all right," he soothed, and Broxton stopped flapping, stopped fighting, and allowed the prime minister to support him while he sucked in badly needed air, heaving it in and out, like a long distance runner at the end of a marathon.

"Lay back, take it easy," Ramsingh said, and Broxton obeyed, floating on his back, putting complete trust in him, allowing the older man to keep him afloat as he stared at the round moon and the slow moving clouds that threatened to take away its light. He'd always thought of himself as a good swimmer, but tonight proved him wrong. And he'd thought himself in fair shape. This night proved him wrong about that, too.

"Better?" Ramsingh asked.

"Yeah, thanks," Broxton said.

"We never give up, we never quit," Ramsingh said, and Broxton felt himself nodding. "That was my campaign slogan," Ramsingh said, his voice soft, slow and rhythmic. "The polls had me so far behind sometimes I wondered why I kept on, but I did, and when things looked the blackest I said that to myself, over and over, like a mantra, 'We never give up. We never quit. We never give up. We never quit'."

"We never give up. We never quit," Broxton said along with him.

"That's the spirit," Ramsingh said, still holding him afloat. "The only thing you have to be afraid of out here is yourself."

"Thanks," Broxton said, breathing easier now.

"You're in control?"

"Yes, sir," Broxton said, and Ramsingh eased his supporting hand away and he began treading water on his own.

"There's a ship out there. Not far, without any lights."

"Not the closest?" Broxton said.

"No, not the closest, but we can stop and rest along the way."

"How do you know?" Broxton asked.

"I've already been out there," he said. Then he started swimming slowly out toward the anchored boats with the easy, graceful strokes of a professional swimmer and Broxton followed. While he swam he thought about what Ramsingh had done. He'd been safely away, yet he'd abandoned that safety and come back for him, saved him from a cold, silent and dark death.

Lightning flashed overhead and the heavens opened as those clouds finally covered the moon. The ocean was turned into a psychedelic supermarket as water pelted the sea, splashing all around him. Visibility was reduced to almost zero and he added a renewed vigor to his strokes, determined not to lose sight of the prime minister.

Then he saw Ramsingh grab onto a dinghy that was tied off the back of a small sailboat and relief swept through him when he saw the prime minister's outstretched arm. He grasped it in a Viking grip and in seconds he was holding onto the dinghy. He started to speak, but Ramsingh held an index finger to his lips and pointed to the boat. Broxton got the message, someone was home.

Ramsingh put his lips to Broxton's ear. "We have to wait for the rain to stop." Then he pulled himself up into the dinghy and Broxton flopped in after him. Both men huddled forward against the pelting rain and just as it seemed like it was going to let up, a brisk wind blew out of the west bringing even more rain.

Then as suddenly as it started, it stopped. The squall had blown through, leaving a star studded sky in its wake. Ramsingh, able to see now, pointed to another boat, bigger, dark with no dinghy tied up to it. Broxton got the message and he stole a few quick breaths as Ramsingh slipped over the side, back into the water, and started swimming toward the dark boat. Broxton was tired, his arms felt like they were weighed down with lead, his legs were spaghetti and his chest was about to explode, the rest had helped, but it wasn't enough. Still the prime minister was an old man recently out of heart surgery, and if Ramsingh could make it, then he bloody well could too.

He let go of the rubber boat and took long, slow, even strokes toward the black ship. At first he grabbed air every other time his right arm dug into the water, but before long he was operating on sheer will and forcing his heavy arms up and out of the water was harder with every stroke. His body demanded more oxygen, so every time the right arm came out of the cold he sucked in air until even that wasn't enough and he had to stop and rest.

The cold no longer bothered him as he flopped over onto his back. He sucked in needed air as the salt water stung his eyes. He wondered if he'd have the strength of mind and body to roll over and continue on his way. What would happen if he stayed on his back forever? Would he drift out to sea, or would the tide take him into shore and into the grip of a killer's hands?

"You're there, Broxton," Ramsingh said. "You've made it." Broxton forced his eyes open. Ramsingh was hanging onto some kind of pipe structure attached to the rear of the boat and once again he was holding out his arm.

"I thought it was all over." Broxton rolled off his back and grabbed onto Ramsingh's arm with another Viking grip.

"Nonsense, you did very well," Ramsingh said.

"You came back for me out there. You were safe and you came back."

"Of course, you're my bodyguard." Ramsingh pulled him toward him, and Broxton studied the bar that the prime minister was hanging onto. It was part of a structure that curved around the stern of the boat, two thick bars, one at the bottom of the stern, another by the top.

"What is it?" he asked.

"Self-steering gear," Ramsingh said.

"What's it do?"

"Uses the wind to steer the boat, and we're going to use it to get out of the water."

"How?"

"Think you can hang onto it and support my weight for a few seconds?"

"Yes, sir."

"I'm heavy."

"I'll manage," Broxton said and he wrapped both hands around the bottom bar, letting his body hang in the water, arms stretched like he was dangling from a gymnast's high bar. "I'm ready," he said, and Ramsingh moved behind him, also hanging onto to the bar. Broxton grit his teeth as the prime minister planted a foot on his back, then another on his shoulder, but he didn't scream out when the sudden shock of Ramsingh's weight pushing down on him stretched his arms like a medieval rack.

"Hurry," Broxton grunted, as Ramsingh struggled out of the sea, using Broxton's back and shoulders as a foot hold. Then he was up and the weight was gone.

"Are you okay?" Ramsingh asked.

"Yeah, now how do I get up?"

"Hang on."

"Very funny," Broxton said.

"There's a swim ladder, I'll lower it." Although it only took seconds for Ramsingh to get the ladder down, it seemed like forever to Broxton, and under ordinary circumstances climbing the four or five rungs from the sea to the safety of the boat would have been as easy as falling out of bed. Now it took all of his remaining strength to get on board.

"We made it," Ramsingh said as Broxton lowered himself onto his back in the cockpit. He closed his eyes, sucking sweet air deep into his belly as he let the evening breeze wash over his chilled body. He was wet and cold and he didn't care, because his body craved rest more than warmth.

"Can't sleep yet, Broxton," Ramsingh said.

"Five minutes."

"No, we have to get inside and get out of these clothes."

"We can't break in." Broxton said, realizing how hollow it sounded as soon as the words came out. Apparently Ramsingh did too, because he picked up something that looked like a hammer that had been in a plastic holder under the winches, and with a few hard strokes he broke open a hard plastic deck hatch.

"Winch handle, very handy," Ramsingh said, sliding it back into its holster. "You want to do the honors?" he said.

"You're doing fine so far," Broxton said.

"I might have a little too much around the middle to slide through that hatch. It'd be better if you did it."

"Then what?" Broxton leaned forward on the cockpit seat.

"Find the tool box. There should be a hacksaw blade in it."

"And."

"You hand it up to me. I cut off this lock," he said, touching the lock that secured the companion way cover. "Then we go to Trinidad."

"You're not talking about stealing the boat?"

"No," Ramsingh said. "We're just going to borrow it. Sort of like you did with that Mercedes."

"Can you sail it?"

"My wife and I wandered the world in a sailboat for fifteen years before our money ran out and I had to come back and take up the law. We'd always meant to go back, but we had kids, and bills, and then politics got in the way."

"You can really handle this?"

"Son, if it sails I can make it dance. You just get me that hacksaw blade and we'll be on our way."

Moonlight showed through the hatch, offering Broxton a glimpse of a small salon below. It's like a motorhome, he thought, as he shifted his position and slipped his legs through the hatch. He dropped onto a settee that reminded him of a sofa in a small living room. "So far, so good," he said, and then he went looking. It didn't take him long to locate a tool box in a cabinet by the engine room. "Found the tools," he said up to Ramsingh and five minutes later the prime minister was using a broken hacksaw blade on the lock, while Broxton continued to search the boat.

When he was a child he'd crossed the country from California to Florida in a motorhome with his parents. Aside from the never ending religious war that was politely fought between his devoutly Jewish mother and his staunchly Catholic father, he remembered the size of the rooms in the home on wheels. Small kitchen, the bedroom in the back, large by motorhome standards, but small compared to a house, the dining table taking up half of the cramped living room. The boat was like that. Compact. There were two small sleeping cabins, one toilet, a salon half filled by the table exactly the way Broxton remembered it in the motorhome, a galley that was slightly larger than the motorhome's kitchen, and an engine room.

He found clothes that fit in the forward cabin, shorts and sweat pants, tee shirt and sweat shirt and several towels. In seconds he had his wet things off and was slipping on the sweatshirt as Ramsingh finished with the lock.

"There's some dry things back here, Mr. Prime Minister," he said.

"Call me Ram, you keep forgetting," he said, as he came in through the companionway.

"How'd you know about the tool box?"

"No properly maintained boat would be without a full compliment of tools," Ramsingh said as he was shucking out of his wet clothes.

Fifteen minutes later Broxton was holding onto the headsail and leaning over the bow, pulpit, with his foot on the windlass button, watching the anchor come up. Ramsingh had raised the main and was behind the wheel. They were going to sail off the hook.

As soon as the anchor broke free the boat started to move backward, no longer secured to the ocean floor. But Broxton kept his foot on the button until the anchor clanked into place as he'd been instructed, then he made his way back to the cockpit, keeping his head under the moving boom as Ramsingh spun the wheel to the right allowing the wind to fill the main.

"Have you ever been sailing before, Broxton?" Ramsingh asked, once Broxton was comfortably sitting in the cockpit.

"Never," Broxton said, "but I served on a carrier in the Navy."

"Doesn't count. This is different. In a powerboat we'd go directly to Trinidad, be there in twelve or fifteen hours, but since we can't sail against a headwind we'll have to make for the mainland and motorsail along the coast.

"How long do you think it'll take?"

"A day, if we don't stop, maybe a little longer. We'll see."

Broxton sat back as Ramsingh let out the jib and the boat picked up speed, gliding through the water like a skater glides over the ice. The moon played off the sea, casting the night in an unearthly glow, and Broxton was reminded of his religious parents, each believing, in their own way, in a God that he'd never been able to find. When he was a child his mother wore her Judaism as a burden and his father, his Catholicism as a cross. But they'd both grown out of religion and into God, coming to peace with each other and their marriage. So Broxton was never barmitzvahed, never confessed, never confirmed. He'd been ignored by two of the world's great religions and as a result God was no more than a word to him.

But still, on nights like this, he wondered.

"You should go below and get some sleep," Ramsingh said.

"I can stay up," Broxton said.

"I don't doubt it, but you shouldn't. We're going

to have to go all night, so we'll need our rest. I'll take the first watch, two hours, then I'll wake you." Ramsingh ran a hand through his long gray hair, pushing it back. "I'll be fine, don't worry."

"Sure you don't want me to take the first watch?"

"I'm okay," Ramsingh said. "The swim was exhilarating."

"What about your heart?"

"It's been six months since the surgery. I'm in better shape than I ever was. I jog every morning. Eat better. Work out in the gym at night. Easy workouts, but I work out. I'll be okay. You're done in. Go below and get some rest. I couldn't sleep now even if I wanted to."

"Yes, sir." Broxton was relieved that Ramsingh was in better health than he'd thought, but he was reluctant, nevertheless, to go below.

"You can sleep in the cockpit, if you wish," Ramsingh said, seeming to understand Broxton's feelings, "but you should sleep."

Broxton stretched out on the cockpit seat and closed his eyes and his thoughts drifted from God and the universe to Dani and Maria. For the first time in his life he had two women on his mind. Their faces kept switching and changing under his eyelids until he drifted off to a dreamless sleep.

"Okay Broxton, it's your watch." He felt Ramsingh's hands gently shaking him and he opened his eyes to the stars overhead.

"Seems like I just closed my eyes."

"Happens like that," Ramsingh said.

"Who's steering the boat?" Broxton asked, stretching and looking at Ramsingh on the cockpit seat opposite him.

"Uncle Dick," Ramsingh said.

"Who?"

"My wife and I had a great friend, Richard McPartland. He sailed with us from Seattle to San Diego. He died shortly after, lung cancer. We carried his ashes to the South Pacific, because he always wanted to go, and spread them along the sand on a small beach on Hiva Oa Island in the Marquesas. Ever since, we always felt that Dick was still with us, so we christened our self-steering gear 'Uncle Dick.' Right now Dick has the boat, all you have to do is stay awake and aware. If it looks like he is going to run us into anything, wake me."

Broxton looked back at the self-steering gear attached to the stern. "You mean that's really steering the boat?" He saw the wheel turn to the right, then back again.

"Sure, the wind moves the windvane, which moves the wheel. Simple and effective, and now I'm going below. Wake me in a couple of hours."

And then Broxton was alone.

The cool night breeze closed over him, sending a delicious spiny chill over his skin. The slight goose bumps pleasured him and the tingling at the back of his neck told him that he was alive. Not living, but alive. There was a difference.

He thought about Ramsingh. He'd saved the man's life and in turn the man had saved his. They'd fled the hotel, stolen a car, been shot at, charged into a night sea, stolen a boat and now they were sailing toward the Venezuelan mainland and the night wasn't even over. The full moon, high in the night sky, the stars, the sound of the boat cutting through a flat sea, all conspired to fill him with awe and he found he envied Ramsingh his years at sea.

High pitched laughter shot through the dark, carried on the wind, and something shot out of the sea, startling him. Then he grinned wide as another dolphin broke the surface, spinning in the air. Broxton stood and watched as the dolphins swam along the bow wake, jumping it and playing in it, letting it carry them along.

Then the dolphin on the right shot up, twirled in the air, then slid back into the water and another took its place, playing and gliding in the bow wake for five or ten minutes. Then it, too, danced away as another took its place and Broxton realized what was happening. They were sharing, taking turns.

The playful animals kept him company throughout his watch and when he finally checked the time he found that he'd let the prime minister have an extra hour of sleep. For a second he thought about not waking him for still another hour, but then three of the dolphins flipped out of the water at the same time, then they sank back into the sea and they were gone.

He called down to Ramsingh.

"I'm awake," he said. "Uncle Dick take care of you okay?"

"He did fine," Broxton said, and again he thought of his parents. He'd never been able to accept their belief in God, but looking out at the night, inhaling the sea air, knowing how it made him feel, he had to accept that there was something, and if he couldn't believe in God or a guiding hand, well then Uncle Dick would do fine. He mentally thanked the unknown Richard McPartland for keeping him safe on his watch.

"Would you like some coffee?" Ramsingh asked from below.

"Yes," Broxton answered, and in a few minutes the pungent aroma drifted up and mingled with the dark morning air.

"How do you drink it?"

"Black is fine," Broxton said.

"Black it is." Ramsingh said, coming on deck with two mugs of steaming coffee.

"There's a light up ahead," Broxton said, accepting one of the mugs.

"That would be Puerto Santos. It's a small fishing village. It's a nice place for us to hide the day away," Ramsingh said.

"I thought you'd want to get back to Trinidad as soon as possible."

"I do, but we're sailing a stolen boat. That's piracy."

"But we had good cause, and you're the Prime Minister of Trinidad."

"Do you think that matters to the owner?"

"I hadn't thought about that," Broxton said.

"And think about this," Ramsingh said. "It probably matters less to the Venezuelan Coast Guard. They're likely to shoot first and ask questions later, just like in your American old west. Remember, I was in Venezuela because their coast guard shot up a Trinidadian fishing boat."

"Couldn't we just call for help on the radio and explain ourselves?"

"We could, but I'd prefer to get to the bottom of this with as little publicity as possible. I'm not too popular with the press as it is. The last thing I want is to give them any more ammunition to use against me."

"Someone tried to kill you. They should be outraged."

"They'd probably criticize his failure," Ramsingh said.

"It's that bad?"

"A lot of jobs were lost when I started shutting down the money laundering operations."

"Honest jobs?" Broxton asked.

"Sure, Billie's Burgers closed down. Six fast food restaurants, twenty jobs each. Coastal Furniture closed down. Two stores, over a hundred jobs each. Four retail stores in the West Mall, six in the Long Circular Mall, all closed down. Two new car dealerships, a bank with four branches and over a hundred jobs. A little here, a little there."

"But they were laundering drug money and calling it profit."

"Tell it to the man who lost his job. Tell it to his wife and kids. Tell it to his neighbors. Tell it to the newspapers."

"I see what you mean. That could put a dent in your popularity."

"Enough that someone might want me dead?"

"We told you we think it's drug related," Broxton said.

"You must be right, because we're not talking lone assassin, are we?"

"No," Broxton said, "we're not."

"I never thought it would come to this," Ramsingh said.

"Who profits most from your death?"

"Nobody, really."

"Think about it," Broxton said.

"I have been. You know I have been."

"Who becomes prime minister?"

"The party would caucus and choose someone."

"Who?"

"Why the most popular man in the party, the most popular man in Trinidad, the old cricket star."

"Who's that?" Broxton asked.

"George Chandee, the attorney general."

"Why am I not surprised? No, don't say anything," Broxton said, holding up his hand. "I'm going below and get some sleep. Just think about it." And Broxton slipped through the companionway and in a few seconds he was asleep. Ramsingh woke him after they were securely anchored in a secluded bay and they had a breakfast of cheese and tomato sandwiches. Not what Broxton would have chosen, but they had to make due with what was available. Then he went back to sleep and slept straight through the day.

They spent the next night motoring eastward along Venezuela's north coast toward Trinidad. They stood two hour watches and Broxton found himself enjoying the night solitude. Ramsingh had the boat on autopilot, and like the previous night when the self-steering gear handled the boat under sail, the only thing Broxton had to do was watch to make sure they didn't hit anything.

The sun came up during his watch, so he was the first to see it. "Big boat, behind us," he said, reaching for the binoculars. "It's a navel vessel of some kind. They've got guns."

"Let me see," Ramsingh said, coming up through the companion way and Broxton handed over the far away glasses. "Venezuelan Coast Guard."

"They be here before we're out of their waters?" Broxton asked.

"Oh, I think so," Ramsingh said.

"Can you fake a heart attack?"

"If I have to."

"How do you work this thing?" Broxton asked, picking up the radio mike.

"Push this button and talk," Ramsingh said.

Broxton picked up the mike and thumbed the push-to-talk button. "Mayday, mayday, mayday. Can you hear me? My father's having a heart attack. I need help. Mayday, mayday, mayday."

"They'll think I'm on death's door," Ramsingh said, after Broxton released the button.

"This is the Venezuelan Coast Guard Cutter *Cuatro de Mayo* to the vessel calling mayday." The man was speaking English with a thick Venezuelan accent.

Broxton clicked the button again. "Are you the big gray boat behind me?"

"We are."

"Do you have a doctor on board?"

"Negative."

"I need to get him to a hospital as quickly as possible and I can't sail the boat. Can you help me?"

"You can't sail?" the voice was skeptical.

"That's right, it's my father's boat. I'm on vacation. I don't know the first thing about sailing. You have to help me."

"Captain Sanchez, Venezuelan Coast Guard, the burly man said, as he boarded. "You have the boat papers?"

"I don't know."

"Why not?" Sanchez asked, twirling a bushy mustache.

"I just came down to spend a couple of weeks with my father. I don't know anything about the boat or its papers. Shit, they could have been stolen during the robbery," Broxton said, improvising.

"What robbery?" the captain asked.

"Last night, while we were ashore in Puerto Santos, someone broke in and stole some money. They came in through there," Broxton said, pointing to the broken hatch.

"That's unfortunate. Some of our people think the yachties are all rich. They don't realize that if they keep breaking in to their boats that they'll stop coming. If that happens everybody loses."

"I imagine it's the same wherever people are poor," Broxton said, wanting to change the subject.

"I imagine so," the captain said. Then Ramsingh let out a yell that sounded like his insides were being ripped out.

"Can you leave someone with the boat and take us to the nearest hospital?" Broxton said.

"Yes, sir," Captain Sanchez said and in minutes they had Ramsingh in a stretcher and were aboard the cutter.

"Two of my men will take your father's boat to Puerto La Cruz, and we'll go on to Trinidad."

"Trinidad," Broxton said, trying to sound shocked, "Can't we go back to Caracas?"

"Trinidad is only a few hours away. Caracas would take us till tomorrow at this time."

"Are the hospitals there any good?" Broxton asked. It wasn't hard for him to sound worried and concerned.

"Not as good as ours, but much better than none at all," the captain said, obviously proud.

"Can you radio ahead and have an ambulance waiting?" Broxton asked.

"It's being done," the captain said.

Four hours later a Trinidad and Tobago customs officer and the crew of the Venezuelan cutter watched as two medical technicians hustled Ramsingh into a waiting ambulance. They were two miles down Western Main Road on the way to Port of Spain with the siren blazing when Ramsingh sat up.

The medic tending Ramsingh in the back of the ambulance dropped his jaw and Broxton fought a smile when Ramsingh spoke. "Driver, turn off the siren and take us to the Red House."

"Holy shit! It's the prime minister," the attending medic said.

The driver looked in the mirror and saw that it was true. "Yes, sir, the Red House, at your service. Sure you want the siren off?"

"Yes off," Ramsingh said. "We don't want any attention drawn to us."

"Yes, sir, siren off," the driver said. He turned it off and drove to downtown Port of Spain.

Outside the Red House Ramsingh told the driver to take Broxton by the American Ambassador's residence where he was supposed to get his clothes, and then, he said, "Bring my new head of security back straight away."

CHAPTER SIXTEEN

THE SUN WAS WINKING over the horizon. Dew still covered the grass. A slight breeze rustled through Woodward park, and though it did little to cool the Caribbean heat, Broxton still shivered. If he was going to kill a prime minister, this would be the perfect spot. The park was in the center of the city, ringed on the north by the Red House, the colonial style buildings of Parliament, built by the British before independence—the south, by Fredrick Street, the main shopping street of Port of Spain, always teeming with people hustling in and out of the many department stores—the east, by the modern Department of Justice building, which stood in stark contrast to the old public library next door—and the west by the Gothic St. Ann's Cathedral, a thousand and one places for a man with a rifle, a security man's nightmare.

He sat on an empty bench and watched the workmen setting up the stage in the old gazebo. Others were connecting up the giant speakers that would pour out the calypso beat from noon to midnight. Twelve hours of live music, guaranteed to make the old, the infirm, and even the recent dead get up and dance.

A scrawny pigeon eyed Broxton from a safe distance, then took a few tentative steps in his direction. Broxton remained motionless, wondering how close the bird would come. It stopped about three paces away and waited, but Broxton had no food for it. One of the workmen started in his direction, stringing speaker wire, and the bird took flight.

"You coming to the festival today?" Broxton asked.

"Wish I could, but I gots ta work, got five kids, all boys," the man smiled, proud, showing off a gold front tooth.

"Gonna be a lot of people?"

"More 'an I can count."

"The park's kind of small."

"You know it. Gonna be peoples here stuffed tighter 'an a maxi taxi at rush hour."

"Lots of people," Broxton repeated as the man shuffled on, stringing his wire. He gazed around the park and tried to imagine how it would be after the festival started, the crowd struggling in the noonday heat to get closer to the bands on stage. The Gazebo was in the southeastern corner of the park, surrounded by shade trees. At least he wouldn't have to worry about the crowd behind Ramsingh. The park was fenced and the high backed stage prevented anyone from moving in behind the bands.

"Hey, mister, coffee?" The voice was deep and friendly. Broxton turned toward it. The man was standing behind a food cart, perched in front of the fountain in the center of the park. Broxton waved and ambled in his direction, taking his time, taking in the morning. Enjoying himself. Enjoying the polite way everybody deferred to him. Yesterday he was a tourist. Today he was in charge of the prime minister's security.

He'd expected flack from the police when Ramsingh proposed it, but he'd received nothing but cooperation. Even Cliffard Rampersad, the police chief, was open and cooperative.

"How you take it?" the vender said.

"Black, and a bag of those honey roasted nuts." Broxton reached into his pocket for some change.

"No charge for the secret agent man," the vender said.

"I'm no secret agent man."

"Gots ta be, otherwise they never bring you out of nowhere and put you over Chief Rampersad. He a proud man an' he can be a mean man."

"How'd you find out?"

"Lord man, nothing happens in Trinidad don't everybody know if they want." The vender stretched his arm across the park toward the stage. "If someone gonna shoot at Mr. Ramsingh today you gonna have a hard time of it."

"How does word get out so fast?" Broxton asked.

"My sister works for Republic Bank," the smiling vender said.

"So?"

"So she works with a woman whose husband's a

big lawyer an' he knows Mr. Rampersad. In Trinidad everybody knows somebody. Nothing stays quiet too long."

"So how would you do it if you were the shooter?"

"Best if you forget about that and spend your efforts trying to make Mr. Ramsingh stay home today. Jus' let the music play and save the politics for another time."

Broxton thanked the man and made his way back to his bench and sat with his coffee and nuts. Some young people were already starting to filter into the park and the music wasn't going to start for another six hours. They were laughing and talking. Having fun on a Saturday morning. He watched while they spread a blanket, five girls and four boys, about fifteen or sixteen years old. A few minutes later more youngsters came and the friendly banter started. If he'd had any illusions about the size of the crowd they were dispelled. The park was going to be packed.

He set the coffee by his side and opened the nuts. They were hot, sweet, and reminded him of Paris. He was fishing in the bag for a second bite when he noticed the scrawny pigeon walking toward him. The bird reminded him of Paris too, only the French birds were healthier, fatter, with feathers bright in the afternoon sun. They ate better. Paris was teaming with outdoor cafes and the French ate a lot of bread. When the birds couldn't get their fill from friendly tourists they happily picked up the local's crumbs. This bird seldom got a meal from a tourist and in Trinidad times were hard, even for the pigeons.

"You'd like Paris, my friend," he said, squeezing the nuts together in his hand, crushing them. Then he tossed them to the bird and watched while it gobbled them from the ground.

Five hours later he was again reminded of Paris as the first of the bands was setting up under the Gazebo. Tammy Drake was opening the show with a few words and a song. He'd seen her perform when she opened for Bob Dylan there in 1980. He'd been nineteen, on vacation and captivated by the young Trinidadian performer. She'd done a mixture of country, rock, and blues that had the audience standing, dancing, stomping and clapping.

The songs were different when he saw her last week, but the timeless appeal of that seventeen-year-old sensation he'd seen in Paris hadn't diminished. She'd held him enthralled in the Normandy's ballroom with the soft bluesy ballads, like she did in Paris when she was belting out her numbers to an audience of thousands. Today she was going to perform Calypso, still a different kind of music. Tammy Drake had been Calypso Queen in the Caribbean for the last five years running, and Broxton wondered if she would scorch his soul with the calypso beat. He was looking forward to finding out.

Then she was on the stage and the crowd went wild with applause. All of Trinidad was in love with Tammy Drake. She was wearing a peasant blouse and a pair of faded jeans. Her pale skin and China blue eyes were framed by a mane of dazzling black hair.

"Hey, hey, hey," she said, holding the mike in her left hand. "Today we dance to the beat," and then she launched into a raucous calypso song that was unlike anything he'd ever heard. This was not like the calypso he'd heard when he was a child. Maryann was not down by the seashore sifting any sand. Tammy Drake's voice was still beautiful, she was still mesmerizing, she still entertained, but the rhyme scheme was repetitious, the band was loud and the lyrics seemed to incite. She was both singing about and raging against the government at the same time, and the audience was shouting its approval. Broxton shuddered. Ramsingh was not a popular man.

And in five hours he was going to appear before them. It was a crazy idea and the man earlier had been right. Ram should stay away, but Broxton knew he wouldn't.

"That's all for now," Tammy Drake said from the stage, "but I'll be back before sundown and I promise you a super long set. We'll do all the favorites, and as an extra added attraction I'll have Prime Minister Ramsingh on stage with me to help us launch the evening portion of the festival."

Her words were met with a chorus of applause and boos. Broxton was sure the applause was for her and the hisses for Ram. It was a crazy situation and there was nothing he could do about it except scan the crowd, and even that was useless. Who could he watch? Who could he single out? Everybody looked like a possible threat the way they were jeering Ram.

Five hours and five minutes later the Sons of Trinidad were finishing their set. In a few minutes Tammy Drake and Ramsingh were going to take the stage. Broxton felt a tight sensation in the pit of his stomach. There was electricity in the air, both from the threatening storm and from the crowd anticipation. He felt the pulse of the crowd as he moved among it. The crowd moved as a single being, swaying, singing, and dancing with the beat, but somewhere among it danger lurked. He tasted it on the evening breeze.

He pushed through the throng till he was at its fringe. The band finished, took their bows, then left the stage. The crowd quieted, gray clouds covered the sky. A cool breeze blew through the park, evaporating sweat, chilling a thousand souls, and chilling his, too. The hair on the back of his neck tingled. His spine quivered. A current ran through him, electric and cold.

He stepped through the north gate and out of the park. He checked his watch. Five to five. Ram was never late. Police surrounded the stage. There was nothing he could do there. Plain clothes police wormed and worked their way through the crowd. That too, was out of his hands. He turned away from the stage and faced the Red House. So many windows.

Then he saw her and his heart jumped. He smiled before he thought. He started to call her name, but checked himself. What was she doing here? She was supposed to be sailing up the islands. Movement caught his eye and he turned to see a pigeon land on the wrought iron fence not far from where he stood. For a brief instant he wondered if it was the same bird he'd fed earlier and again he thought of Paris. Dani was in Paris when Aaron Gamaliel was shot. Why did he think of that? She was in Zambia when President Jomo Seko was shot, too. Coincidence? Why was she here? Then he knew why the assassins in Venezuela were told to spare him.

She started to turn toward him, almost as if she knew she was being watched, and he stepped back through the gate. He could see her through the iron bars, but she wouldn't be able to make him out. She studied the street, raised an arm and gave proof to his thoughts when she greeted the man he'd seen from the water in Venezuela. The big man with the Texas accent. The man who had tried to kill Ram.

He shuddered. A terrifying thought rippled through him. The plane, the hotel. She hadn't used a rifle. She had no rifle now. She was standing just outside the park with the Texan, not to shoot but to watch. To watch the blast. It was going to be another bomb.

He turned toward the gazebo on the other side of the crowded park. In a few minutes Ramsingh would take the stage. He wondered if it was set on a timer or if she was here to detonate it via remote control. He looked toward Dani again. She had a clear view of the stage from where she was standing, safely outside the park. She'd be outside the panicked throng. She could just walk away while the crowd fought to get out the gates.

He looked around for a policeman. They were all in the park, surrounding the gazebo. For a second he thought about charging toward Dani, but Ram was going to take the stage shortly. Besides, the Texan could hold him off while she punched the remote. If she had a remote. If the bomb was on a timer there was nothing he could do. But if she was holding her finger over a button there was a chance.

And he took it. Turning away from Dani and the Texan, he charged into the crowd, yelling, "Move aside! Emergency! I'm a doctor! Please, step aside!"

The people at the edges of the crowd parted as he pushed and forced his way through in his mad dash for the stage.

"Hey, watch it," a giant of a man yelled when Broxton slammed into his back.

"I'm a doctor, the prime minister is ill."

"I'll get you there," the big African Trini yelled

back to Broxton. "Get out of the way! Mr. Ramsingh needs his doctor!" The man hurled himself into the crowd, shoulder forward, as if he was blocking for a quarterback.

Broxton kept his head down and his eyes on the broad back as the giant cleared the way, shoving people aside, shouting, "Doctor coming through! Step aside!" Then they were in the center of the crowd, people packed together. He smelled their sweat, felt their anticipation, touched their souls. The parting corridor the big man cut through the throng closed as soon as he'd pushed by. He was but a part of the pack, a single cell in the living, breathing, swaying and crushing crowd.

People started applauding. Something was happening. He couldn't see.

"Tammy, Tammy, Tammy," the crowd chanted, excitement rising.

"Out of the way," the big man yelled louder, trying to be heard above the applause.

"Tammy, Tammy, Tammy," the crowd shouted as one.

"Hurry," Broxton pleaded.

"Coming through," the giant shouted, but the closer they got to the gazebo the slower the going. People were jammed together, back to front, shoulder to shoulder, but still the big man grunted, shoved and pushed. "Let the doctor pass," he wailed, and to their credit, as tightly bunched as they were, people tried to get out of the big man's way.

"Ladies and gentlemen," Tammy Drake's amplified voice boomed through mammoth speakers, "it's good to be back. It's going to be a wonderful evening." The crowd went wild, yelling, clapping and whooping, drowning out the giant's voice.

People jumped, some swayed, some danced, some called out, they all clapped. Everybody in Trinidad loved Tammy Drake.

"Doctor coming through!" The giant pushed into the mass of people, shoving his way to the stage.

"It's my great pleasure to bring Ramish Ramsingh up to the podium."

The crowd was muffled, but there were no catcalls, they remained respectful. Ramsingh wasn't popular, but the audience wasn't going to let politics ruin this musical night.

Then they were at the stage.

"You, stop!" Broxton heard a rough voice scream. The giant dropped his shoulder and Broxton saw four uniformed policemen guarding the steps up the gazebo, all holding truncheons in hand, all raising them to strike. The giant spread his arms and dove into them, grabbing the center two and taking them down. The two on the outside swung their clubs, but the nightsticks hit only air as the big man rolled safely through.

Broxton saw his opportunity and vaulted over the melee, landing on the stage as the prime minister took the podium. He felt a strong hand grab his arm, another wrapped around his neck.

"Hold," Ramsingh said.

The policemen relaxed their grips, but still held on to him.

"It's all right," Ramsingh added. "It's Broxton. He's in charge of security, remember?"

"Sorry, sir," one of them said, as they released him. "We didn't recognize you."

"What's going on?" Ramsingh said. The crowd, sensing something ominous, quieted, all eyes on the stage.

224

"Your wife is ill," Broxton lied. "We have to go."

"I'm sorry, ladies and gentlemen. Please forgive me," Ramsingh said. "I have to leave. I hope you understand."

Broxton looked across the park as he put his arm around Ramsingh's shoulder, and he locked onto Dani. She had her armed linked with the big Texan. She was too far for him to see into her eyes, but he knew she was boring into him. The Texan was holding something in his hand and Broxton didn't think it was a Sony Walkman. He shivered, wondering if she would let him push the button.

"Is she all right?" Ramsingh asked, breaking Broxton's concentration.

"We have to go," Broxton said.

"All right," Ramsingh said as Broxton, turning, pulled the prime minister toward the back of the stage and down the back steps of the gazebo. Cool sweat dripped from under his arms and his neck hairs were prickling. Any second it could all be over. All she had to do was give the word and the podium, the stage, the gazebo, and several people would vaporize. He knew the truth of the thought as surely as he knew his own name.

CHAPTER SEVENTEEN

"YACHT CLUB, Yachting Association, Drake's," the youth shouted at Dani. The sun was still up, it was still hot. She wiped sweat off the back of her neck with her left hand as she signaled the young man with her right. "Yacht Club?" he yelled at her.

"Drake's," she yelled back to him."

"This is crazy," Earl said as she took his elbow and motioned for him to cross the street. The large green building on the corner across from the Globe Theater gave the place its name, *Green Corner*, and Dani was leading Earl to the maxi at the head of the line. There were already four people in it. The driver was waiting for six more.

She passed it and climbed into the van second in

line, taking a seat behind the driver. Earl jumped in and moved beside her. She leaned forward and put her mouth next to the driver's ear as she draped a hand over his shoulder. "Go now," she said, "and don't pick up anyone on the way."

The driver, a thin Rasta man with dreadlocks past his shoulder, snatched the blue hundred from her hand. "We're gone," he said, and Earl slid the door closed as the van shot away from the curb, barely missing the maxi in front.

"Want a fast trip?" the driver asked. Earl recognized the Texas accent as he moved to the seat in back.

"Fast as you can and still get us there alive," Dani said, getting up and moving to the back with Earl.

"Fucking crazy," Earl whispered to her. "We're making our getaway on a bus."

* * *

"It's Dani Street," Broxton told Ramsingh as they made their way out of the park.

"What?"

"She's the one behind the attempts to kill you. It explains why they wouldn't kill me. She doesn't want me hurt. And right now, I think she's headed toward the ambassador's yacht. She's supposed to be taking it up island."

"What are you going to do?"

"Go after her."

"I'm going too," Ramsingh said. Then he motioned to a young policeman standing next to a blue and white police car. "I'll be taking the car, Gary."

"Sir," the policeman said.

"Mr. Broxton and I are going to use the car." He

offered the policeman a bright smile. The officer stood fast.

"I'm supposed to drive it."

"Gary, I'm sixty-two years old. I know how to drive."

"Not the point. I'm supposed to drive."

"Look at me, Gary." The policeman looked into Ramsingh's hard gray eyes. "I'm the prime minister and I'm taking this car. Tell your sergeant that I gave you no choice. Then tell the president I'll be out of touch for a day or so."

"Sir?"

"Step aside, Gary."

"Yes, sir," the policeman said, as he opened the driver's door and moved out of Ramsingh's way. Broxton jumped in the passenger side and in seconds they were driving away from the park, the concert, and the thousands of fans who never knew how close they came to witnessing the assassination of a prime minister and possibly becoming victims themselves.

"Warren keeps his boat docked at the pier in front of Drake's Shipyard. It's a sixty-five foot sloop. Very fast. We'll play hell trying to catch them. I don't know if we can," Ramsingh said, as they passed the maxi stand at Green Corner. They didn't see Dani and Earl climb into the second maxi. They didn't notice the maxi bolt from the curb. And they weren't watching as it followed them down Western Main Road.

"We can't have her arrested," Broxton said.

"Don't I know it," the prime minister said.

"What are we going to do?" This time it was Broxton asking the question.

"Follow her and see where she goes. Play it by ear."

"How are we going to do that?"

"I keep my boat at the yacht club. Not big and fast like *Sea King*, and the yacht club's five miles this side of Drake's so they'll have a head start, but I'm a sailor, and Dani's not. She'll reef up, we won't. We might get lucky."

"Reef up?" Broxton asked.

"It'll be dark soon. It's blowing like stink out there. I know, I check the weather every morning, old habits die hard. She'll be cautious and reef. That means she'll bring most of her sail in."

"What if she's in a hurry?"

"She'll be afraid of being overpowered. When the weather's bad, you reef. Too much sail up and you can put your mast in the water, or worse you could roll the boat. It makes for a much safer and more pleasant ride if you reef when it starts to blow hard."

"You think we'll be able to catch her?"

"Maybe, if she reefs, like I said. The wind will be at her beam, the best point of sail. She'll cook. Seven, eight knots, even if she is reefed, but it won't be fun with the kind of weather that's out there. And there's no place to hide in the Caribbean, too many yachties these days. There's no such thing as a quiet or private anchorage anymore."

"She won't hide," Broxton said. "She knows I saw her, but she also knows I'd never do anything to hurt Warren. Plus she thinks I'm still in love with her. She'll be convinced I'll keep my mouth shut. No, she won't run or hide. She'll think she's in the clear. It would be just like her to take a leisurely cruise up the Islands, drinking, dining and dancing in the most public nightspots all the way to the Florida Keys."

They were quiet for a few seconds, then Broxton asked. "What do we do when we catch up to her?"

"That's a good question."

"She tried to kill you."

"We don't know that for sure," Ramsingh said. He stopped at a red light, looked both ways, then ran it.

"She was with the man I saw in Margarita. That's why I charged the stage. I'm convinced they had a bomb ready to blow."

"And you thought if you were on the stage she wouldn't set it off?"

"Yes."

"But what if it wasn't remote controlled? What if it was on a timer?"

"I didn't think of that," Broxton lied.

"Sure you did," Ramsingh said. He waited through another few seconds of silence then added, "Thanks. I doubt any of my men would have taken such a risk." Then he looked in the rearview mirror and changed the subject. "The maxi behind ran the light, too, with a police car in front," he said.

"People don't respect the law here," Broxton said. "That's part of your problem."

"We have a long way to go," Ramsingh said. Then he turned into the yacht club, oblivious to the maxi that sped around him and continued north on Western Main road toward Drake's Shipyard.

* * *

"Fuzz is gone. Now we can move," the Rasta driver said and he stepped on the gas.

Earl watched the scenery fly by, fascinated by the rain forest that edged up to the road. He imagined monkeys, snakes, big cats and cannibals inside the dense jungle and shivered as he thought of witch doctors throwing bones and voodoo priests jabbing pins in lifelike dolls.

"Got snakes in there?" he asked the driver.

"Got plenty, man."

"Poisonous?"

"Real deadly."

"Monkeys?"

"Most died off, some kind of fever."

"Cats, like lions and tigers?"

"No man."

"How about voodoo?" He knew better than to ask about cannibals.

"We got that."

"Shit," he said, glad they were heading out of the country.

"I hear ya," the driver said, then he turned on the radio, cranked it up loud and started singing along with a calypso song.

For the next five or six minutes Earl stared at the lush, green vegetation as it whizzed by the window, wondering why they were leaving. The prime minister wasn't dead yet. He turned from the window, leaned toward her and whispered, "Where we going?"

"Grenada," she said, whispering back.

"But we haven't finished it."

"Relax, Earl. We'll be in Prickly Bay shortly after sunup. We'll check in, go to town, be seen, talk to a few yachties and then we'll board a plane and come back and finish the job. I don't like doing it that way, but my father expects the boat to be in Grenada by tomorrow and that's where it's going to be, besides it's a perfect alibi."

"Won't they have a record of us leaving the country?"

"You said you travel with a couple of extra passports, well I do too."

"But everybody here knows you."

"Earl, really," she said. "Think about who I am and what I've been doing for the last several years. Don't you think I can get by a customs officer without being recognized. Shit, I can be eighteen or eighty and I have a passport for every occasion.

* * *

The guard left the guard shack as the police car pulled up to the gate. His uniform was pressed and the visor on his hat was as spit shined as his shoes. He wore the uniform like he was proud of it, but his stomach spoke of too many beers when he was off duty.

"Trouble?" he said, seeing the police car and looking in the window.

"No, Cletus, I'm just going for a sail."

"Mr. Ramsingh, sir." The guard stepped back.

"Would you call the president and tell him I went sailing for a day or so. Tell him I'll call him tomorrow and explain everything."

"I can't call the president."

"Sure you can," Ramsingh said. "Get your clipboard and I'll give you his private number."

"I thought you were the prime minister," Broxton said a few seconds later as Ramsingh put the emergency brake on in the parking lot.

"The president's the head of state, like the Queen in England, and like in England the prime minister's the head of the government. I'm elected, he's not."

"How's he get the job?"

"The prime minister appoints him. He serves for five years, that way his term overlaps the election. In theory he's not beholden to the prime minister or party in power. He's supposed to be above politics."

"Is he?"

"Usually."

The day was fading away as they made their way through the bar toward the dock. There were a few tourists and locals gazing toward the setting sun, hoping to see the green flash, a group of yachties playing cards at one table, a foursome playing bridge at another. Palm trees swaying in the breeze grew along the fence that guarded the north side of the club, a rich housing development bordered on the south and with the road behind and the gulf in front, the yacht club was truly cut off from the daily grind of Trinidad. It was a world unto itself.

"My boat's at the end," Ramsingh said as they left the bar and stepped onto the main dock.

Halyards clinked against aluminum masts, wind generators hummed, a local was hammering a board into the dock, replacing one that had rotted away. These sounds Broxton understood, but there was another, like a west Texas coyote howling long and high in the distance. He stopped and cocked his head, curious.

"It's the wind blowing through the roller furled mainsails. Spooky sounding. I don't like it," Ramsingh said. "I don't know why people have them. I can see a roller furled headsail, but what do you do in a blow if the gear jams or the sail bunches up and you can't get it through that slot in the mast?"

"I don't know," Broxton said. He didn't understand a word Ramsingh was saying.

"Exactly," Ramsingh said. "Give me a main you haul up and reef at the mast any day. It's the only way."

"Sure," Broxton said, convinced the prime minister was talking to build up his courage, because Ram had to know by now that he didn't know the difference between port and starboard.

"There she is, *Gypsy Dancer*."

"That's it?" Broxton said.

"That's her," Ramsingh said.

"You're kidding? We're not taking that out there," Broxton said, pointing to the ocean.

"Yes we are."

"It's so small."

"Not so small. My wife and I sailed her around the world."

"Shit."

"She's twenty-seven feet and she sails like a witch."

"Shit," Broxton said again.

"Not scared are you?"

"Yes."

"You'll get over it," Ramsingh said as he jumped onto the boat. "You'll have to undo the lines, take them off those cleats as soon as I start the engine."

"Sure," Broxton said. He shivered when the small inboard sprang to life, but he unwrapped the line from the cleats and jumped on board. They motored from the yacht club and Ramsingh pointed *Gypsy Dancer* toward the setting sun. When they were in deeper water he turned the boat back toward the club.

"Are we going back?" Broxton said, almost wishing they were.

"We have to face into the wind to raise the main."

"Oh, yeah, I forgot. Want me to take the wheel?"

"Yes," Ramsingh said, and he stepped up on the deck when Broxton relieved him. At the mast he fed the main halyard into a self-tailing winch and cranked it up. The snapping sounds the sail made as it flapped in the wind reminded Broxton of gunfire and he shuddered.

"All right take her around," Ramsingh said, stepping back into the cockpit.

Broxton spun the wheel to the right and kept the boat in the turn till the wind was at their back and Ramsingh shut off the engine. They sailed like that for a few minutes, the main powering the boat at three knots over a calm sea toward the glow on the horizon where the sun had been.

* * *

"The end of the line," the Rasta driver said as he pulled up in front of Drake Road.

"Take us all the way in. Right up to the dinghy dock," Dani said.

"Your wish is my command," he said, turning left onto the dirt track that led into the shipyard.

"You're not from here, are you?" Earl said.

"Dallas, born and bred."

"Why here, driving a taxi bus?" Earl asked.

"They're not so up tight here. Live and let live. Try that back in the States." The driver stopped the van in front of the dock.

"I still don't get it," Earl said as he stepped out of the van.

"Jah is love. It's all I need," the Rasta driver said, then he put the van in gear and sped off.

"Holy shit, that's some boat," Earl said, as they were approaching *Sea King*.

"Two million dollars of sixty-five foot steel boat. She really is the King of the Sea. Wait till you see the state room."

"It would be gorgeous if it wasn't for those two giant hook things hanging off the ass end."

"Those are the dinghy davits and yes they do kind of ruin the lines, but my father wanted them as an extra safety feature, because he doesn't believe in life rafts."

"Say that again."

"He doesn't believe in life rafts. They have no motor or sails, you have no way to steer them. All you do is float around in the ocean and hope someone finds you. Those poles on each side, by the oars, connect to form a mast. Under the forward seat is a mast step that my father had build into the dinghy. The sail is under the rear seat. Those giant hooks, as you call them, are designed to raise the dinghy with an electric motor. In an emergency we can grab our get-a-way bags, lower the dinghy and be in it in seconds. So although the dinghy davits ruin the lines of the boat, I've learned to like them. Besides, it makes raising the dinghy oh so easy."

* * *

The sun was down and stars were dotting the sky as Ramsingh unfurled the jib and they sailed downwind past the Five Island group. Then he turned so that the wind was crossing the starboard side at twenty knots. Gypsy *Dancer* responded by heeling over and her speed increased to seven knots.

"This is pretty much our top speed," Ramsingh said. "Once we get out there it'll be choppy and we'll be fighting a cross current. We'll have bigger wind, spray in the face and maybe a little rain."

"Swell," Broxton said.

"You might want to take your shoes off."

"Sure." Broxton kicked them off.

"Okay, why don't you take the wheel while I go below and get the life jackets and tethers." A few minutes later Ramsingh was back. "All right, slip this on," he said, handing Broxton a blue inflatable life vest. Broxton put it on. "If you wind up in the water, pull on the chord and the vest will inflate, but it won't make any difference, you'll die anyway, because I won't be able to find you in the dark, so don't fall off."

"You're just full of glad tidings," Broxton said.

"And to aid you in staying on board we have these," Ramsingh said, and he clipped a line to the front of his vest. Broxton watched as he clipped the other end to the binnacle. "Now you're secured to the boat."

"You went around the world tied to the boat?"

"Only when we were on deck after dark or in bad weather. Tonight we're going to get both."

* * *

Earl looked at the darkening sky as they motored toward *Boca del Monos*, Monkey's Mouth, the westernmost and smallest of the four openings between Trinidad and Venezuela that separated the Gulf of Paria from the Caribbean Sea. This was his first time on a sailboat, but he'd raced plenty of speedboats across Lake Dallas, so he wasn't worried about the crossing to Grenada. Nothing bad could happen on a boat that topped out at ten to twelve knots.

He settled himself back in the cockpit. Soon, he thought, they'd be through the opening and into the sea. Then they could put the boat on automatic pilot, go below and screw till sunup. Life was good and it was getting better.

"You want to take the wheel while I let out the sails?"

"Sure," he said, getting up.

"Just keep it pointed to the slot between the land on the right and the small island on the left."

"Gotcha," he said.

She pushed a button and he heard the whirring of a powerful electric motor. He watched, fascinated, as the mainsail pulled out from inside the mast. The boat picked up speed as the sail came out and she kept her finger on the button until it was out all the way. The boat heeled over a little and Earl felt the apparent wind as it soothed across his face. He glanced at the knot meter. Seven knots. It seemed faster.

"Now the jib," she said and he watched her as she took the lines off the large starboard winch and let it lay slack. Then she moved over to the port side and pushed another button and the port winch started turning.

"Are all the winches electric?" he asked as the sail came out.

"No, just the two big ones. They have the jib sheets on them."

"What?"

"The lines that control the big head sail. It's too big to handle by hand."

The jib filled as it unfurled, and she kept her finger on the button until it was all the way out. *Sea King* heeled over more and for a second Earl thought he was going to fall off, but he held onto the steering wheel and grabbed another look at the knot meter. Nine knots. He turned his attention back to her, long hair flying around her face as she pulled the jib sheet tight into the jaws of the self-tailing winch. He looked at the wind instrument. Twenty knots. Twenty knots of wind and they were doing nine knots over the water. He tightened his hands on the wheel. He felt the adrenaline zip through him, lighting up the hair on his arms, sparking across his skin, tingling at the

back of his neck. His palms were sweaty on the wheel
and the wind was whipping across his face.

"You okay, Earl?" she said.

"I had no idea nine knots could be so fast."

"We'll do eleven or twelve once we pass through
the Bocas."

"Shit," he said.

It seemed like they were flying. And they were
still in the gulf. And then it was calm as they entered
the narrow channel between Trinidad proper and
Monos Island. *Sea King* moved flat across the water,
powered by the motor, the wind useless as it blew
over Trinidad's high mountains, ignoring the sailboat
below.

Earl used the calm moments to catch his breath.

"You want a drink?" Dani asked.

"Shot of tequila and a beer if you can," Earl said.

"Okay, just keep her pointed through the center
of the channel," she said, before going below, leaving
him alone with the boat, the sea and the night.

"What the—" Earl said, ducking as something
flew by his face. Bird, he thought and he raised his
head as another one whipped by and he knew it
wasn't a bird. "Bats!" he yelled as another one, then
another flew by. He felt his skin crawl, he wanted to
swat at them, but he was afraid to take his hands from
the wheel. Another zipped by, inches from his face,
and he followed it with his eyes. "*Jose y Maria*," he
said, staring wide-eyed at the bats swarming around
the boat. There were hundreds, thousands of them,
silently flapping above the water, over the deck, and
back to skimming the sea again. It was a miracle they
didn't get caught in the sails.

Then as quickly as they'd come, they were gone,
flocking toward a small bay off to the right and again

Earl was alone in the dark.

"You say something, Earl?" Dani said as she popped up from below, holding onto the boat with her right hand, balancing a shot glass and a beer in her left.

"No, nothing," he said, staring at the salvation in her hand.

"Here you go," she said, stepping up to him. He downed the tequila in a quick gulp and then took a long pull on the beer.

"Aren't you having anything?" he asked.

"No."

"Look ahead," she said and Earl followed her pointed finger.

"Holy shit," he said, staring at the boiling seas, three foot swells coming from all directions, churning as evil as any witch's caldron.

"Confused seas where the Caribbean meets the Gulf," she said. "We'll keep the motor on till we're through it."

The first hint of breeze started to fill the sails before she finished her sentence and in seconds they were full and *Sea King* was bucking and thrashing through the end of the churning passage. Earl held the wheel with a tight right handed grip and tossed the beer can over the side with his left.

"Keep her straight, Earl," Dani said.

"Yeah."

"And stay away from the rock on the left."

"What rock?" he said. Then he saw it, large, dark and forbidding, hogging the center of the channel.

"A little to the right," she said, her voice calm, reassuring.

He pulled the wheel to the right and felt the boat turn.

"Too much, come back a little."

He obeyed, feeling the sweat dripping down his back as they sailed up to it. He checked the knot meter. Eight knots. Eight point two, three, five, seven. *Sea King* heeled back over and Earl pulled the wheel sharply to starboard, convinced they were going to hit the rock, then they were past it and into the choppy, churning, open sea. Sails full, wind whipping his face, knot meter reading ten-five and rising.

Huge swells, made more powerful by the current, slammed into the side of the boat. *Sea King's* bow bucked to port with each hit, then jerked back to starboard. The wind, howling now, kept the boat heeled over so far to port that her rails were in the water. Spray slapped his face, salt stung his eyes, and sheer terror stabbed at his thumping heart.

Then they were past the bubbling, boiling seas and had only the swells, the wind and the current to contend with. The rails were still in the water, sending spray shooting over the side, showering them like they were under a giant sized salt water spigot, and Earl watched, horrified, as Dani white knuckled the stainless steel bimini supports in an effort to keep herself from going over the side.

"We're in trouble," she shouted.

"No shit," Earl shouted back.

"I have to reef it in."

"What?"

"I have to take in some sail."

"Do it!"

Dani pushed the furling button for the main. The motor whirred, then whined in protest, but the sail stayed full.

"Head up some," she shouted back to him.

"What?"

"Turn a little to the right."

He did and some of the wind spilled out of the sail. She hit the button again and sighed as the sail started to wind itself into the mast, but again the motor screeched in protest. She let up on the button, afraid she was going to burn it out.

"Turn all the way into the wind," she shouted, pointing.

Earl pulled hard on the wheel, spinning it, feeling the boat shudder and quake. Would he ever see land again.

"More," she shouted and he obeyed, turning the wheel till they were headed directly into the wind and the waves.

The jib cracked like an amplified thunder blast.

"Shit, shit, shit!" Dani jumped to the large port winch, where she took the jib sheet out of the self-tailing jaws. Then she grabbed a winch handle from a plastic holster in the cockpit, jammed it in the furling winch and started grinding, bringing in the heavy sail. The jib cracked again, sending the jib sheets whipping and twisting, smacking the deck, the shrouds and the sails with enough force to maim, or to kill.

"Down!" Earl screamed.

Dani dropped over the winch like she'd been shot. The boom whipped over her head, breezing her hair in its killing arc. Now the main was thunder-snapping as the boom whipsawed from port to starboard and back again with the fury of a log riding the rapids.

Once the jib was halfway in she stopped grinding and pulled out the winch handle. Now she had to tackle the swinging boom. She thrust the handle into the mainsheet winch and started grinding on it. Earl could see that she was almost done in, but he didn't know what he could do to help. He was at her mercy. If she succeeded and got the boat under control, they might make it. He had no doubt about what was going to happen if she didn't.

Once the mainsheet was tightened and the boom's violent motion curtailed, Dani went back to the button that operated the main's roller furling gear. The boat was still rocking and slamming, but a lot of the fury had been tamed. He watched as the main again started to disappear inside the mast. Then it stopped.

"It's jammed," she said.

"Oh, fuck," Earl said. The main was three quarters of the way in and still flapping.

"I'm going to have to let it out and try again," she shouted.

"Hurry," Earl shouted back.

She pushed the opposite button and the sail came out a bit. Then she pushed the other one and Earl sighed loud enough to wake the dead as the sail retracted into the mast. "Are you taking it all the way in?"

"No, we'll need to keep some of it out for stability," she shouted, but the ripping sound told them that the sail had gotten caught again, only this time the motor overpowered the canvas. There was nothing for her do to but to keep her hand on the button and get as much of the torn main in the mast as possible.

CHAPTER EIGHTEEN

"I TALKED TO A FRIEND of mine on the radio this morning," Ramsingh said. "He'd just made the crossing between Trinidad and Grenada."

"You're a HAM operator?"

"Not licensed, but I use it every now and then to keep track of my cruising friends."

"Isn't that against the law?"

"Not for the prime minister."

"What did your friend say?"

"He said that it was the worst crossing he's made in the seven years he's been in the Caribbean."

"Swell," Broxton said.

"This isn't going to be like our last sail together. Then we were on a much bigger boat and the wind was just horrible. Tonight will be a lot worse."

"How much worse?"

"You can't imagine."

"But you can?" Broxton said.

"Sure. I've lived a good part of my life on boats, remember? I've sailed around the world twice, been in three hurricanes, several tropical storms and more squalls than you can count."

"Hurricane winds out there tonight?" Broxton asked.

"No."

"Tropical storm?"

"No."

"Then I'd say I'm in pretty good hands."

"I was twenty-five years younger."

"Are you trying to scare me?"

"No, just trying to prepare you. It'll be a fast crossing for *Gypsy Dancer*. We won't reef, so we'll be fighting the wheel the whole way, so I think it will be a good idea if we take hourly shifts throughout the night. That seem okay to you?"

"Sure."

Ramsingh smiled. "Keep her pointed northwest. We'll go between the point and the prison island. Then we'll head straight for the first Boca," he said, before going below.

Broxton looked toward the prison island, Trinidad's version of Alcatraz. It was less than a quarter mile from shore, but the current between the small island and the mainland was so treacherous that only one man had ever survived the swim. And he was caught as soon as he hit the road, picked up hitchhiking by a prison guard.

Forty-five minutes later Ramsingh started the engine as they approached the Bocas. "We'll lose our wind for the next fifteen minutes, then we'll hit confused seas, so I'll take the wheel till we're clear. Then I'll show you how to ride the waves without putting the mast in the water."

"You're the boss." Broxton relinquished the wheel. He sat down in the cockpit, staring at the giant rock in the center of the channel.

"The deeper water's on the right side," Ramsingh said and he maneuvered the boat dead center between the giant rock and the mainland. There's supposed to be a flashing light on the rock, but apparently it's out."

When they were abreast of the rock Broxton saw the boiling sea ahead and the swells beyond. "We can sail in that?"

"We can," Ramsingh said, then they were past the shelter of the mountains and the wind filled the sails. Ramsingh switched the engine off and they were in it.

* * *

"Turn to port, left, left, left!" she shouted and Earl started cranking the wheel, bringing the boat around toward their original course. "Too far, back, back," she said, and he pulled it back a little to the right. "Good, that's good, hold it there." His hands shook on the wheel and although it was cold as a Texas winter sweat still dripped down his back, his hands were clammy and a river was leaking from under his arms.

The boat was heeled to port again, but not like before. Earl didn't feel like he was about to fall off. The rails weren't in the water, but a quarter of the torn main was hanging out of the mast, cracking like thunder, sending chills to the back of his neck. He didn't know if he'd be able to stand it all night.

He cast a shivering look over his right shoulder and saw a wave coming toward him at eye level. He thought it was going to capsize them, but the boat rode over it. The bow broke to port, but he pulled it back on course. A few seconds later another wave rode under and he pulled it back on course again. Then another, taking the bow to the left, he corrected, then again, then again. He was going to be plenty tired by sunup.

She moved back toward him, bent low, holding on to the cockpit combing as she scooted along. She straightened and grabbed onto the binnacle and faced him. "I'm going to swing around next to you and set the autopilot," she said, her face inches from his.

"Fine by me," he said.

She kept one hand on the binnacle as she moved behind the wheel. He saw numbers dance across some of the instruments as she started pushing buttons.

"You can let go now, the autopilot has us." Earl obeyed, amazed as the wheel turned back and forth. "It'll take it a minute or so to figure out the wave pattern," she said. Earl stepped away from the wheel and grabbed onto the backstay for support. The wheel turned less with each wave until the boat was making steady headway. "The autopilot is programmed into the GPS, and I've set in the lat and long for Grenada. Barring problems, our job is over. We're passengers now."

"But it's so rough."

"I screwed up. I had too much sail out. This is a strong boat, she can handle seas a heck of a lot rougher than this."

"Seems plenty rough to me," Earl said, looking out at the black waves, and as if to punctuate his thoughts, a wave crashed over the side, showering them with spray.

Then she shut the motor off.

"Why'd you do that?"

"We don't have enough fuel to motor all the way to Grenada."

"What?"

"Relax. It's a sailboat, remember?"

Earl looked up at the torn and flogging main.

"It's not our only sail. We'll make it just fine with the jib alone."

"How come we didn't gas up first?"

"Because my father doesn't like to buy diesel from the fuel dock, he thinks it's dirty fuel. He has a man jerry jug diesel from a gas station whenever the tank gets low."

"Who does he think you're sailing with?" Earl asked, as she grabbed the binnacle again and swung around it so that they were facing each other with the wheel between them.

"Friends, he's not worried. I've sailed up island and back without him before. He plans on flying up to St. Thomas and sailing on back with us."

"But you don't have any friends on board?"

"I have you."

"You know what I mean."

"I'll tell him they left for Europe on another boat, it won't be a problem."

"Then it's your fault we got no gas."

"Has anyone ever told you that you have a one track mind?" She was staring straight into his eyes, their faces inches apart. He saw the fire there, felt the chill in her heart. This was not Maria and he sure as hell didn't want to piss her off.

"Sorry," he said. "This is all new to me and I don't think I like it too much."

"It'll be all right, Earl, you'll see. Let's go below and get out of these wet clothes," she said. He saw some of the fire melt. He was going to have to be careful with her.

He followed her below and walked into bedlam. It was like he was in an amusement park fun house. Because the boat was heeled, the floor was about thirty degrees out of kilter. Up wasn't up. He wasn't able to stand, so he slumped down onto the settee on the down side. He felt like he was being sucked in, like he was on an airplane during take off. The flogging main ricocheted through the boat, like he was inside a giant base drum. The wind whistling through the shrouds and the halyards raised the hair on the back of his neck, reminding him of every ghost story he'd ever read. The swinging hurricane lamp sent shadows and light spinning out of control. The back and forth seesawing of the boat as the waves flung it to port and the autopilot brought it back to starboard set his stomach churning, like he'd had too much to drink. The whole thing sent his pulse pumping. And he didn't like it.

"It looks like we're not alone out here tonight," she said. She was sitting at a table, staring at a dark screen with green shapes on it. Radar.

"What do you mean?"

"Another boat, about six miles back, just came through the Bocas."

* * *

"They're about six miles ahead of us," Ramsingh said, looking at his radar screen, "and they're doing about six and a half knots. If our luck holds we'll catch them by morning."

Broxton looked toward the star-filled sky.

"Beautiful, isn't it?" Ramsingh said.

"I've never seen anything like it."

"Just an average night sky for a cruiser."

"Cruiser?" Broxton asked.

"That's what we're called, us boat people. We live on board and travel the world, going where we want, when we want. No government, no boundaries, no rules, except the law of the sea, the wind and the rain."

"Kind of an unusual statement coming from you."

"Yes."

"Now you are the government."

"Ironic, isn't it?" Ramsingh said.

"I'd say," Broxton said, then he ducked as spray splashed over the side.

"It just proves that you never really know what the future holds in store for you. When I was your age I wandered the world, now I'm leading a nation. I won't run for re-election. I just decided that."

"Why not?"

"I'm not very popular, but that's not the reason. The kids are grown, the youngest is going to the States in a few months to start college. I'm going back."

"Going back?"

"Back to the sea."

"In this?" Broxton asked, raising his eyebrows.

"No, this is a boat for a younger man. I've got some savings. Some retirement pay coming, and we're selling the house. I think I'll buy a forty-five footer and head toward the Pacific."

"Really?"

"Yes, sir, really," Ramsingh said, stepping back as more spray came over the side.

"I can't believe I'm having a conversation in these

conditions."

"What conditions?" Ramsingh said, laughing.

"This." Broxton waved an arm, gesturing toward the sea.

"It's a little rough," Ramsingh said, "but not dangerous."

"I'll take your word for it," Broxton said. He checked his watch, thirty minutes till his shift. "If you get tired, you'll let me know, right?"

"I will," Ramsingh said, but he didn't. Both men spent the night without sleep. Every hour, as soon as he'd finished his turn at the wheel, Ramsingh checked and charted their position and made note of the closing distance between themselves and *Sea King*.

"I see a light up ahead," Broxton said, an hour before dawn.

"That'll be them," Ramsingh said, from behind the wheel. "In an hour we should be within shouting distance."

"Then what are we going to do?" Broxton asked.

"You're the policeman."

"I've never arrested anybody. Besides, we're in international waters. How do we arrest them here?"

"We can't," Ramsingh said. "And we can't call the coast guard, not without ruining the ambassador's career. I guess the only thing we can do is follow them into an anchorage and see if we can overpower them tonight. Then maybe we can find out who's behind it all. Maybe Dani will tell us when she finds out we're not interested in arresting her."

"Somehow I don't think she'll tell us anything," Broxton said.

"She'll talk," Ramsingh said. "She's just a girl."

"She's Scorpion," Broxton said.

"Shit," Ramsingh said. It was the first time

Broxton had heard him swear.

"You know about the Scorpion?"

"Aaron Gamaliel was a friend of mine. I know." Broxton saw Ramsingh tighten up on the wheel and looked into his steel gray eyes.

"It's not going to be easy," Broxton said.

"But we have to see it through," Ramsingh said, "now more than ever."

"You still don't want to call the coast guard?"

"No."

* * *

"That boat back there's a lot closer," Dani said, looking up from the radar. She was naked and Earl was grinning as he took in her slender form.

"Come over here, babe," he said, still hard, still excited. He was lying on the settee in the big salon, and like Dani, he was naked

She looked back at the screen. "It could be anybody," she said. "Probably nothing to worry about."

"But I'm worried," Earl said.

"Yeah, about what?"

"About this thing sticking up between my legs. You gotta do something about it or I'm gonna be condemned to go through life with it sticking out in front of me like a flagpole."

"Don't you ever get enough?" she said, laughing and coming toward him.

"Not of you, babe. I'll never get enough of you."

"Lie back and close your eyes," she said.

He obeyed. This wild night had been the night of his dreams, any man's dreams. The boat had been rolling and swaying from side to side throughout the night. The wind had been howling. The torn main had been flapping. It was like a night in a stormy cemetery. And all night long they'd been making love. She was a demon in bed, a mad loving demon. Her perfect white body glistened in the moonlight that filtered in through the overhead hatch. Her firm breasts stood erect with hard nipples that begged to be kissed. Her silky thighs quivered when he touched them.

"I love it," he said, when she took him in her mouth. And now it was his thighs that were quivering as she used lips, teeth and tongue to bring him to a climax. He fought to hold back and when he couldn't fight it any longer he let it go. "Fucking wonderful," he said as she swallowed. Then the autopilot failed and the boat slammed into a wave. "Shit," he screamed when she bit into him, just before she went flying from the settee.

"God dammit!" He doubled over, grabbing himself. You could have bit it off." He looked down, "Shit, I'm bleeding."

"Here, let me look." She bit her lower lip to keep from laughing.

"It's not funny," Earl said.

"I know, I know, I'm sorry," she said, prying his hand away. "It's only a scratch."

"What if it gets infected?" he said, as another wave crashed into the side of the boat.

"I'm going to have to go up and see what happened," she said.

"What about me?"

"You'll be fine, Earl, really. Trust me." Then she pushed herself from the settee and went topside. He followed her up.

"What's wrong?" he asked, holding onto his throbbing penis with one hand and the binnacle with the other.

"No more fun and games. The autopilot's not working. We have to steer it manually."

"I had no idea," Earl said, looking out over the ocean. "It didn't seem so bad down there." Six foot breaking seas were slapping into the side of the boat and the wind sent shivering goosebumps crawling over his skin.

"It's not bad, Earl. Just a little choppy." She swung the wheel to starboard as a wave approached, then back to port as the boat rode over it.

"It's scary is what it is," Earl said. "I'm in the middle of a stormy sea, it's dark, and I'm naked."

"It's not stormy, just choppy," she said, turning the wheel to starboard and back to port as she took another wave.

He watched her handle the boat for a few minutes and started to feel more secure. The early morning cold prickled his skin and made him shiver, but the pain in his penis was subsiding. He took in a deep breath and turned toward the east and the rising sun. "Fucking beautiful," he said.

"It is," she said.

He took in another deep breath and swept the horizon with eyes. "Boat behind us," he said.

She turned. "I forgot about them," she said, staring at the small boat. "They're sailing with everything out. They must be in a hurry."

"Maybe after us," Earl said.

"I doubt that." She picked up the binoculars from their stand on the binnacle. "Hold the wheel a second while I have a look."

"You got it, babe," he said, sliding behind the wheel.

"It's Ramsingh, and my childhood sweetheart is

with him. And he's watching me as I'm watching him." She held her hand up and waved.

* * *

"She waved," Broxton said, putting down the binoculars. "And they're naked."

"It seems they had a better night than we did," Ramsingh said.

"It seems so."

"You're sure about her?" Ramsingh asked. "You're positive you're not making a mistake."

"I'm sure," Broxton said. "The guy with her is the man I saw on the beach when we were swimming for it in Margarita. The man with the Texas accent."

"And about this Scorpion thing? You're sure she's the Scorpion?"

"Yes," Broxton said.

"She's heading right for the Porpoises. If she doesn't watch it she'll be in trouble."

"I don't understand," Broxton said.

"A group of rocks. In calm seas you can see them sticking two or three feet above the water, but they're invisible in this."

"We should get on the radio and warn her,"

"Let's wait and see what happens," Ramsingh said.

CHAPTER NINETEEN

"IT LOOKS LIKE she's cleared the rocks," Ramsingh said. Broxton hadn't slept in over twenty-four hours and he was cold, but he was as alert as he'd ever been. He felt like he could go on forever. Tension, anticipation, excitement all rippled along his skin, competing with the cool, wet wind.

"I don't see them." He looked over the sea, then back at Ramsingh. The prime minister's badger gray eyes sparkled. He was grinning, showing his top teeth. His long, silver hair, usually in place, was flying about, like he had been charged with a cartoon electro-shock machine. The adrenaline was flowing through him too.

"Just off her starboard side."

"What?" Broxton shouted. They were approaching the south coast of Grenada and the early morning wind was whipping along the coastline, in and out of its many bays, stirring up the seas, making it hard to hear.

"They're there," Ramsingh said, voice raised, but not shouting as he pointed ahead and to the right. Then he said, "Take the wheel."

"Sure," Broxton said, slipping by to take control of the boat. "What are you going to do?"

"Tighten sail." He slapped a winch handle into a winch and started grinding in the jib sheet. The boat heeled over more as the rails slid into the water. "Turn a little to port." Broxton stared at him, but didn't respond. "Your left, just a little, off the wind."

"Yes, sir," Broxton said.

"I want to gain speed and stay well away from the rocks."

Broxton spread his legs wide, to keep his balance, and gripped the oversized wheel with both hands. It was a chilly gray morning. The sea was snapping whitecaps and spitting foam over the deck. The wind whistled through the shrouds. The sun was hidden by cloud cover. It started to sprinkle. He tightened his hands on the wheel and squinted against the rain, straining to see the boat ahead.

"Okay, they should be up ahead, between one and two o'clock," Ramsingh said, pointing. Broxton followed Ramsingh's finger.

"I see them." The sea broke around the rocks, the white caps shooting higher than the surrounding seas. "How many are there?"

"I don't know," Ramsingh said. "You're only seeing the tips of them."

"Any boats ever been sunk on them?"

"I imagine that's how they were discovered," Ramsingh said, and Broxton shivered as a breaking wave hit the rocks sending foam high in the air. He pictured a tall ship breaking apart, its hands jumping over the side, grabbing at broken pieces of the boat, grabbing at each other, grabbing at crowded life rafts, and being pushed back into the cold, cold sea.

"Frightening," Broxton said.

"Very," Ramsingh said.

"What's she doing?" Broxton said, eyes again on *Sea King*.

* * *

"What are you doing?" Earl called out. He'd watched her from behind the wheel as she circled the port jib sheet around the big electric winch.

"Go below and get the gun," she shouted to be heard above the crashing waves, "we're going to jibe."

"What's a jibe?"

"Just get the gun."

"You got it," he said. He let her have the wheel and he scurried below, appearing seconds later, pants on, gun in hand. "What's a jibe?" he asked again.

"We're going to do a turn with the wind behind us. Normally I wouldn't do it in weather like this without a more experienced crew, but without the main it isn't a big deal."

"What are you talking about?" He was holding the gun, looking over her shoulder at the boat behind. It was gaining on them.

"No boom to come around," she said. "Take the wheel and crank it to the right when I tell you. When we come abreast of them, start shooting."

"Yes, ma'am. Do you still want me to spare Broxton?" he asked.

"No," she said. "Shoot them both."

"Yes, ma'am," he said again. These were orders he understood. At last she was over her thing with him. If she'd let him deal with Broxton in Venezuela it would all be over now. They'd be on some tropical island somewhere drinking rum punches and lazing the days away. But *mas vale tarde, que nunca,* better late than never. And the Spanish phrase reminded him of Maria. He was finished with her now, but he'd seen that son-of-a-bitching bastard Broxton with her, the two of them cooing like love birds out by the pool. He'd sure enjoy turning his lights out.

Dani went back to the port winch and took off a loop of the line. "All right!" she yelled. "Jibe ho, start turning." Earl turned the boat as she went to the starboard winch and took the line all the way off of it. Then she was back at the port winch, with the port jib sheet in her hands. "Turn, turn, turn," she yelled, as she hauled on the line, pulling it, as Earl brought the boat around. The sail came across the deck and billowed on the other side as the wind hit their backs. She threw two more wraps on the winch, tugged the line into the self-tailing jaws and used the electric motor to power the sheet in. "All the way!" she wailed.

Then with the turn complete she took the wheel. "I'm going to sail close enough so that you can see the dirt under their nails. You think you'll be able to hit them?"

"You get me a shot, I'll do the rest," he said.

"I want them both."

"I'll get them both. Don't you worry."

* * *

"She's jibing," Ramsingh said.

"What?" Broxton said.

"Turning." Ramsingh's voice dropped an octave, like he couldn't comprehend what was going on. But then he grabbed hold of the situation and started issuing orders. "Keep on a steady course, I'm going below for a second." Ramsingh slipped down through the companionway and in a few seconds was back with two large square sections of wood about three feet by four feet.

"What's that?" Broxton asked.

"Sections of the cockpit sole, the boat's floor. Teak, three quarters of an inch thick. I think we might need it up here."

"Why?"

"Shields."

Broxton nodded, then turned his attention to the boat in front. *Sea King* had completed her turn and was now headed back toward them. Broxton adjusted the wheel slightly. Turning a bit to the left, mindful of the rocks.

"My guess is she'll sail by as close to us as she can get, shooting away as they pass," Ramsingh said.

Broxton didn't say anything. He kept his eyes on the boat in front. It looked like she was planning on coming along their left side. His emotions were whirling out of control. She'd been a large part of his life. Still was. He was in love with her. At least he thought he was. He didn't want anything to happen to her, yet he couldn't let her get away. He wanted her stopped, but he didn't want her arrested. It would ruin Warren.

He turned the boat a little more to the left. Ramsingh met his eyes, but didn't say anything. *Sea King* was charging toward them, jib billowing, heeled over, slicing through the waves. She turned a little to her right, to avoid the collision course Broxton had put them on, but he turned a little to the left, keeping the boats nose to nose, racing toward each other, like two great animals about to do battle.

She turned again.

Broxton matched it. Once again he was playing chicken, but these weren't kids on Cherry Avenue. Dani was on that boat and she had more nerve than anyone he'd ever met. If she perceived it as a contest between them, she wouldn't flinch, she'd hold course and sail that boat right into them and damn the consequences.

He would turn aside, but not till the last minute, not till she was sure he was intent on playing out the game, not till she was bracing for collision, then he'd turn.

"After I set this up, I'll set the self-steering gear and we'll go below," Ramsingh said. Broxton smiled. The prime minister was laying the hatches across the cockpit seats.

"We're not going to hide behind your wooden shields?"

"Of course not," Ramsingh said, "but they're going to think we are." Then he went below and seconds later returned with a bagged sail. Broxton watched while he propped it under the teak floor covering. Now instead of lying across the two cockpit seats, the floor covering rested on the port seat and on the sail underneath.

"This way it'll look like we're hiding behind, under the wood, and hopefully they'll shoot where we're not." He moved behind the wheel to set the self-steering gear.

"Don't set it," Broxton said. "You go below. I've got other plans."

"Mr. Broxton," Ramsingh ordered. "We're going below."

"No, sir," Broxton said. "I have the helm now. My job is to keep you safe. I'll be all right." There was something about the way he said it that made Ramsingh smile.

"Right, I'll go below." The prime minister slipped down the companion way, but kept watch as Broxton kept *Gypsy Dancer* on a collision course with *Sea King*.

"Any minute," Broxton yelled.

"What's going on?" Ramsingh said. From his position looking up and out the companionway he could see Broxton behind the wheel, but not much else.

"Ramming speed," Broxton said, as *Sea King* bore down on them, looming large in his vision, like a hulking monster ready do devour them.

"Oh, God," Ramsingh said.

A wave or slight wind shift altered Broxton's course, but he corrected, keeping his eyes on the vee of the approaching vessel. *Sea King* was slicing through the water like a sharp razor through soft skin. For a second he thought about playing the game out, but he knew his rival and he couldn't imagine Dani giving up. He tensed his right hand on the wheel in anticipation of the turn. Then *Sea King* broke to his left. She was turning. The amazement zapped him like a cardiac arrest. She wasn't interested in besting him. If she was, she could have held out longer. She didn't want to take the chance and guess which way Broxton would turn. She wanted them off her left side and there could only be one reason for that. Ram was right. The Texan was in position to shoot at them as they sailed by.

Broxton turned, not away from her as he'd

planned, but toward her. He kept them on a collision course. *Sea King* turned more to his left and he corrected, keeping *Gypsy Dancer* aimed at the bigger boat's bow. There was no doubt in his mind who'd lose in a collision. The basic laws of physics favored the larger vessel and he had no desire to test those laws. He moved the wheel slightly to the right when *Sea King* was only a few yards away.

He heard the skin crawling sound of the two boats scrapping hulls, but he didn't see the damage they were causing each other, because he was busy scurrying around the wheel. He dove under Ramsingh's teak floorboard shields as the Texan opened up. The first two shots went wild. The third thunked into the teak. Broxton crouched low, hugging the sail. The fourth ricocheted off a winch. The fifth slammed into the teak, followed by the sixth. Then the screeching, scraping and shooting stopped and they were temporarily out of danger.

"It's all right," Ramsingh said, coming up through the companionway. "They're behind us and out of range."

"Sorry about your floor." Broxton stood and set the floor hatches on the port cockpit seat.

"Sod the floor," Ramsingh said.

"And your boat. It's probably pretty scratched up. It sounded like it was coming apart."

"You're alive. They missed. That's all that counts," Ramsingh said.

* * *

"You missed," Dani wailed and Earl almost cringed from the fury in her eyes. He had no problem hearing her above the sound of the flapping main or the choppy sea. But as suddenly as the anger was upon her it seemed to pass. "All right," she said. "We'll just have another go at it."

"We're not going to fool them again," he said.

"We didn't fool them last time. Broxton faked me out with his chicken game and he had some kind of cover rigged up to hide behind. It's not going to be so easy."

"What are we going to do now?" Earl asked.

"What I should have done the first time. We're going to ram this boat up their ass and sink them."

"What about us?"

"*Sea King* is a steel boat. Strong and sturdy. Ramsingh's boat is made of fiberglass. When steel crashes into plastic, plastic loses."

"You should have rammed them then."

"I thought I said that," she said, glaring at him. This was one woman he never wanted to cross, he thought. Not ever.

"Take the wheel," she ordered, and Earl obeyed. "We're going to jibe around and finish it." Earl watched as she looped a turn of the starboard jib sheet around the winch, then she turned back to him. "Just the opposite of what we did before. When I yell, "Jibe ho," you crank it to the left. Stop your turn when you have the ass end of that boat sighted across the bow. Got it?"

"Got it," he answered.

She waited a few seconds, judging distance and speed, Earl thought, then she yelled out, "Jibe ho," and Earl started spinning the wheel as she slacked the port jib sheet from its winch. Halfway through the hundred and eighty degree turn she started hauling in on the starboard sheet, taking in the line, hand over hand, a demon possessed. Muscles rippled along her bare arms. Sweat glistened on the back of her neck and ran down her naked back. Her hair flew in the wind, and he felt an animal power flow from her. She was like a great jungle cat, everyone else was just prey.

She cleated off the sheet, then ground some more of it in with the winch. "I'll take the wheel now," she said, and Earl let her have it. Then she reached over to the engine panel and pushed the ignition button. Earl heard and felt the rumble of the diesel as it started up. "I don't think we can catch them without the main, but with the help of the engine they won't have a chance of getting away."

"I don't think that's a problem," he said.

"Why not?"

"I don't think they want to get away."

* * *

"They're turning around," Broxton said. He was back at the wheel. Ramsingh had just come back up from below, after having replaced his damaged floor hatches.

"I spend all of my spare time on this boat," he said. He was talking loudly, but Broxton heard the sigh in his voice. "It's more than a hobby."

"I'm sorry about hurting it," Broxton said.

"It's not your fault," Ramsingh said. "You were doing your job, but I'm taking over command now. I know you're trying to keep me alive, but I don't think *Gypsy Dancer* can take much more of your methods."

Broxton nodded, meeting Ramsingh's eyes. There was a grim determined set to his jaw, a sturdy, unafraid timbre to his voice and a sad, soulful look in those eyes. He'd made a decision and Broxton wasn't sure he wanted to know what it was, but he had to ask. "What do we do now?"

"We let them catch up to us."

Ramsingh let out some of the mainsheet and the boat slowed from seven to five knots. "Look, there," he said, pointing, "those are the Porpoises, right off our starboard side."

Broxton turned to look. They were close to the rocks and he still had trouble seeing them. If Ramsingh hadn't pointed them out he'd have missed them completely. He looked behind. "They've completed their turn."

"Look at the island ahead," Ramsingh said. "We're headed directly for the south coast. When I tell you, turn to starboard, to the right. Keep turning till the island is off the port side. That'll be a ninety degree turn. Hold that position till I tell you differently."

"But the rocks?"

"We should be by them by then."

"Should be?" Broxton said.

"Should be," Ramsingh answered.

Broxton checked behind them again. He didn't have to tell Ramsingh they were getting closer. He turned away and eyed the coastline, looked again toward the rocks, but they'd moved past and he couldn't see them through the rising swell.

"What are you doing?" he asked, as Ramsingh let out more of the mainsheet.

"Slowing the boat down even more."

"They're coming awfully fast."

"I think she wants to ram us."

"Won't she go down, too?"

"Good possibility, but she's thinking she's got a steel boat. We're fiberglass, she's bigger. She probably thinks she'd survive a collision and we wouldn't. She'd be wrong. Fiberglass is a lot tougher than it looks, and that thin skinned steel boat isn't as strong as she thinks. Anything can sink, even the Titanic went down, and that boat's no Titanic."

Broxton looked over his shoulder. They weren't far behind now and they were rapidly closing the distance. "Shit," he said, staring at the stainless steel bow roller. Two heavy anchors rested in it and to his eyes they looked like great steel tipped battering rams charging up the ass end of their small boat. He gripped the wheel in a fit of panic.

"Don't!" Ramsingh yelled. "Not yet."

And Broxton stayed his hand. He'd been about to turn out of the way, but there was something about the authority in Ramsingh's voice that screamed out to be obeyed.

"We don't turn till the last possible moment. We want her to think we're running like frightened jackals. If she even suspects what I have in mind we could all find ourselves swimming." So Broxton kept a steady hand on the wheel as Ramsingh fiddled with the lines, making ready for the turn.

He grabbed another look behind. The twin anchors seemed to be aimed right between his eyes, chromed and glistening, so polished that they reflected, like a mirror, the few rays of sunlight that managed to sneak through the gray clouds.

"Hold steady your course," Ramsingh said, as the monstrous form of the boat behind filled his vision. "Eyes front," Ramsingh said, and Broxton turned away from *Sea King* and faced Grenada's south shore. "Steady, steady," Ramsingh cautioned. Broxton felt like there were a million eyes shooting laser-like pin pricks up his back, but he held the boat steady as Ramsingh commanded.

"Now!" Ramsingh screamed, and Broxton spun the wheel to the right as Ramsingh played the sheets.

The wind from behind filled the jib and the boat heeled and picked up speed. Broxton risked a quick look back and shivered. *Sea King* slipped by, missing them by less than a yard.

"Two strikes!" Dani yelled out across the space between their two boats. Broxton shivered again. She had been his friend his whole life through. He loved her. She was all he wanted. If only he could make her see the light. But the fleeting look he caught from her eyes as they flew past told his heart what he already knew in his head. There was no going back. Though he and Dani both lived, their friendship was dead. He loved her still, but there was nothing he could do about that.

"We're going to turn right again in a few minutes," Ramsingh shouted, "so be ready." He heard the voice, nodded to let Ramsingh know he understood, but he kept his eyes on *Sea King* and watched as Dani rushed around the wheel. The Texan took her place as she struggled at a winch, making ready to turn and give chase.

"Did you make out what she said?" Ramsingh asked.

"Two strikes," Broxton said. "It's from baseball."

"We play cricket here, but I know what it means."

"They're coming around," Broxton said.

"And so are we. Turn now, right again, ninety degrees," and again Ramsingh was at the sheets as the little boat bucked and turned through the churning seas. When the sail had come around to the other side and they had the land directly at their backs, Ramsingh said, "Turn a little more right, not too much." Broxton obeyed as Ramsingh tightened sail. He stole a look at the knot meter. Seven and a half knots. The wind was across their left side now, blowing strong. They were heeled over, rails back in the water, headed back toward Trinidad, seventy-eight miles away, going full tilt, as fast as *Gypsy Dancer* was able to take them.

"Will we be able to out run them?" Broxton said.

Ramsingh didn't answer. His eyes were on *Sea King* as she made a clumsy and wide turn. But instead of stopping at ninety degrees as they had done, she kept coming around.

"No!" Broxton screamed.

One second, *Sea King* was slicing through the water, a dangerously beautiful sight as she moved through the choppy seas, and the next she was stopped dead as she slammed into the rocks.

Ramsingh slackened sail and *Gypsy Dancer* straightened up and slowed to four knots. "Three strikes," he said. "She's out."

And Broxton understood. Ramsingh had gambled that she would be so caught up in the chase that she'd forget about the rocks. While she was changing places with the Texan and struggling to turn the ship around, Ramsingh had him circling around the rocks. She'd been too busy to notice what they were doing.

"We have to go back," he said as the boat floundered.

"No," Ramsingh said, and Broxton watched in horror as a gaping hole opened in *Sea King's* bow. In seconds she was on her side. Ramsingh looked away, tightened sail and cleated off the sheets. "We're going back to Trinidad," he said.

"We can't leave them," Broxton said.

"Sometimes a prime minister has to make life and death decisions," he said. "This is the first time for me, and I hope the last. I hope in the end God will judge that I acted properly."

"She'll die," Broxton said.

"And her father will go on to serve his president and the world. The Scorpion will kill no more. Warren will mourn his daughter and you and I will keep our silence. A beautiful young woman has died and the Scorpion has gone into retirement."

"I loved her," Broxton said.

"I know you did, son," Ramsingh said, "and that saddens me, but it was the only way."

Eleven hours later they sailed back into Trinidad racing the setting sun. The waters around the Bocas were unusually calm, the sea inside the gulf clear and flat, the wind silent. A yellow-orange sky greeted them as they dropped anchor. The sound of cheerful pan music floated across the anchorage, but it failed to lift Broxton's heart.

Dani was dead and he'd had a hand in the killing. There was no other way. He knew that, but still she was gone. He felt like the light had gone out of the world.

CHAPTER TWENTY

"HEY, HOW'S IT GOING?" Broxton said. "I called your room. When you didn't answer I thought I'd come out here and check." Maria was finishing dinner at a table by the pool. Two of the other three chairs were full of shopping bags and there were more under the table. He pulled out the empty chair and sat down.

"I'm getting by. I got on with Iberia. I start in a week." Her smile was genuine. She looked happy. "How's the protection business?"

"Finished," he said. "They got the bad guys, so they no longer need my services."

"Where does that leave you?"

"They've offered me a field assignment. Here. I'll be working out of the embassy for a year. Then I suppose they'll rotate me."

"So you're a field agent now?"

"Looks like it."

"How do you feel about that?"

"It's what I've always wanted."

"Then I'm glad for you."

"Enough about me. What did you do, buy out the city?"

"No, it's all fabric. I'm a seamstress in my spare time. I make quilts."

"So much," he said, looking at the bags.

"Port of Spain must be the fabric capitol of the world. I've never seen so many fabric shops. I couldn't help myself. Give a girl a credit card and you know what happens."

He laughed as he subconsciously took the ring out of his pocket and started playing with it.

"There's that ring again," she said.

"I guess I've given up on her," he said.

"Really?"

"Yeah," he said. Dani was dead, but there was no way he could tell her that. He turned toward the pool.

"You're not?" she said.

"I am," he said, and with a flick of the wrist he sent the engagement ring spiraling and sparkling toward the deep end of the pool.

"That was very foolish," she said.

"Better to have loved and lost."

"But you haven't lost yet," she said.

"Ramsingh has a mantra he repeats to himself when the going gets tough. 'Never give up. Never quit,' but the battle has to be winnable."

"What do you mean?"

"Dani and I were best friends growing up. She was one of the guys. She was the one I could tell everything to, but I think that's all we were ever meant to be, best friends. Even that's over now."

"Never lovers?" Maria said.

"We never were," Broxton said.

"Really? I thought—"

"Can you think of a better way to ruin a perfectly good friendship?"

"I think maybe it can make a friendship even stronger. Something that can last forever. What could be better than your lover being your best friend? I think that would be very nice."

"I suppose, if you found the right woman. Dani obviously wasn't the right one for me."

"Can you help me carry these up to my room?" she asked.

"Sure," he said.

"Then let's go," she said, pushing herself from the table. She stood, brushed her hair back with her fingers, then picked up several of the bags. He picked up the rest and followed her toward the lobby and the elevators.

At her room she slipped the plastic card key into the door. She reached out to open it when the green light on the lock told them it was okay to enter, but the door jerked open before her hand touched the knob.

"Bring the bags inside and set them down, then walk to the bed and put your ass on the mattress, Mr. Broxton. You too, Maria." The voice commanded obedience, and the gun in his right hand backed it up.

"You?" Broxton said.

"Me," Earl said. "Surprised?"

"Very," Broxton said.

"You know each other?" Maria said.

"He's the man that tried to kill Prime Minister

Ramsingh in Venezuela," Broxton said.

"He's also my husband," Maria said.

"Curious," Broxton said.

"And that's the way you're going to stay," Earl said. Broxton tensed his legs and gauged the distance between them, two quick steps, but Earl seemed to be daring him to try it and Broxton knew he'd be dead before he closed half the gap.

"Sit," Earl said. "Only you, Broxton. Maria, get a glass of water out of the bathroom."

"Get it yourself."

"Come on, baby, we both know I can be difficult if I get upset, so don't get me angry and make me do something I'll be sorry for." He was talking softly, but he was a man on the edge and any second he was going over.

"Do as he says, Maria," Broxton said, sitting.

"You don't scare me anymore, Earl."

"Baby, if you don't hustle your buns into that bathroom, I'm going to put a bullet into lover boy's stomach, then we'll see how much I can scare you."

She went into the bathroom and got the water. "What do you want me to do with it?"

"Put your ass next to his," he said, as he fished a bottle of pills out of his shirt pocket. "These won't kill you, but they'll put you right out." He tossed the bottle toward them and Broxton snatched it out of the air with a quick left handed catch. "Four for you, Mr. Broxton. Two for my wife."

"How do we know they're not poison?" Maria said.

"You don't, baby, but it's the pills or a bullet."

"What are they?" Broxton asked.

"How should I know? She gave 'em to me and told me if you got in the way to drug you up till it was over. She wants you alive, remember?"

"She tried to sink us," Broxton said.

"That was then, this is now."

"How'd you get away?"

"You were so busy turning tail and leaving us to die that you didn't notice when she lowered the dinghy into the water. We grabbed her get-away-bag and sailed into this nice little bay. Three hours later we were on a plane for Port of Spain. We probably beat you back."

"She's well known in Trinidad, by now Ramsingh knows she's back. He's probably got every cop in the country looking for her."

"Think again, you'd never believe the shit she had in that bag. She's a master of disguises, you're old girlfriend. I thought I was flying back to Trinidad with my mother. She sailed through customs, a little old lady from Boston, coming down to Trinidad to visit her son who works for one of the oil companies. She even had the accent down."

"I don't believe it."

"Believe it," Earl said, then he gestured toward the pills in Broxton's hand. "Now, eat up, I don't have all day."

"I'm not very hungry."

"Mr. Broxton, we can do this easy, or we can do it hard. I got no instructions about my wife. You want her to stay alive you eat the pills," Earl said, as he moved the barrel of the gun till it was pointing at Maria. "Well?"

Broxton poured four of the pills into his hand and swallowed them dry.

"Now you baby."

Maria took the bottle from Broxton and tipped it to her lips, swallowing the last two pills, then she drank the water. "I hope they kill me, Earl," she said. "That way I'll never have to see you again."

"Baby, death is the only way you'll ever get rid of me," he said.

"Now what?" Broxton said.

"Now we wait," he said, looking at his watch. "Tomorrow evening, at five straight up, Ramsingh will be getting his and it'll all be over."

"She's going to hit him during the dedication speech?"

"Yeah, in front of an army of cops, pretty fucking ballsy. I almost with I was doing it, but it's her show now. I'm out of it."

"It's not too late to really be out of it, Earl," Broxton said. "Let us go and I'll keep you out of it."

"Climb up on the bed, lay down on your backs and stare at the ceiling," Earl said.

"You don't have to do this," Broxton said.

"You're wasting your breath," Maria said, and she scooted on her rear till she was in the center of the bed and lay down with her head on the pillow.

"Now you, Broxton," Earl said, and by the time he was stretched out next to Maria she was asleep and he was out a few minutes later.

The slight breeze blowing through his hair told him it was a dream. He tried to reach a hand up, to touch it, to pull on it, to feel its texture, but his hands were locked at his sides. He opened his eyes and looked down, wind rippled through his loose clothes, tickled his bare feet and helped to keep him aloft.

"Dani," he moaned. He was floating above her nude body, gently coming down on top of her. He felt her breasts pushing against his bare chest, felt himself getting hard. He tried to bring a hand up to caress her, but his arms were locked iron tight at his sides.

He felt her hand take him and guide him into her. After all these years, it was happening at last. He felt her grind up to meet him and he was thrilled. He never wanted to wake, the dream was better than any reality, better than life.

He was so hard, but he couldn't seem to find release. The dream had him in its grip and he slowly pumped into her. He came so close, but the pleasure he craved was just beyond the edge. He tried to grind into her faster and harder, but he was crippled without the use of his hands and so he was forced to match her slow, sensual rhythm and she held him on the edge of forever with her steady rocking, stomach tightening, thigh clenching motion, seeming to suck him deeper and deeper into her until he felt like his heart was going to burst.

Then she pumped her pelvis up to him to catch him as the greatest release he'd ever known ripped through him. He went and went and went and he thought he'd go on forever. "Dani, Dani," he moaned, then he was sinking in dark waters, the surface fading away. There were sharks here, danger near, and he was moving blindly out of control, buried in black, shivering and shaking, cold one second, hot the next. He tried to see, but pain plagued his eyes, the lids weighed heavy, covering an ache that caromed through his head. To open them would be to invite in the hot chills that ravaged his body. He felt like he'd been crucified and tossed into a whirlpool, and it was sucking him down into the pit.

Reality was spinning away as the varying shades of red running inside his eyes turned into flames dancing over hot coals, leaping out from behind his eyelids and wrapping hot tongues of fire around the back of his neck, hot and clenching, choking his breath away as his lungs exploded. He gagged, trying in vain to suck air through lips that refused to part. And then he passed out again.

Later he came awake, shaking in a cold sweat. He was covered in pain. His legs felt like an army of assassins were beating on them with flaming torches. His arms were frozen, hands still nailed to the cross. Ice dripped from his armpits instead of sweat. His face was buried in snow. His mouth was nailed shut, cutting off air. The red flames inside his eyes had turned into frozen hands of clutching ice. Wicked hands, long nails digging into the back of his neck, digging deep, drawing blood, squeezing, clutching, seizing his spinal chord, snatching it away, pulling it through his throat.

Somewhere someone moaned, then his body started shaking, arms and legs vibrating and shuddering. He sensed that the source was from outside of himself, and he was powerless to control it. His right arm shot upward and came down hard, hitting himself in the leg. He felt a stab of pain as his arm was going up to attack himself again and he stiffened himself and fought against the force, slowing the attack. His midsection started jerking, spasms from outside of himself, flesh against him, pounding and rubbing, slippery and slapping. He wanted to see, but was choking, struggling to take in air, and he passed out again.

The cold was gone when he woke again, the clutching hands replaced by a dull headache, greater than a hangover, but bearable. The pain in his legs was gone, but so was most of the feeling. His bladder was screaming, but he couldn't relieve himself. He was aching, stiff, and his tongue lay flat, dry in his mouth. He tried to move it, tried to swallow saliva and couldn't. He had a kink in his left foot and tried to move it. Like his tongue, it was immobile. He opened his eyes.

Her eyes were inches from his own, staring unblinking. He tried to jerk away, but he was frozen in place. He fought to reclaim his raging pulse. He tried screaming, but the sound was killed in his mouth. He squeezed his eyes closed and tried to fight the fright building inside. He was attached to her and she was dead. He shivered and gagged on another scream, then his arm shot up, out of his control, and he slapped himself in the leg, but he kept his eyes closed, hoping beyond hope that he'd slipped into a nightmare and not cold reality.

He slapped himself again and he opened his eyes.

She blinked.

She was alive.

He stared into her eyes and forced his fear aside. Her nose was touching his, he could feel her warm breath on his face. She had gray duct tape stuck over her mouth. He tried to move his lips, moved his parched tongue between them, touched and tasted the tape covering his own mouth. Cold fear crept up his spine.

He closed his eyes again and inhaled a long slow breath through his nostrils. When he open them back up she was still staring at him. She cast her eyes down the length of their bodies and he followed her look and the fear so recently calmed burst through the surface, screaming and sending spikes of ice into the base of his neck.

Their arms and legs were duct taped together,

wrapped several times, mummy like. They were naked, her breasts were flat against his chest, her pelvis pressed against his, their breath intermingled, their eyes sharing their combined fear. They couldn't move, he couldn't sit without breaking her back, she couldn't without breaking his, but there had to be a way, he thought. There was, it was at the edge of his mind, but the drugs riding the blood through his veins dulled him and he found himself drifting into semi consciousness.

But there was a way out, he thought, as everything faded to black.

He felt the sun warm on his neck as he woke again, craving water, still stiff, still unable to move, and she was still staring, eyes so close to his. He tried to blink her away. He was still groggy from whatever drugs that were working on him, and it took a few seconds before he realized that this was no dream. He tried to talk through the tape, but his words, "Are you all right," filtered through his dry mouth, the drug haze, and the duct tape, and came out like a cross between a moan and a groan and he knew they were as unintelligible to her as they were to himself.

He closed his eyes for a few seconds, to think, but he opened them quickly when she raised her arm up, pulling his along with it, and slapped him in the leg. He got the message and nodded his head. He wasn't going back to sleep.

Then he remembered the dream and he knew that it had been no dream. It wasn't Dani he'd made love to, but Maria. He stared deep into her eyes, felt her sweat mingled with his, felt her heart beat racing and rippling through her to him, tingling his skin and his soul. They were trapped and taped to each other as one, and he felt all the love he had to give flowing through him, passing into her.

She picked his arm up again and he shook his head. She didn't have to slap him anymore to get his attention. He was awake now and he was thinking. He looked past her to the clock on the nightstand beyond. Two-thirty, two-and-a-half hours to prevent an assassination, but first he had to get free.

Then he remembered something he thought about as he fell back into unconsciousness He knew how to get free. The phone. All he had to do was get a message to the operator and help would come running, but first he had to get the message to Maria. They had to work as one or they'd never get free.

"Phone," he tried to say through the tape, but it came out as ome. "Ome, ome," he repeated.

She shook her head, indicating *no*. She didn't understand.

"Hone," he said, empathizing the H part of the sound.

She shook her head and he raised his and looked beyond her, at the nightstand, the clock and the phone. Then he looked back into her eyes, then beyond her, then back into her eyes, then beyond her again. She blinked and scrunched up her nose. She understood, he wanted her to see something, to see what he saw and then her eyes lit up like a kid's in school and he knew she got it.

"Phone," she said and he heard her distinctly through the tape. He wondered how come she could talk better than him and then he saw it. The tape over her mouth wasn't on very well. He stared at it. She saw the direction of his eyes and blinked several times letting him know she understood.

She moved her head forward and he ran the side

of his face against the tape, pulling it down with his chin and his cheek. One sweep of his face and the tape started to peel away, two and it gave way some more, three and it was hanging off her mouth and she could talk.

"Help," she screamed. Help us." Her voice was loud and full of desperation and it was the sweetest thing he'd ever heard. "Hurry, help us, help us," she screamed again.

"It's going to be okay," she said to him. "Someone must have heard me. We'll be free soon."

He blinked at her.

"They're going to kill the prime minister at exactly five o'clock."

He blinked at her. He remembered her husband saying that.

"Help," she screamed out again, but nobody came.

"Ome," he hummed through the tape.

"Yes, the phone," she said. She was breathing hard, panting heavy, like she'd just finished a race. "Let's roll toward it and see if we can't knock it off the hook. Ready, now," she said, and he rolled with her toward the right side of the king-sized bed.

He was on the bottom now and she stretched her neck, trying to reach the telephone. Then she stopped. "It's unplugged," she said, staring at the wire dangling over the nightstand.

He sighed, breathing out through his nose. Any minute his bladder was going to cut loose and he didn't want to do that.

"My husband's gone off the deep end," she said. "I think he's going to kill us."

Broxton nodded. He wasn't surprised.

"The tape on your mouth isn't like it was on

mine. It goes all the way around, two or three times. It looks tight, that's why I couldn't understand you, but I think I can get it off. Hold still."

He felt her teeth on his cheek as she bit into the tape that was wrapped around his neck. After a few attempts she had a firm grip and he winced as she worked the tape downward. It was tightly wrapped, but it stretched and he felt it pull away from his mouth. Then it was down past his upper lip and he drew in a great gulp of air. She wasn't able to get it past his chin, but his mouth was halfway uncovered and he could talk.

"Thanks," he said, his voice a raspy whisper.

"Now what?" she said. She was on top of him and they were both looking at the phone they couldn't use. He felt her flex her fingers and then she squeezed his right hand with her left.

"It wasn't a dream?" he said.

"No, it wasn't," she said.

"I'm sorry, I didn't know what I was doing."

"You were drugged."

"He didn't tape our hands. If we had something sharp we could cut our way free."

"Like a broken glass," she said. They were both looking at the nightstand and the glass sitting next to the phone. The same glass that not so long ago washed the pills down Maria's throat.

Broxton ran his tongue over his parched lips as he looked at the little bit of water left in it. "Think we can reach it?"

"If we turn sideways, maybe," she said.

"Yeah," he said, eyes locked on the water in the glass.

"Which way?"

"Feet over the side of the bed, I think."

"Okay," she said, and together they squiggled around so that they were on their sides and then they gradually slid, like two slippery snakes, over the side of the bed until they were both struggling to keep their legs dangling in the air and themselves from falling over.

"You roll on top," she said, and once he was over he stretched his arm, bringing hers along with it, but he was inches short.

"We have to get closer," he said.

"All right," she said, and they slipped and scooted sideways until Broxton was able to grab the glass with two of his fingers.

"Got it," he said, and he clamped his fingers together and raised it up.

And dropped it.

"Shit," he said. The glass landed and rolled onto the carpeted floor.

"Over we go," she said, and without giving him a chance to think she rolled and twisted, jerking him along with her, and then he was falling.

CHAPTER TWENTY-ONE

DANI SURVEYED THE SITE. The street below was teeming with the usual early noon crowd. People were pouring out of the buildings, grabbing an early lunch. Others were hunting for that hard to find parking space, still others were rushing to the stores for some quick shopping or doing a myriad other things that make an active city like Port of Spain bustle even in the heat of the day.

And the city wouldn't sleep until long after the sun went down. Bars, restaurants, jazz clubs, rock clubs, calypso clubs, whorehouses, movie theaters and fast food joints all stayed open late to service the throng that entertained itself along the Brian Lara Promenade.

Brian Lara. Dani smiled at the thought of the new name for the Promenade, a wide walking park that could be counted on to be full of people out walking their dogs or themselves, greeting their friends, playing chess or checkers, or just people watching from the benches, all out enjoying the evening and the night. Brian Lara was Trinidadian and arguably the best cricket player in the game today. She loved it that the Promenade was named after him. She loved it because George hated it. Ten years ago he was the best, and today he was the attorney general and the most popular politician in Trinidad. He'd had his friends argue that the Promenade should bear his name, but popular as he was, he was yesterday's hero. Brian Lara was today's.

Looking down from her perch atop the Caribbean Bank Building, she held her arms out straight, palms wide, facing downward, thumbs extended toward themselves, the way a movie director might frame a scene. She imagined she was holding the rifle. She'd only get one shot, but it's all she'd need. Ramsingh would be in her sights at five o'clock, by five-oh-one he'd be dead.

She'd get him before he said a word about the new treaty with the United States, before he had a chance to praise the efforts of the DEA in Trinidad, and before he spoke about the drug-fighting efforts of the Trinidadian police. The dedication of their statue would show the people just how incompetent the police and the security forces were, when the man dedicating it was gunned down in front of it.

Satisfied that she'd have a clear shot, she stood and walked across the roof. When she did the actual shoot she'd be one floor below. Cliffard Rampersad, George Chandee's handpicked choice for the head of the security forces, would be on the roof. She smiled. The bait was set, the trap was ready.

She left the roof via the inside stairway, amazed that it wasn't guarded. But Ramsingh was just the prime minister of a small third world nation, not the President of the United States.

She exited the stairway on the second floor and walked out in the middle of the bank's busy loan department. No one noticed her enter or leave. She was just another young woman in a blue Caribbean Bank uniform heading downstairs for her lunch hour. Several people were seated in the waiting area to her right, waiting to conduct foreign business. What took only a few minutes in an American bank could take up to an hour here. People were talking, drinking coffee or tea, and passing the time of day. No one was in a hurry. It was the Trinidadian way.

She took the escalator to the street level, passed through the crowded lobby and in seconds she was through the double doors and out in the street.

"Everything set?" Earl asked, holding the door open for her.

"Couldn't be better." She slid into the passenger seat of her new Porsche. She didn't mind Earl driving, in fact she liked it.

He moved around the front of the car, slapping the hood as he passed, and she smiled. He was enjoying himself. In some ways the man was a child, but he had nerves and he'd call a bluff every time. He overflowed with courage, but he didn't understand caution. She'd have to work on that.

"You're really something," he said, "you enter the bank looking like my mother and you come out looking like junior high school jailbait."

"You like them young, Earl?"

"I like you anyway I can get you. Where to now?" He started the car, smiling.

"Lunch at the Yacht Club."

"You think that's smart? What if Ramsingh shows up?"

"Think he'd recognize me, Earl?" She watched his eyes as he turned to look at her. She flicked her hair over her shoulders. The wig was hot, but she liked the way the blue-black hair matched the green contacts. She thrust her shoulder's back, her breasts were larger, her smile was bigger, her face was innocent.

"Your own father wouldn't recognize you."

"Then let's go to the yacht club."

"Show me the way and I'm gone," Earl said.

"Okay let's go over it again," she said. Their lunch had just been served, they were both having the special, meatloaf, potatoes with gravy, and plantain on the side.

"Ramsingh takes the stage at five o'clock," Earl said. "We know he'll be on time, because he's never late. You shoot, depart via the stairway, leaving the rifle. I run up screaming, 'He's down below, right under you.' Then I make sure Rampersad goes into the room. Naturally there'll be no prints on the weapon and when Rampersad sees it's his gun he'll pick it up, 'cause he's dumber than dog shit."

"Then what?" she said.

"Then I blow before the place is crawling with cops."

"You sure you can do your part?"

"Hey, I'm a lot of things. Sometimes I drink too much, I swear when I shouldn't, I bend the rules more than I should, sometimes I slap my wife around, but I ain't no fuckup."

"Earl, you have a way with words." She turned toward the yachts in their slips and pulled her long hair out of her eyes. Then she turned back toward him. "You'd never think about slapping me around though, would you, Earl?"

"No, ma'am," he said, grinning like a schoolboy.

"Why not?" she asked, unable to hide the humor in her voice.

"'Cause you'd probably cut it off and make me eat it before you killed me," he said, grinning even wider.

"And don't you forget it," she said.

"I never would."

She watched him as he dug into his food. In a few hours he'd be doing his part in the assassination of a prime minister, and now he was tucking into his lunch like it was the only thing on his mind. He had nerves of steel, nerves like hers.

He set his fork down and took a long drink of water. He was still holding the glass in his hand when he said, "The bodyguard won't be a problem tonight."

"What have you done?" she said.

"I caught him with my wife. They came up to the room for a little hanky panky."

"Earl, you're being obtuse."

"Not fair to use words normal people don't know," he said through a good ol' boy Southern smile.

"Just get to the point, Earl," she said. She couldn't help herself, she still cared for Broxton. She hoped he hadn't done anything rash.

"Relax I didn't hurt him. I got the drop on them and tied them up."

"Where?"

"In her room at the Hilton."

"Shit. Now he knows we're still alive. He'll try and get Ram to call off tonight's speech."

"You think you're dealing with a twelve-year-old here? He's not getting away. I made them take the pills, then I stripped them and duct taped them together, arms to arms, legs to legs, several wraps. Then I taped their mouths. They're not going nowhere. Shit, they probably won't even wake up till it's all over."

"You're sure?"

"Sure I'm sure."

"What do you plan on doing with them?"

"That's up to you. It's still your show as far as I'm concerned. You want I'll call the hotel after it's over and Mr. Broxton and my wife can live happily ever after, have ten kids for all I care, long as you think you can keep him from talking. Or if that's not to your liking, I'll stop by the hotel on my way to Rampersad's and pop them both. It's for you to decide."

"You'd do your wife?"

"She's been getting it on with your friend Broxton. She doesn't mean anything to me anymore. No loyalty."

"Loyalty means a lot to you?"

"Yeah."

"But you weren't loyal to her."

"That's different."

"How do I know you'd be loyal to me?"

"That's different too."

"How?"

"You've earned it. She never did."

"You mean you're afraid of me and you were never afraid of her?"

"That too," he said, smiling. "But afraid or not, after tonight it's fifty-fifty. Fear don't run my life and you're not gonna either. I pay my way and I take my chances. We can be a team, you and me, but we ain't ever gonna be anything else. If that don't work for you, tell me now and after tonight, I'm outta here. I got enough stashed away that I can live real good down in old Mexico and I'm the kind of guy that the señoritas really go for."

"What about the money I promised you?"

"I can live without it. I'd like it, but I ain't gonna push. In fact if truth be told, I'm kinda thinking about walking away after tonight no matter how it comes out."

"Why?"

"It's your line of work. Someday someone's going to walk up behind you and put a bullet in your brain and anybody that's close to you is liable to go down as well. Eventually you're gonna be expendable."

"I'm impressed, Earl. The average man would have said that eventually I'd get caught."

"There's that, too, but I'd worry more about the other."

"Kevin was my control," she said.

"I wondered how you did it, but then it wasn't my business."

"I met him in Israel years ago. He wrote that book defending the Hezbola's right to take hostages."

"I remember the guy," Earl said. "I thought he was a jerk."

"Yeah, that's him. He was a reporter with an idea for a book. He sent me the proposal and I was intrigued. He also sent me the price of a round trip ticket and that intrigued me even more."

"So you went to Israel?"

"Yeah. I liked the idea for the book, but unfortunately he couldn't write anything longer than a news story, so I helped him with it. While we were working on it one thing led to another."

"And you wound up in bed."

"Yeah, but that's not what I'm talking about. Kevin had all these inside contacts with the Hezbola and I saw a story developing that would make me a fortune. I was running all over the country interviewing all the wrong people and drawing the attention of the Israeli government. One night while Kevin and I were driving near the Golan Heights a couple of soldiers stopped us. They wanted Kevin to get out of the car, and when he wouldn't they jerked him out and started using him for a punching bag. It was the last thing they ever did."

"What do you mean?"

"Kevin kept a forty-five automatic in the glove box. I knew this, the soldiers didn't. They were so intent on teaching him a lesson in Middle Eastern politics that they forgot about me."

"You shot the soldiers?"

"And afterward Kevin turned me into an assassin. You could say that our roles became reversed. He became my agent. He'd hand me cash and a name and I did the rest. The incident with the soldiers turned me into a rabid supporter of any Arab cause. I killed to further their aims and got paid well in the process. After a few years it didn't matter anymore. I was in too deep to quit, and besides I enjoyed my work. I got hooked on the challenge, the adrenaline and the adventure. They never knew who I was. Kevin kept it that way, both to protect me and to see that he never got aced out of his cut. But now he's dead and they have no way to contact me. As far as the world's concerned the Scorpion has gone into retirement."

"Jesus," Earl said.

"So what do you think, now that I've bared my soul to you?"

"I think that now you don't have to do Ramsingh."

"Think of the money. You can take Kevin's place training the troops and heading up Chandee's security. He's already agreed to it. In a year we could leave here richer than our wildest dreams. You and me Earl. Forever. Do I still have your loyalty?"

"Always," Earl said. "Till death."

"And the money? What about that?"

"I'd love being richer than God, but do we need it? I've been a crooked cop a long time. I've got enough for us to be happy. Let's just go to Mexico. You'd love Cabo. We'll lay on the beach, drink margaritas, windsurf and dance till dawn everyday for the rest of our lives."

"I want this Earl," she said. She had plenty of money too, probably a lot more than he did, but she wanted more than plenty of money. She wanted it all. She'd worked for it, she'd earned it, she wasn't going to walk away now.

"Okay, babe. I'll stick with you," he said. She sighed. She'd been right about him. He was the man for her. Together they'd be unstoppable.

"It'll be great, you'll see," she said.

"There's your man," Earl said. She turned and watched as George came into the restaurant from the dock.

"Look, Daddy it's George Chandee, the Attorney General," she said in a perfect White Trini accent, loud enough for everybody to hear. She jumped out of her chair and went up to him. "Mr. Attorney

General this is an honor," she blushed.

He smiled at her. "I'm sorry, I'm pretty busy right now."

"What's the matter, George, don't you have time for your friends," she said, lowering her voice and dropping the accent as she took his hand. She turned to Earl, added the accent and said, "Daddy, Minister Chandee is going to have a drink with us."

Chandee looked confused as Dani led him to the table. Earl stood and pulled a chair out for him. "Nice to meet you," he said.

"What the fuck's going on?" Chandee said, ignoring Earl and glaring into Dani's eyes. He'd never seen her in disguise before, but he was adjusting fast.

"I didn't want to talk on the phone."

"You blew it at the park. Again. Then Ramsingh takes off, God only knows where, on that boat of his. Now he's back, Broxton's out and everything's back to normal. What's going on?"

"This is Earl," Dani said, ignoring his last question. "I don't believe you've met."

Earl offered his hand and Chandee shook it. "So you'll be taking Underfield's place?" Chandee was talking through pursed lips and clenched teeth. He wasn't a happy man.

"Seems so."

"Not if you two don't get it right tonight. It's your last chance."

"It's taken care of, George. Don't worry," Dani said.

"That's what you said last time and I'm still worrying."

"He goes down at five straight up. This time I'm pulling the trigger. There'll be no mistakes.'"

"It's about time," Chandee said, looking visibly relieved.

"I guess you two got business, so I'll be on my way." Then he turned to Chandee and offered his hand again. "Been a real pleasure."

"Same here," Chandee said.

Earl released his hand, turned and made his way to the old Indian Trinidadian sitting on the hood of his taxi in the parking lot.

"Earl," Dani called after him. He stopped, turned. "You forgot the key."

"Yeah, stupid of me," he said.

She left the table and headed toward him, smiling as his eyes played over her body. "You'll need this, unless you want to break a window," she said, slipping the key into his hand.

"I'd have got the job done, but this makes it easier."

"Be careful, big guy," she said.

"I'll be careful," he said.

"One more thing."

"Yeah."

"I've been too sentimental about Broxton."

"Kind of wishy washy," Earl said.

"Exactly, but not anymore, it's time I grew up. Go by the hotel and finish it. No bullets, make it look like a double drug overdose. George will make sure the cops buy it."

"You got it, babe."

* * *

Earl cursed the old Indian under his breath. The bastard drove slower than his mother's molasses. He checked his watch as he got out of the cab. He wanted to go up and finish it now, but he was pinched for time. Maria and her loverboy were going to have to wait till after it was over, but he wasn't worried, the pills would keep them out. They weren't going anywhere.

He gave the valet his room number and studied a tourist map of Port of Spain while he waited for his rental car. Cliffard Rampersad, the chief of police, lived in the rambling string of Victorian houses along the Savannah, not far from where Dani lived with her father, the American Ambassador. He was still studying the map when the valet honked the horn.

He jumped in the car and took off, grabbing a look in the rearview as he spun the wheels and laughed. The valet's eyes were bugging out. Well, let him stare, Earl thought, because he didn't tip valets.

Ten minutes later he parked in front of Rampersad's house. High fence, decorative and deadly. Spikes on top. Rottweiler at the gate, eyeing him as he got out of the car. The house was at the southeastern end of the Savannah, not one of the stately homes farther up the road. Not a rich man's home, but not a poor man's home either. "You wanna win the game you gotta make the rules," he said as he slipped out of the car and started up the walk like he lived there. He opened the gate like the Rottweiler was no more than a puppy. The big dog met his hand as he slipped a steak into its mouth and he made a friend for life.

Dogs smelled fear as your adrenaline flowed. Earl wasn't afraid.

He knocked on the front door and waited.

No answer.

He waited and watched as the dog wolfed down the steak. Dani had been right, there was nobody home. Rampersad would be at the Red House going over security for this evening's dedication speech. His wife spent her afternoons at the country club, tennis and swimming. There were no children and the police chief had no servants.

Piece of cake.

He opened the front door with the key and stepped into the entryway. A couch, two chairs, new and covered with plastic were the only furnishing in the sitting room on his right. The hardwood floor was covered with a fringed Persian carpet with plastic runners over it. Earl wondered if they took the covers off when they received guests. He passed through into a larger living room. This must be where the family spent most of its time, he thought, looking at the well lived in furniture and the giant screen television. He moved through the room quickly and into a dining room. A large table surrounded by six chairs set off the center of the room. The dining set looked new, a sharp contrast with the living room furniture, but the teak wood wasn't covered.

From what Dani had told him the kitchen was the door to the left and Rampersad's office was the door on the right. The rifle would be in the gun rack behind the desk. He pushed the door open and smiled as a hinge squeaked. It was a man's room, floor covered in rich brown wall to wall carpet, walls covered in oak paneling, the paneling covered in trophies, lion and leopard from Africa, tiger from India, jaguar from Brazil, puma from America, buffalo, elk, kudu and deer. Rampersad was a hunter.

He spent a minute admiring the trophies. He was a hunter himself. Then he turned his attention to the back of the room and the large teak desk facing toward the door. The darker Trinidadian teak stood out like a throne against the lighter American oak.

The chair behind the desk was also teak, but the gun rack the chair was touching was oak and glass. And in the rack, the hunting rifles. It was the World War II Springfield thirty-ought-six he was after.

Dani had told him all about the gun, but his hands trembled slightly as he opened the case. He looked at the weapon with a mixture a fascination and religious awe. Sometime, long ago, a gunsmith had put a lot of time in on it. It had a custom stock with a modified pistol grip so that the hunter could wrap his hand completely around it and still have a loose and easy trigger finger. It was the perfect hunter's rifle and a flawless assassin's weapon.

The bolt action would only suit a man confident and competent enough to hit what he was shooting at the first time. And Rampersad was such a man, if one were to believe the trophies decorating the walls were all brought down by him. He checked out the other six rifles in the case as he lifted out the '06. All bolt action. Earl believed it.

He heard the unmistakable sound of a car pulling up into the driveway. Shit, he thought, as he replaced the rifle in the cabinet and eased the glass door closed. He remained behind the desk for a second, wanting to be sure, then he heard a key inserted into the front door, heard the door open, then close. There was a door on the right side of the room and Earl moved toward it, opened it and found a full bathroom complete with tub and shower.

He heard footsteps crossing through the house and his instinct told him that soon they'd be coming his way. He had only one choice. He moved into the bathroom, eased the door closed, pulled the shower curtain aside and stepped into the tub. Was it Rampersad or his wife? And if it was Rampersad, was he armed? He heard someone set something down. He heard the heavy steps of a heavy man coming through the dining room.

"Elizabeth, are you home?" It was a male voice. Rampersad.

Then there was quiet, followed by the familiar sound of water running in the kitchen telling him that Rampersad hadn't stumbled on to his presence. Yet. The sound of the refrigerator door opening and closing told him he was getting something to eat, or maybe ice for his water. He strained for any drop of sound. He heard the scrape of a kitchen chair against the floor. He was sitting down at the kitchen table.

For a long few seconds no sound came. He was alone in the shower-tub with only his labored breath. The chair scraped against the tile floor again, sending shivers of ice over his skin, cooling the sweat on the back of his palms. Rampersad was getting up.

He heard the footsteps as they left the kitchen. They were getting closer. The squeaking hinge told him that Rampersad was in the den. He leaned back against the tile wall, willing his heart to quiet as the bathroom door opened. He closed his eyes, and survived by taking baby breaths, silent from even God's ears. Every sound Rampersad made was magnified by the small room and his shooting imagination.

Rampersad belched and Earl silently shuddered, but stayed quiet. He heard the creak of tiny hinges as he opened the medicine cabinet. He heard him take out something, heard the rattle of pills in a glass jar, heard him pour them into a beefy hand, heard a sound like a drain being pulled on a tub full of dirty water as he gulped them down. He almost screamed when Rampersad closed the cabinet door.

Earl heard him leave the den, heard him leave the house and then he heard the car start. A close call, he thought, as he stepped out of the tub and left the bathroom. Back at the cabinet, he opened it again and lovingly took out the weapon, this time admiring the scope. It was a variable power piece of optics with a top magnification of thirty-five. He put the rifle to his shoulders, sighted through it, looking through the crosshairs, and whistled. A man, or woman, with steel nerves, and something to mount the weapon on, like a tripod or a window sill, would be a dead accurate shot at five hundred yards.

Ramsingh was a dead man, he just didn't know it yet.

In an oak chest next to the gun rack, Earl found a leather rifle case for the weapon and the ammunition. He slapped a five round clip into the rifle, but didn't chamber a round. Then he stuffed the weapon into the bag. "Mission accomplished," he said. Then he remembered his friend out front and stopped at the refrigerator, where he liberated two pounds of hamburger. At the door he fed the grateful guard dog, then he whistled his way to the car.

He was still whistling when he pulled out into the traffic. He had the murder weapon.

CHAPTER TWENTY-TWO

DANI EYED THE CROWD below and wiped the sweat from her forehead. The room was air-conditioned, but it didn't matter, she sweat before a hit, she always had. She was ten stories up, but she felt like she was down there with them. She tried to imagine the panic that would ensue when the prime minister went down.

A little less than two hours to go and they were packed in almost as tight as they were at the calypso fest. Already people were pushing and shoving, trying to get as close to the stage as possible. Everybody loved the cricketeer. It had to gall Ramsingh. To get an audience to listen to him he had to have George Chandee on the podium with him. Had to let him speak second if he wanted the crowd to stay through his own speech. Ah, Ram, Dani thought, turning away from the window, life isn't fair.

But that's what makes it so interesting. Who would have ever thought that she'd fall for a backwoods southern sheriff? Well, maybe not backwoods, but definitely not the type of man who was going to be invited into the Washington social scene. She'd miss the parties, the gowns, the gossip, walking with power, being in on the cutting edge of crisis, but she'd missed it for the last year and survived.

She dry fired the rifle, pulling the bolt back and shoving it home again, and squeezing the trigger. It was a heavy weapon, heavier than she preferred, but she'd make it dance in her hands in a very short time. Ram would die, George would have his country, and the Salizars would have no more problems laundering their money.

She moved her gaze back to the throng beneath her. The sun peeking through a moist, partially cloud covered sky painted the crowd below with a friendly brush. From her perch the people looked freshly scrubbed in the tropical afternoon. The lively and bright Caribbean colors—vibrant reds, bright greens, crystal yellows and razor sharp blues—worn by the average man and woman mingled with the dull grays of the light weight suits worn by the office workers, lawyers and politicians, to give the crowd both a sober and a festive look.

She was shaken from her reverie by a light knock on the door, three rapid taps, two slow, Earl's signal. She lay the rifle down and shut the blinds, shutting off the outside. The blinds were efficient. A little light squinted in from the sides, but none squeezed through. She'd always liked the dark, felt at home in it. She'd always been an observer and the dark of night helped her to merge into the background while she watched.

She raised herself from the chair and went to the door. She tapped lightly, one time, Earl tapped back twice and she opened it.

"Rampersad's on the roof. Alone," Earl said.

"Arrogant. He should have some officers with him."

"Dumber than dog shit."

"He thinks he's a prince and he doesn't want to share his princely perch," she said.

"Lucky for us."

"Unlucky for him."

"The name on the door, 'Martel's Magic,' what's that?" Earl asked.

"Michael Martel the Magic Man. He manufactures magic tricks here in Trinidad. He exports all over the world. He also smuggles cocaine and launders money for the Salizar drug cartel," she said.

"How do you know that?" he asked.

"Trinidad's a small place, not many secrets."

"What about the cops?"

"George owns the cops."

"Yeah, I forgot," Earl said. She watched him as he digested what she'd said. She liked it when he put his mind to work. She could almost smell the electrical impulses snapping in his brain as he worked it over. Then he smiled and she knew he got it. "You're sending a message to George Chandee. You're saying, 'Don't fuck with me.' I like it, but what about Martel?"

"About now he's listening to my father tell him

why he can't ship his tricks to the States duty free. Dad will keep him tied up for about another hour, then he'll give in sometime after Martel agrees to contribute substantially to the president's next campaign."

"How do you know they won't finish early?"

"If they do, they'll celebrate over drinks till dinner. I'm supposed to be the hostess, we're having Peking duck. The Magic Man likes Chinese."

"So the prime minister gets killed by the police chief, shooting from Martel's window. Your friend George is gonna be one pissed off motherfucker."

"The money laundering operation will come to a standstill. It'll only be a temporary setback but it'll remind them that the Scorpion has a lethal stinger."

"An hour-and-a-half to go," Earl said, looking at his watch. "I'm gonna go and grab myself a quick snack. You want me to bring you back something?"

"No, I'm fine," she said.

"Okay, I'm outta here," Earl said, and she went back to the Magic Man's desk and sat in his plush swivel chair, resuming her vigil at the window, as Earl went out the door.

* * *

"Are you okay?" Broxton asked.

"I think so," Maria said, gasping for breath. "Just got the wind knock out of me. Can you see the glass?" They were lying on their sides, his back against the bed.

"Arm hurts, can you ease off it?" he said. Both their arms, his right and her left, were under her side. She arched her body and moved so that their arms were lying between them. He bit into his lower lip, against the pain. "I don't think it's broken," he said.

"Sorry," she said. "I just wanted to get to the glass. I wasn't thinking."

"It's okay, I see it. I'm going to have to roll on top of you."

"Go," she said, and when she was on her back he reached out and picked up the glass. He raised their hands and cracked the glass against the edge of the nightstand just like he'd crack an egg against a frying pan

"Damn, cut myself," he said, biting back more pain.

"Where?" she said, turning, straining to see.

"My hand."

"I see it," she said, and now it was her turn to reach out their arms. She picked up a sharp piece of the glass. "If it sliced into you that easily it ought to slice through the tape." They were slick with sweat as she brought her left hand through their bodies and sliced at the tape that bound their wrists together, and in seconds they each had an arm free. Then she handed him the glass and he cut through the tape binding their other arms. In a few more seconds they had the tape off their legs and were sitting on the floor, backs against the bed, panting heavily.

"Want me to turn away?" Broxton said. Although they'd made love, they hadn't really seen each other naked, and despite the situation, he was embarrassed.

"Shit, that's the last thing I care about," she said, and she pushed herself to her feet using the bed for support."

"Can you help me up?" he asked.

"Your arm's swollen," she said, taking his offered left hand and helping him up.

"Thanks." He looked at the clock, two-and-a-half hours till five, plenty of time.

"I need a quick shower," she said, but first I think I ought to splint and tape that arm, just in case it's broken. She went to the closet, took down a wooden coat hanger, broke the tops off it and tossed them aside. "This might hurt," she said. He nodded, sitting on the end of the bed as she used the bottom of the hanger as a splint, taping it to his arm with duct tape. He shivered when she pushed the wood hard against his forearm, but he didn't cry out.

"Doesn't hurt as much."

"You're lying," she said.

"You're right, it hurts like hell, but you did a professional job. Were you a nurse in a past life?"

"First aid training goes with the job. I'm going to take that shower now."

"Wait, I gotta use the head first." He hustled into the bathroom and relieved himself, sighing as the pain in his bladder eased. Finished he headed toward the phone as Maria passed him on her way to the bathroom. But when he reached it he saw that it wasn't unplugged, the line was cut. He heard the water go on and he looked around for a weapon in case Earl came back. He settled on a vase. He picked it up in his left hand, hefted it, then turned it over, spilling the flowers and water onto the rug. If Earl came back now, he'd get a face full of vase the second he entered the room.

The water in the bathroom stopped running and in seconds she was coming out the door, toweling off. "The sooner I'm out of here, the better," she said.

"Right," he said. "The phone's been cut. We'll have to get to another one, but we've got plenty of time."

She looked at the clock. "It's stopped," she said. He must have unplugged it when he cut the phone.

He whipped around and looked at the time. Two-thirty, about the time they'd come up to the room yesterday. "You're right. I don't know why I didn't see it," he said, as she was pulling on a clean pair of panties. She picked a watch up off the bureau. "Four-fifteen, you don't have much time."

"Shit we have to hustle."

"Not me. I'll be on the eight o'clock flight to Miami. Tomorrow I'll be in Madrid. It's been nice knowing you, Broxton, but I'm going."

"Don't go," he pleaded.

"I'm sorry. I need my own life for awhile."

"I love you," he said.

"I believe you think you do, but it was your girl's name you were moaning through that tape last night."

"Please," he said.

"Don't beg, Broxton." She crossed the room and kissed him on the cheek. "You're bleeding from that cut," she said, then she added. "Give it a couple of months. If you still think you're in love with me, give me a call. You'll be able to reach me through Iberia in Madrid."

* * *

There was a crowd around the reception desk. Broxton recognized the uniforms of an American Airlines flight crew mingled with a group of tourists, all smiling, talking and waiting to check in.

"Excuse me," he said, going to the front of the line and speaking to a young woman behind the counter. "I have an emergency situation and I need to use a phone." The words *emergency* and *phone*, coupled with Broxton's taped and swollen right arm, and the blood crusting on his left hand immediately quieted the crowd.

"This way, please." The girl was quick to recognize that he needed medical attention. She raised the counter and held it till he passed behind. "We have an emergency here," she said as she opened a door to an office behind the reception area. She didn't enter, but she left the door open. She was curious.

"How can I help?" a young man in a white shirt and tie asked. His wide smile and close cropped hair reminded Broxton of himself when he was in high school.

"I need a phone, it's a life and death situation."

"Right there," the man said, his smile gone.

Broxton saw the phone sitting on a wide desk next to a stack of computer print outs. He pulled out a chair and fell into it. There were two other young people in the office besides the man with the tie, both girls who couldn't be much over twenty. The three youths and the girl at the door all regarded him with a mixture of excitement and fear. His shaved head, glazed eyes, bandaged arm and bloody hand, all added up to daring and danger, and they, along with the tourists and flight crew waiting to check in, were intrigued.

He scooped up the phone, and then he had to think. Who was he going to call? Ramsingh had given him his direct line, but the chances that he'd be there with less than an hour before his speech were slim. Still, anybody who answered would take him seriously. He picked up the phone and punched the buttons. He spent twenty rings drumming his fingers before he hung up.

"How do you call the police?" he asked.

"999," the young man said.

Broxton punched the numbers, more finger

drumming and fifteen rings before someone answered. "Police Emergency, Officer Gopaul speaking." The voice was male and he sounded bored.

"My name is William Broxton. I have information about an assassination attempt against the prime minister."

"Yes, and when is this going to happen?" The boredom was stiff in the officer's voice.

"Tonight at five o'clock, during the dedication speech."

"I'll make a note of it. Where are you calling from?"

"The Hilton Hotel."

"That is unusual, usually you people don't leave your address, but I suppose you could be making it up."

"What's the matter with you?" Broxton said, his voice rising. "I've just told you that somebody is going to kill the prime minister and you're accusing me of making it up. Don't you think you ought to call Ram and warn him?"

"So you're on a first name basis with the prime minister?"

"Yes," Broxton said, and then he heard a loud click as Officer Gopaul hung up. "Shit," he said. He punched the numbers again. This time he didn't count the rings, but it took longer than the first call for Gopaul to answer.

"Police Emergency."

"Just listen to me, Gopaul," Broxton said. "I'm a American DEA officer working for the prime minister. In thirty minutes someone is going to put a bullet into Ramsingh's head. Just get a hold of him and tell him Broxton says not to speak tonight."

"No, you listen. For the last couple of months

we've been getting these kind of calls every day. We no longer take them seriously. The prime minister is unpopular right now, that is a fact, but he is safe tonight. He is dedicating the Police Services Statue and almost every policeman in Trinidad is on hand. Only an idiot would try anything against him there.

"Just call him," Broxton said.

"I don't know if you're just another hateful citizen or if you're for real, but if you are for real your information is wrong. Prime Minister Ramsingh is safe tonight, believe me."

"Call him, please."

"No. Now, if you have nothing further, I'm going to hang up again. Please don't call back, this number is for real emergencies only."

Stunned, Broxton replaced the phone in its cradle. "He doesn't believe me," he said to nobody in particular.

"The police have been getting a lot of calls like that. It's been on the news and in the papers," the girl at the doorway said.

"Would you like me to call you a doctor?" the young man with the tie said.

"He didn't believe me," Broxton said again, and he looked up into the young man's brown eyes and saw that he didn't believe him either.

"I'm sorry, sir," he said, "but we have a lot of work to do."

Broxton looked at the two girls in the room. They were trying hard to smile, but he saw fear in their eyes, and it made him shudder. He spun his gaze to the girl at the door and to the crowd of people waiting to check in. They'd all heard him. They were all staring at him and most of them looked disgusted. To them he was no more than a beggar on the street who'd bullied his way to the front of the line and he was inconveniencing them all with his antics.

"Doesn't anyone believe me?" he said, and he realized the words were raspy in his throat. They probably thought he was drunk.

"Is there a problem here?" Broxton looked up and saw a beefy security guard.

"No, Jerry," the man with the tie said. "This gentleman was just leaving."

"Do you want me to help him out?"

"That's all right, I can find my own way," Broxton said. He moved away from the desk and started for the door. The guard stood aside, letting him pass. Outside of the office he ducked under the counter and started across the lobby toward the exit.

"Sir?" the doorman said.

"I need a taxi," Broxton said.

"One should be by just now." The door man took in Broxton's disheveled appearance and shook his head.

"I'm in a hurry."

"Everybody's in a hurry these days," the doorman said.

"I believe you, Broxton." He turned. Maria was standing there, carry-bag on her shoulder. She looked like a crisp green-eyed angel. "I have a car. I can get you where you need to go."

"Thank you," he said.

"This way," she said and she took off running. Broxton started off after her. She sprinted through the empty taxi rank and made a quick right into a parking lot. He saw her fish into her purse as she ran and by the time she reached a bright yellow Toyota she had her keys in hand. The doors were unlocked by the time Broxton made the car and she had the engine running by the time he slid into the passenger seat.

"He's speaking at the Brian Lara Promenade," Broxton said.

"I know the way." She dropped the transmission into low and laid rubber as she spun out of the parking lot. She made a right onto the access road down the hill toward the Savannah without taking her foot off the gas. She drove like she knew what she was doing.

"Is the time right?" he asked, looking at the dashboard clock.

"Yes."

"Then we only have twenty minutes."

"We'll make it," she said, but Broxton saw the traffic ringing the Savannah and he wasn't so sure.

CHAPTER
TWENTY-THREE

DANI WENT BACK to her place at the window and peered out. The crowd was quiet now, everybody was settled in, waiting for the unveiling of the statue, the speech and then the cricketeer. Dani remembered her father taking her to see Bobby Kennedy in downtown Long Beach when she was a little girl. He was running for president and everywhere he went he was mobbed. Men, women and children offered him a sea of hands, all wanting to be touched. Magic had touched Bobby at that time, that magical and tragic year. She remembered her father holding her up and she remembered shivering when the electric energy flowed from his hand and tingled through her. These Trinidadians felt the way about George Chandee that

Americans felt about Bobby in 1968.

But Bobby was good, she mused. George is not. If ever evil sparked out of the eyes of a man, George Chandee was that man. For a few instants she thought about what she was going to do. In the grand scheme of things it made no difference, but this was the first time that she was going to put a man like George in power. Always before, her hits had been political, even the one in the United States. Maybe the successors to power in those third world nations weren't always suited to the task, maybe they were fundamentalists, leftists, or idealists, maybe they wanted to stop a civil war, or maybe they wanted to start one, but in the past those that paid her always had an agenda that they felt justified murder. George's only agenda, if it could be called that, was to amass as much money as possible, in as short a time as possible.

And if she thought about it, she had to admit that Ramsingh was unlike any man she'd ever hit. He wasn't a fanatic, he wasn't leading his people in a bloody war, wasn't lining his pockets, wasn't forcing them into slavery, didn't have death squads, abysmal tax rates or even an insufferable personality. He was just a good man who would have been a fine prime minister about fifty years ago. But he was out of his league in a world of drug smugglers who were richer than God and still wanted more. They wanted his country and no power on earth was going to keep it from them.

She pictured his face, the craggy eyes, bulbous nose, crooked grin and that thick shock of gray hair. She'd never had to do a friend before. He was a man to her. A good and kind, but terribly incompetent man. For a second she was having second thoughts, but she banished them. Ramsingh was going to die in a few minutes and she was going to be the instrument of his death. That's just the way it was.

She heard applause outside and lifted the blinds an inch. She looked down upon the square, and balled a fist in irritation. George had taken the podium and was waving to the crowd. Damn him, that wasn't in the script, but it was just like him. He wanted to be on the stage when Ramsingh was hit. He wanted blood on his shirt, like Jackie in the limo. He wanted to rage against the assassin. He wasn't satisfied with the charisma of a Kennedy, he wanted the power of a messiah.

She watched as George held his hands above his head, trying to quiet the crowd. He was clearly enjoying the applause. He beamed his best false smile and the crowd went wild. Mothers were holding up infants and she was again reminded of Bobby. Young girls screamed and swooned like he was a rock star. Young boys applauded. He was their idol, he was from them, one of them that made it.

"I want to introduce a friend of us all. A true son of Trinidad and Tobago. A man who has given up much to serve his country. A true national hero. Let's give a warm Trinidadian round of applause for my best friend and your best friend, Prime Minister Ramish Ramsingh." George was screaming into the microphone, caressing it like it was part of him. "Ram is always here for us, let's always be there for him," he wailed, almost singing the words and the audience burst into a screaming round of clapping and foot stomping applause for a man they didn't like, a man they all wanted to step aside. George could make them do anything.

Then to her horror Ramsingh stepped up to the

podium and waved to the crowd. What the fuck was George doing? She wasn't ready. He knew she was going to pull the trigger at five. Why was he bringing up Ram now? Why was he forcing her hand? Did he know she was going to implicate Rampersad or was he just stupid? She thought about it for a second. No, he couldn't know. He didn't know where she'd be shooting from. He was just being himself, trying to shake her up, trying to maintain control, trying to force her hand, even if only by fifteen minutes. Maybe he could, maybe he couldn't. She had to hit him before he said anything about the treaty with the United States, that was the deal, but she didn't have to pull the trigger a second before. She'd wait and watch George sweat.

* * *

Maria spun around the corner, took one look at the cars ringing the Savannah, saw a gap between the traffic and stomped on the accelerator, shooting between three lanes of cars. "Hold on," she said, and Broxton threw his good arm against the dash, bracing himself. The protesting sound of squealing brakes shot through to his soul, but nobody came close to her as she flew between bumpers and fenders. "Going to cut across," she said, and she gunned the rented Toyota and jumped the curb.

"Look out," Broxton said, and Maria spun the wheel, barely avoiding a pair of evening joggers. Then she was past the jogging path and churning up dust as she steered the car across the vast park.

"Are you going around the cricket game?" Broxton asked.

"Going right through," she said. She was charging toward the game without a thought about the brakes.

Broxton saw one of the players point. The bowler turned to look. He yelled and the players started to scatter as the Toyota ripped through the field, kicking dust and throwing rocks from the rear wheels as the players shouted at them when they flew through.

Seeing the players in their white uniforms reminded Broxton of the attorney general, George Chandee, and that niggling thought that if something happened to Ramsingh, Chandee would be the next prime minister. He remembered Chandee's hard look on the plane, his flash of temper, and the look in his eyes when Ramsingh called him on it. He hadn't liked Chandee from the get go and he wondered why the man was so popular.

Maria slammed the car into low and slid into a left turn.

"What are you doing?"

"I just remembered the road around the Savannah is one way. If I cut straight across we'll be facing the wrong direction, we'd have to go all the way back around." She stopped talking and gripped the wheel, hands tense as she sat rigid in the seat. She was approaching another cricket game in progress. This time the players were children and they weren't bedecked in white uniforms. Maria laid on the horn, and some of the kids turned to look, but unlike the adults, they didn't scatter. She jerked to the right to avoid a grungy kid with a defiant look on his young face, and then she was shooting, like a well batted ball, headed straight for the bowler, a wide eyed youth too frightened to move.

She turned the wheel a fraction, and they sped by the young bowler, showering him with dust. "Hey," the batsman yelled as the car gobbled ground in his direction, and he swung the bat as he dodged the rampaging car, connecting with the front window as he was jumping back. Spider webs flashed across Broxton's sight, but the safety glass didn't break. Then the Toyota bowled over the stump and the sound of the bumper colliding with the wood was like an explosion inside the car, but Maria kept her foot on the floor as she headed for the stands.

They were empty now, but Broxton could imagine them full and wondered what they were for.

"Carnival bands go through here. Hundred thousand people, big laughing party. Only ghosts in the stands now," she said as she threaded the car through the bleachers toward the ramp. Broxton tried to imagine the stands full of gaily dressed people as Carnival marchers paraded before them in their scanty, bright costumes. He'd heard so much about the ultimate party, but he never imagined he'd be taking the revelers' route in a speeding car, witnessed only by phantoms.

Then the Toyota was climbing the giant concrete ramp between the stands, putting on a show for no one, as the speed steadily climbed, till they topped the incline and they were speeding over the long stage built to handle over a thousand marching, romping, stomping people at a time.

"The ramp at the end is gone," she said.

"That's not good," Broxton said as he realized what she was saying. The cement stage was about five feet high and as long as a football field, but they'd cut away the ramp on the end, probably to enlarge it, but the why didn't matter. The only thing that mattered now was that the end ramp was gone.

"Don't stop," he said.

"Right," she said, and she kept her foot to the floor as they sailed over the end.

"Hail Mary!" he screamed.

"Yeah!" she screamed back. They were airborne and the engine was howling in protest, then they slammed into the ground, front tires first, then the spinning rear tires. The car bounced and jerked left, but she whipped it back to the right and kept it pointed toward the Savannah ring road.

"Good driving," he said.

"Miracle the tires didn't blow," she said.

"Almost there," he said.

"Hold on!" she shouted, spinning the car to the left as they slid across the jogging path and then over the curb. She aimed between two cars on the ring road and for an instant Broxton thought she was going to make it into the traffic okay, but the driver of a beige pickup saw the car about to cut him off and accelerated. Broxton braced himself for the crunch as the Toyota's rear end smashed into the front fender of the pickup, sending it spinning into an accident in the adjacent lane. Horns honked and people shouted from both the jogging path and moving cars, but Maria didn't stop. Instead she stepped on the gas and took the first exit off the ring road and headed for downtown Port of Spain.

"Ten till five," he said.

"We'll make it," she said, but the traffic was heavy and they were already slowing down.

He was afraid that she was wrong.

* * *

Dani slipped long fingers through the blinds and eased the window up about six inches. There was a touch of a breeze and they rippled slightly, but not enough for anybody below to notice. She lifted a hand to the dangling cord to bring them up, but decided to wait. She could raise them, sight in on Ram and pull the trigger all in less than fifteen seconds. She'd wait till after his opening and his customary few jokes. Usually he spent as much as five or ten minutes trying to warm up his audience, and lately, because of his sinking popularity, sometimes longer.

She watched as he raised his hands, asking the crowd to quiet down enough so that he could be heard. The applause was for Chandee, but Ramsingh was basking in it like it belonged to him, while Chandee stood just behind the prime minister and to his right, gently clapping, as if he was leading the ovation.

"Ladies and gentlemen, Trinidadian's all," Ramsingh tried to start, but even with the mike he wasn't able to project himself above the din. He smiled, looked from left to right and lowered his hands. There was nothing he could do but ride it out. He wasn't a big man, but standing at the podium, with the breeze rippling through his silver hair, and the sun at his back casting long shadows, he looked larger than life.

Chandee stopped his applause, apparently realizing that he was keeping the crowd going, but they didn't stop with him. He started shifting from side to side. Ram was bathing the crowed with confidence, while the hero, the cricketeer, squirmed like a five-year-old in church.

George, she thought, always so confident on stage. The perfect snake oil salesmen, slick enough to sell taxes to the poor. Calm down, you're giving yourself away. But Chandee couldn't read her thoughts. She watched as he clasped his hands together in front of himself, almost like he was praying. She smiled as she looked down on him. He was afraid she'd shoot him. She liked thinking about it, but she wouldn't do it. There was too much money riding on this, and it was all about the money. She'd be richer than her wildest dreams.

Part of her said, shoot now, get it over with, but another part enjoyed seeing the sweat around Chandee's hairline. He'd wanted to push her into shooting early, wanted to play a little power game with her. She looked at her watch. Eight minutes till five. She'd wait. Let George shiver in the fear of his own making. If it looked like Ram was going to announce the drug treaty she'd do him early, but if not, she wouldn't pull the trigger till five.

Then she saw Michael Martel pushing his way through the crowd, headed for the Caribbean Bank building, the building she was in, probably going to his office, the office she was in. She picked up the gun. Damn you, Daddy, you were supposed to keep him busy. She reached out and took the cord with slippery fingers and eased up the blinds a few inches. Then she slipped the barrel out the window, resting the stock on the window sill and she sighted in.

* * *

"Seven minutes," Broxton said.

"We'll make it," she said.

The traffic was poking along and Broxton felt his nerves crawling through his skin. They were so close and so far, there was no way. In seven minutes she was going to pull the trigger and Ramsingh would fall. "Hurry," he said, "please, hurry." Ramsingh was more than a job, he was his friend, and more than anything he didn't want to fail him.

"We'll make it," she said, and she jerked the wheel to the left, punched the horn and stomped on the gas.

"Shit," Broxton said as the car shot over to the other side of the street, charging into the oncoming traffic. She kept one hand on the wheel, the other on the horn as she bobbed and weaved her way through the approaching cars leaving Port of Spain. Broxton wondered why the traffic going into the city was so dense. The rush hour traffic should all be going the other way. Then he saw the accident up ahead.

"There," he said.

"I see it." She maneuvered the car so that she was racing down the center line, forcing the oncoming cars to turn out of her way. A policeman standing by the wrecked cars blew his whistle and pointed at her, then at the curb, indicating that she should pull over. Instead she swerved to the right to avoid the oncoming traffic and pointed the car at the whistle-blowing cop.

"Look out," Broxton said.

"He'll move," she said as the policeman jumped out of the way. They both felt the slicing sound of metal scraping against metal as the Toyota brushed one of the damaged cars. Then she was back on her side of the road with a clear path toward downtown Port of Spain.

"Almost there," she said.

"Maxi," he said, and she swerved to miss the mini van full of people, running the light on Park Street. "Another!" he shouted. She slammed on the brakes, skidding to a stop and allowing the maxi to pass in front of her, then she was back on the accelerator only blocks from the Brian Lara Promenade.

* * *

Dani watched as Martel stopped and talked to a

shapely woman. Ram had started his speech and she was torn between listening to him, watching Martel, and keeping an eye on the clock. Earl would be expecting her to shoot at five straight up and she wanted to stick to the plan. Martel turned away from the woman, but she grabbed his arm, still talking. He looked pained, like he didn't want anything to do with her. She was yelling to be heard above the applauding crowd, peppering her speech with rapid gestures. She was mad about something.

Dani checked her watch. Five to five.

* * *

"Five minutes," Broxton said.

"End of the line," she said.

Broxton looked up from the clock. There was a blockade across the street and police cars were parked in front of it, but there were no policemen in sight. They must all be with Ramsingh, he thought. He hoped they were watching the crowd and not the prime minister, but he remembered when Reagan was shot and how the Secret Service men had been looking the wrong way, watching their chief instead of scanning for potential assassins, and he shuddered. The Trini police force was no Secret Service.

She pulled up behind the blue and whites and he was out the door and running before she brought the car to a complete stop. She grabbed her purse and was only a second behind him. Neither of them had bothered to close their doors.

He heard Ramsingh's voice booming through the square before he saw him on the podium. The crowd was huge but well mannered. "Police emergency," he said, pushing into the throng. "Move aside." It was the calypso concert all over again, only this time the giant man wasn't breaking trail for him.

"Emergency, emergency, please step aside," it was Maria's voice behind him. "Police emergency, please step aside." Her voice carried the authority that his lacked and people started to move.

"Move, move," he said, squirming through the living, breathing crowd. He was sucking air like a race horse straining for the home stretch, struggling like a salmon swimming upstream, pushing people aside with his bad arm, oblivious to the pain, adrenaline sparking through him, giving him the energy of the Gods. He sliced through the throng like a heavyweight through school children.

* * *

Dani looked at her watch. Two minutes. Martel was pulling away from the grabbing woman, heading toward the stairs. She kept her eyes on his bald spot, the evening sun gleaming off it.

"And it's with the unswerving support of men like George Chandee that we have been able to get this far," Ramsingh was saying, "And with his help and others like him we'll be able to lower this horrible fifteen percent VAT. A value added tax is wrong. It hits the poor and the lower income people the hardest. I'd like to drop it immediately, but unfortunately I can't, but what I can do is lower it to ten percent, starting tomorrow and I can promise you that before the next election, not after, I will replace it completely with a graduated income tax that will hit all of the people of our country fairly. And if the rich and the well to do don't like it, they are going to have a fight the likes of which they've never seen before."

What was he saying? This was not the anti-drug, pro-American speech George had told her to expect.

Ram was singing her song, echoing the words she'd used against him so often. She couldn't believe it. He'd finally seen the light. Maybe he was a man for the future after all.

She moved the sight away from Ramsingh, toward Chandee, thought of the money, then moved it back. What difference could he make anyway? They would never let him get away with it. He'd be run out of parliament by the end of the month.

She relaxed her trigger finger and looked toward Martel's shiny bald spot. The woman had him in her grip again and he was visibly agitated, struggling to get out of her grasp.

She saw movement in the crowd. "Damn you, Broxton," she muttered. He was seconds from the stage, charging through the crowd like a mad bull.

Martel finally succeeded in pushing the woman away and she lost sight of him as he entered the building.

She put her eye back to the sight. Ramsingh and the money, she asked herself, or Chandee and the future? She had all the time in the world. Money or honor? Her finger tightened around the trigger.

* * *

The two policemen on the steps going up the podium had their eyes on Ramsingh with their backs to the crowd. Broxton burst through them, knocking them aside. Now there was nothing between him and Ramsingh, except George Chandee.

"Ram!" he screamed. He slammed into Chandee, sending the attorney general careening into Ramsingh and knocking the prime minister aside as gunfire exploded in the square and blood exploded above Chandee's heart.

THE BOOTLEG PRESS CATALOG

RAGGED MAN, by Jack Priest
ISBN: 0974524603
Unknown to Rick Gordon, he brought an ancient aboriginal horror home from the Australian desert. Now his friends are dying and Rick is getting the blame.

DESPERATION MOON, by Ken Douglas
ISBN: 0974524611
Sara Hackett must save two little girls from dangerous kidnappers, but she doesn't have the money to pay the ransom.

SCORPION, by Jack Stewart
ISBN: 097452462x
DEA agent Bill Broxton must protect the Prime Minister of Trinidad from an assassin, but he doesn't know the killer is his fiancée.

DEAD RINGER, by Ken Douglas
ISBN: 0974524638
Maggie Nesbitt steps out of her dull life and into her dead twin's, and now the man that killed her sister is after Maggie.

GECKO, by Jack Priest
ISBN: 0974524646
Jim Monday must rescue his wife from an evil worse than death before the Gecko horror of Maori legend kills them both.

RUNNING SCARED, by Ken Douglas
ISBN: 0974524654
Joey Sapphire's husband blackmailed and now is out to kill the president's daughter and only Joey can save the young woman.

NIGHT WITCH, by Jack Priest
ISBN: 0974524662
A vampire like creature followed Carolina's father back from the Caribbean and now it is terrorizing her. She and her friend Arty are only children, but they must fight this creature themselves or die.

HURRICANE, by Jack Stewart
ISBN: 0974524670
Julie Tanaka flees Trinidad on her sailboat after the death of her husband, but the boat has a drug lord's money aboard and DEA agent Bill Broxton must get to her first or she is dead.

TANGERINE DREAM, by Ken Douglas and Jack Stewart
ISBN: 0974524689
Seagoing writer and gourmet chef Captain Katie Osborne said of this book, "Incest, death, tragedy, betrayal and teenage homosexual love, I don't know how, but somehow it all works. I was up all night reading."

DIAMOND SKY, by Ken Douglas and Jack Stewart
ISBN: 0974524697
The Russian Mafia is after Beth Shannon. Their diamonds have been stolen and they think she knows where they are. She does, only she doesn't know it.

TAHITIAN AFFAIR: A ROMANCE, by Dee Lighton
ISBN: 0976277905
In Tahiti on vacation Angie meets Luke, a single-handed sailor, who is trying to forget Suzi, the love of his life. He is dashing, good looking, caring and kind and it looks like her story will have a fairytale ending. Then Suzi shows up and she wants her man back.

BOOKS ARE BETTER THAN T.V.

The bootleg Press Story

We at Bootleg Press are a small group of writers who were brought together by pen and sea. We have all been members of either the St. Martin or Trinidad Cruising Writer's Groups in the Caribbean.

We share our thoughts, plot ideas, villains and heroes. That's why you'll see some borrowed characters, both minor and major, cross from one author's book to another's.

Also, you'll see a few similar scenes that seem to jump from one author's pages to another's. That's because both authors have collaborated on the scene and—both liking how it worked out—both decided to use it.

At what point does an author's idea truly become his own? That's a good question, but rest assured in the rare occasions where you may discover similar scenes in Bootleg Press Books, that it is not stealing. Writing is a solitary art, but sometimes it is possible to share the load.

Book writing is hard, but book selling is harder. We think our books are as good as any you'll find out there, but breaking into the New York publishing market is tough, especially if you live far away from the Big Apple.

So, we've all either sold or put our boats on the hard, pooled our money and started our own company. We bought cars and loaded our trunks with books. We call on small independent bookstores ourselves, as we are our own distributors. But the few of us cannot possibly reach the whole world, however we are trying, so if you don't see our books in your local bookstore yet, remember you can always order them from the big guys online.

Thank you from everyone at Bootleg Books for reading and please remember, Books are better than T.V.

JACK STEWART
PORTLAND, 2002

Printed in the United States
105460LV00001B/18/A

9 780974 524627